BRIGHTER THAN *Fear*

BECCA SEYMOUR

RAINBOW TREE PUBLISHING

BRIGHTER THAN FEAR

FANGS & FELONS
BOOK THREE

BECCA SEYMOUR

RAINBOW TREE PUBLISHING

Zone Defense

No Take Backs | No More Secrets | No Wrong
Moves | No Backing Down

Fast Break

Rules, Schmules! | Facts, Smacts! | Regular
Smegular! | Easy, Schmeasy!

True-Blue

Let Me Show You | I've Got You | Becoming Us
| Thinking It Over | Always For You | It's Not
You | Our First & Last | Next For Us

Outback Boys

Stumble | Bounce | Wobble

Fangs & Felons

Thicker Than Water | Weaker Than Instinct
| Brighter Than Fear | Stronger Than Fate

Stand-Alone Contemporary

Not Used To Cute | High Alert | Realigned |
Amalgamated | Under the Blazing Stars |
Best Kind of Awkward

For information, contact the author:
HELLO@BECCASEYMOUR.COM

EDITING: HOT TREE EDITING

COVER DESIGNER: BookSmith Design

PUBLISHER: RAINBOW TREE PUBLISHING

E-BOOK ISBN: 978-1-922679-64-2

PAPERBACK ISBN: 978-1-922679-65-9

CHAPTER 1

FLYNN SMYTHE

W ITH THE LOUD THROB OF MUSIC PULSING through my EarPods, the thud of rubber on concrete provided an extra beat as I finished my run. It drove me forwards and urged me to keep up the pace.

One more kilometre, and I could collapse and crawl into the shower before finally starting my day.

I pushed myself harder, focussed on the pavement ahead, on the apartment block I called home since graduating from the SICB—Supernatural Investigation & Crime Bureau—Academy seven months ago.

My condo was situated on the edge of the hustle of Sydney CBD. Just close enough to experience the vibrant offerings of the city—which one day I hoped I'd be able to find time to enjoy—and the location was perfect for work.

With just a fifteen-minute drive, I could be at the secure doorstep of the Infiltration Tactical Unit—the official location rather than the kick-arse "lair" my boss, Agent Lucas, created.

I zeroed in on the building's entrance, my breathing shallow despite my piss-poor attempts at controlling it. The door beckoned me, practically mocked me.

Just twenty more metres.

I slammed my hand against the wall next to the door and gasped, losing all semblance of control as I pulled in ragged breaths. Hanging my head, I inhaled deeply, wincing at the cold air hitting my teeth and making them ache.

How being a human in this world I lived in both sucked as well as kicked arse was a quandary I contemplated daily.

My teeth being sensitive to the biting edge of the winter's morning air was almost winning top spot of things that sucked.

Obviously, the top spot belonged to me having to work my backside off exercising twice as hard as my fellow agents of the supernatural variety.

But it was a duty I took on willingly.

And I had the best bloody job in the world to

remind me that each shuddery breath and aching muscle was worth it.

The door opened, taking me by surprise.

I held back my humourless laugh when I smiled at Macca, the guy from apartment 4, as he headed out for his day on whatever construction site he needed to be at. Because, yeah, not having supernatural hearing or reflexes or any superpowerful senses also sucked monkey balls.

The human plight wasn't something I wanted to get caught up in. Life was far too amazing for that.

The warmth of the entrance hall embraced me as I stepped inside. While it offered a welcome relief, I still had to get my butt up to the third floor, and the lift remained broken.

With a sigh and a few grumbles, I made it up the staircase and unlocked my apartment door. Less than two minutes later, hot water sluiced down on me, easing my burning muscles.

Absorbing the heat and stillness, I centred myself before going over my itinerary.

On top of some initial investigative research I needed to pull for Michaels, one of the field agents in our unit, my day ahead looked intense.

Running point as the lead handler for a case Chris was working meant I'd been running on adrenaline for almost two weeks. Hell only knew how field agents, deep in infiltration, dealt with the mounting stress and pressure.

I suspected all field agents fit the mould of an adrenaline junkie and were slightly unhinged. A smirk formed on my lips as I thought about my friend Shaw's reaction to the assessment. No doubt he'd be in complete agreement.

I washed, dried myself off, and downed my premade smoothie. As I settled into my car, my phone buzzed. I started the engine, using it to distract myself from the uptick of my pulse.

Right on time.

I ignored my shaking hand as I opened the encrypted messaging app. My heart stumbled, just like it did every single morning at 7:12 a.m.

And fuck if I could hold back the twitching of my lips when I read the name selected for today's exchange.

```
SPARKLESORCERER:
Why did the hacker stay
calm during the
cyberattack?
```

Every day the jokes got worse. But at least today, it was one about hacking rather than unicorns.

Was I frustrated that I couldn't figure out how the unicorn hacker had discovered our inside ITU joke about the name that stuck? Quite possibly. Especially as I'd asked more than once but never received a straight response.

AGENTTECH:
Do I want to know?

Was it possible to flirt in a text when you didn't even know who the person on the other end was? Hell, I didn't even know if it was a man, but fuck, I really, really hoped it was.

I'd had too many horny dreams featuring a faceless man over the past few months—occasionally with the not-as-disturbing-as-it-should-be addition of the unicorn hacker fucking me hard with a unicorn-horn-shaped dildo.

Since I had practically zero experience bottoming, it was one hell of a dream.

Though maybe one of my dreams when the unknown hacker actually had a "real" horn protruding from his head as I debased him should have been more concerning. Especially when I'd woken panting and wishing I could drift back to sleep to ride the horn as he jacked me off.

It said a lot about my life and state of mind that the

thought of riding a unicorn horn got me revved up.

I shook my head, trying to push away the visual.

Everything about this exchange was wrong on so many levels.

It would likely be the reason I got my arse fired or even arrested one of these days.

> SPARKLESORCERER:
> Because they had CTRL of
> the situation!

I snorted. How could I not?

> AGENTTECH:
> Bad… oh so bad.

Every single time I responded to the unicorn hacker, I was one step closer to being in a whirlwind of trouble. But I couldn't stop.

Nor did I want to stop.

It wasn't like I was hooked on our exchanges.

My eye twitched at the thought, and I called bullshit.

A new message cut off my spiral into weighing up the odds of right and wrong.

> SPARKLESORCERER:
> Before you drive away,
> are you ready…?

I'd been freaked the first five or so times they'd said such a thing—explicitly implying that they knew what I was doing or where I was. But now, a shiver of awareness rippled over my skin. Errors flashed, and warning signals begged for me to take notice, but I was blind to them. Ignored every single alarm.

Being in so deep, pushing too far made me feel alive.

Reckless.

Forbidden.

Perhaps I was on the brink of a system crash, and everything I'd worked for would short-circuit and blow up around me, but in the rush, the charge of something "more" was too addictive for me to ignore.

```
SPARKLESORCERER:
I'm the science of
atoms, reactions, and
more, mixing elements
and compounds, that's
for sure. When you study
me, you'll surely be
vexed. Tell me, what
comes after "chemistry"?
What's "next"?
```

Fuck, how I loathed and thrilled at these frustrating riddles I got from the hacker.

The app shut down, just like it always did when

they signed off. It was my cue to pull away and drive to work.

Disappointment weaselled its way through my system, a familiar feeling lately.

I swallowed down my self-loathing at just how needy and pathetic my crazy crush was and focussed on getting to work, my thoughts not straying far from the final words in our exchange.

Whatever they meant, I suspected by the end of the day, they'd make sense.

They always did.

All that meant was, the unicorn hacker knew what I was working on and had information I'd yet to figure out for myself.

Did I feel resentful? Envious? I sighed as I passed through the first security barrier at the official office, showing my ID and passing the retina scanner.

Guilt shifted in my chest as I realised I didn't feel either of those emotions. I wasn't sure what that actually said about me.

Instead, I was impressed as hell by the hacker and fell a little deeper.

I was one giant push away from being swallowed whole by the illegal exchanges I'd been having.

But hell if I was willing to stop.

It didn't take long to settle in at my workstation

and become absorbed in my tasks. With a deadline looming, I stayed focussed, or as much so as Shaw would let me.

"What do you mean, you've never had a birthday cake?"

Shaw looked so perplexed that I reached out and patted his shoulder. It wasn't enough to distract him, though.

My mortification grew when he said, "Seriously, Flynn."

My eyes widened. Shaw never first-named me. Shit had apparently just got real.

"What? It's no big deal." I willed my cheeks not to turn beet red, hating the attention, especially when it was about something as silly as a birthday cake.

"Mate, not a big deal?" He parted his lips, his brows shooting so high, I started to cringe in expectation.

"Smythe."

I jumped to attention at the sound of my boss calling my name. I was always eager and never one to drag my feet. My speed would give Shaw a run for his money when in panther form. "Coming," I hollered towards Mathew Lucas's retreating back.

The interruption couldn't have been timed better if I'd orchestrated it myself.

"Don't think this conversation is over." Shaw's disgruntled voice followed me, but I wasn't too concerned about him accosting me when I stepped foot back in the main hub of our base of operations.

Michaels, a senior agent who was also Shaw's boyfriend, was due back any time now. It meant they'd disappear somewhere to suck face for at least half an hour.

Entering Lucas's office, I offered a tentative smile. So far, I'd never been in his bad books. Never pissed him off enough that I feared for my jugular.

I suspected that if—though *when* was more likely —he found out about my communication with the unicorn hacker, that would change.

But from the expression on his face—soft smile and questioning gaze—I figured I was safe for another day.

"Why don't you take a seat."

Following orders had become the norm. Two years at the academy drilled that into me. The almost seven months working for the SICB's elite covert Infiltration Tactical Unit—the ITU—made the whole rule-following aspect as natural as breathing.

Something I thought my boss appreciated, especially since not everyone on the team was all that great at following directives. They did provide hefty entertainment, however. It helped that they were incredible agents. Though if it was possible for vampires to go prematurely grey, I suspected Lucas would be a total silver fox by now.

As soon as my butt hit the soft leather of the visitor's chair, I relaxed my shoulders, my attention on Lucas as I waited for him to begin.

"Any update on the Kaldone case?"

"Yes," I was pleased to report. "I've followed a trace to Melbourne. Found four offshore accounts, at the last count. I'm just formalising the data to send up the chain of command."

"That's great. I'll catch up with Kent this afternoon."

Contentment fluttered in my chest, all soft wings and gentle calm.

Kent, my mentor, was a vampire who apparently didn't pull her punches. Except with me. Since meeting her during my last few weeks at the academy— when I was brought onto the team early with Shaw— Kent had seen something in me that nobody really ever had before.

Not even my parents.

Potential.

Not only that, but she'd also sort of dragged me into the close-knit unit with a threatening glare and a sharp tongue directed at anyone who dared to underestimate me.

It was a hell of a thing and made it impossible not to lean into her special kind of acceptance.

My weekly dinners with her and her wife, Jada, simply cemented my place in her family.

Aware Lucas remained quiet, silently studying me, I focussed hard on controlling my breathing.

Every day I surrounded myself with supernaturals. I had done so for years, even before joining the academy. It didn't make that natural fight-or-flight instinct any easier to ignore.

As a human in a world filled with supernaturals who had far superior strength, speed, and reflexes, I learned at an early age to rely on my intelligence. It was the reason I'd come so far.

My affinity with computers came easily. There was little I couldn't navigate or figure out. Few digital loops and routes I couldn't travel. And with both Lucas and Kent being literal geniuses, too, every day I learned from and was supported by the best.

With the exception of one person I couldn't figure out—species unknown—who continued to perplex us all. Truth was, they ran circles around us.

Of course I was back to thinking about the unicorn hacker. They were never far from my mind.

Being intrigued was one thing—acceptable and understandable, even. It would be a whole other ball-game if anyone realised just how much I was crushing on the mystery person.

Not sure how anyone would react to that news.

With the way Lucas stared at me, I suspected where his thoughts lay.

"And the"—he winced, and I managed to bite back my lip twitch—"unicorn hacker?"

My boss detested the name coined for the hacker who'd not only infiltrated our system eight months or so ago but had also created a program so terrifying and mind-blowingly ingenious—Mirrormat coding—that it put us all on edge.

It was only because of the hacker's immediate removal of the software—after we no longer needed it—and the fact that there hadn't been any satellites pulled out of the sky or complete blackouts around the world that Lucas hadn't organised an all-out mission to find the hacker and bring them in.

Would we even be successful if that was the direction Lucas or the bureau's director wanted to go?

I suspected not.

Swallowing my guilt, I kept my voice steady. "Nothing. The last communication was three months ago." There was no need to add that we only suspected it was the unicorn hacker who'd fed us intel on Captain Hornell, a piece-of-shit villain responsible for heinous experimentation and bloodshed.

Unfortunately, while the intel proved fruitful in closing down a small lab in Perth, Captain Hornell had been long gone. Again.

The man took the role of dastardly villain in a frustrating and worrying direction.

As such, Hornell occupied the top spot on the bureau's most-wanted list.

That didn't mean, however, that we could focus only on his case. The director fed us a fast stream of cases. Most demanded the specialised infiltration skills of the unit—requiring hours, days, and sometimes weeks of work—though sometimes, easy cases came our way.

Those were fun, and we could theoretically handle them with our eyes closed.

I suspected they came our way due to the speed our unit worked. Being a covert unit came with a wonderous assortment of red-tape-snipping abilities.

The Kaldone case was one that required them.

"Okay, just keep me apprised of any changes or suspicions."

I bobbed my head. "Absolutely, sir."

Lucas smiled, not trying to correct me for the

millionth time by telling me to call him by his surname. I'd tried. Truly. Every time, the discomfort made me itchy.

Taking that as my cue to leave, I exited his office and made my way to the kitchen tucked to the right of the open office space. A quick coffee fix, and then I'd get those reports completed and sent to Kent. It should only take an hour.

After that, I had two leads to follow for Chris's case—one for a possible location, and the other should lead to money. The sooner I gathered the information for him, the sooner he could close the investigation on the BloodRush drug ring.

He was in deep and had been for two weeks.

It was time he came home—something the whole unit agreed on.

Not that anyone had expressed a specific concern.

As an experienced agent, Chris could hold his own. No doubt about it, he could handle the case. Compared to other investigations I'd witnessed in my short time being here, this one wasn't especially taxing.

The knowledge didn't help the flurry of nerves threatening to solidify and take hold whenever I thought about the mission, though. *Our* mission. Because I was acting as Chris's point of contact. As his digital ears, his safety net, it was my job to always have an eye on and ear open for anything and everything surrounding his mission.

It was my first flying solo.

That the team trusted me filled my chest with pride while I simultaneously battled nausea and self-doubt.

My daily reports to Kent indicated she was happy with everything I was doing. While that gave me the brief relief of reassurance, I wanted the mission over and Chris safe.

By the time I'd inhaled my coffee at my desk, I'd sent the data report to Kent and was now focussing on my screen.

This aspect of my work—following digital foot-prints, navigating through the labyrinth of possible pathways—I loved. The challenge fed my anticipation, charged my excitement, and powered my synapses.

Rather than listening to music, I took comfort in the soft, familiar hum of my computer—a Lucas special. The man lived for electronics and had built some ingenious security tech over his long years. And his computer-building skills were particularly impressive.

While I was a dab hand myself and had fun creating tech, I much preferred working with it.

Determination thrummed in my veins as I pulled

up the database, passed through the high-spec security measures, and flexed my fingers. The money would be an easy trail to follow.

It usually was.

After spending a few moments sifting through the behemoth of data, searching for the right coding, I grinned. There it was. A giant red flag. The data might as well have had flashing neon lights.

I grabbed the data and pulled out the coding, looking for the seven numbers and three letters that would tell me exactly what I needed to shut down.

Once the money became untouchable, there'd be a reaction in the organisation responsible for the BloodRush ring. That would be the first cue for Chris.

He'd previously fed me the information, having finally managed to pull some records from the ring's offline database.

Tomorrow would be when I pulled the trigger so he could make his move.

But there remained one more detail I needed to locate before he could do that so we could get Shaw and Michaels out there to assist.

When I opened the main folder to which I'd been periodically adding content, a cascade of subfolders spilled out. Hours had been spent working through the many pages of data, all carefully arranged into these subfolders.

Today, I focussed on the content of one in particular.

Locating the supplier of one of the key ingredients of BloodRush was just as significant as the money trail. Cutting the drug ring was one thing, but another would just pop up.

Cut the head off the proverbial snake—or "wolf," based on Chris's intel—by going for the chemical supplier, and the operation would collapse like a tower of playing cards.

Chemical supplier.

With my heart skipping a beat, the message from the hacker bounced around in my brain.

I'm the science of atoms, reactions, and more, mixing elements and compounds, that's for sure. When you study me, you'll surely be vexed. Tell me, what comes after "chemistry"? What's "next"?

Of course they'd known I'd be focussing on the chemicals—a.k.a. the "chemistry"—today.

My cursor flew across the screen as I scrolled and searched. With no supernatural sight or speed, it was a painstaking process, but I was fast.

I'd sure as hell given the nonhuman trainees at the academy a run for their money.

Double-clicking on a piece of code, I dragged it to a secondary screen. From there, I ran it through the decoding program the SICB had developed a few years back—well before my time. But this version had a few key adjustments I'd made. Ones approved by Kent and Lucas.

Dabbling and fine-tuning was not only fun but second nature.

The program now ran lightning-fast and separated coding to identify broken and illegal backdoors.

Data flooded my screen, dancing and jumping as the program ran through its final stages. The whole time I watched, scanning all that I could.

There it was.

I snapped the Return key, pausing the program.

My heart raced, a warm flush settling in my chest.

Holy fuck.

The unicorn's riddle smacked me in the face. The words "chemistry" and "next" danced on the screen in the form of NexChem, a chemical manufacturer based right here in Sydney.

Or at least their main office was.

"What have you got?"

There was no concealing my rush of excitement as I cut a glance to Kent as she joined me. Not with a vampire present. Or most supernaturals, truth be told.

My focus returned to the screen as she stood by my side. "I found the string. Just transferring it now."

Every chemical created contained some sort of fingerprint—a type of chemical coding. In this instance, the additive revealed exactly who the manufacturer was.

A few clicks and I verified that the company NexChem was above board. In fact, it was a government-approved manufacturer. A search provided no intel that even hinted at corruption.

It gave us the lead we needed to trace the supplier from there.

"I've got an in at NexChem." Kent's fingers flew across her phone screen. "I'll see what intel they can get me."

That Kent had a contact there wasn't much of a surprise.

I bobbed my head. "What do you want me to do?" Time was creeping on. We didn't have the hours to spend on waiting to see if Kent's connection could provide information. If the plan remained in place to shut the operation down tomorrow, sitting on our arses and twiddling our thumbs while relying on someone else to gather additional data wasn't an option.

I had enough info that I could bypass NexChem's firewall and search for it myself if needed.

"I've just sent the chemical coding assigned to BloodRush that Chris obtained. With each batch having its own unique fingerprint, it shouldn't take her long." Kent focussed on her computer as she spoke.

In these instances, the government, for all its Big Brother ways, had established some useful protocols. Branch and production coding being a couple of them.

I waited, my gaze on Kent. A ping on her phone followed.

Making eye contact, Kent set her jaw, instructing, "Break through their firewall."

Sounded good to me. Sitting on my hands never felt right.

"On it." My fingers immediately flew across my keyboard, adrenaline fuelling my speed. I lived for this shit.

"Check the batch yourself," Kent ordered, her face a mask of stoicism.

Her expression told me all I needed to know: whatever I found was likely going to piss her the hell off.

"See which department was involved, who signed off, where it was meant to go."

"Understood."

Even as I did so, I couldn't help but wonder who her contact was and why the shift in her tone. Based on her directive, it left little doubt there was something more going on.

Kent having tucked me under her proverbial wing meant I'd grown familiar with her tells. Not that she had many. Unless Callen, the division leader, was around. Then she tended to devolve into this spiral of sharp-tongued, sarcastic banter. As well as hilarious, Callen getting under her skin was fascinating to watch.

I'd mentioned it once to Jada—only when Kent was nowhere near hearing distance.

With a small, knowing smirk, Jada had taken great delight in telling me it was because Callen and Kent were scarily alike. I suspected Kent would tear the head off anyone—except her wife—who dared to voice such an opinion.

"I need to speak to Lucas. Do you have this covered?"

With my focus on the screen, I nodded. "Yeah. I'll let you know the second I find anything."

The squeeze of my shoulder no longer took me by surprise. It did pull a smile from me, though.

My parents were never affectionate. It went deeper than them not buying or making me a birthday cake. It made every kind word or touch of approval and gentleness I received more meaningful.

Especially coming from Kent, a renowned hardass.

With my gaze bouncing between the two screens, my fingertips warmed up as they barely broke free from the keyboard. The security measures, while standard, contained some interesting code. I smiled, enjoying the challenge.

The cool glow of the screens, familiar and welcoming, flickered as I navigated through the virtual wall. Between the rhythmic clicking of the keys and the hum of the servers, I relaxed into my search, barely holding back a fist pump when the barrier started to crumble.

The lines of coding changed.

I had to hand it to the company. Whoever had installed the security measures had done a decent job. A few more clicks and I'd find the signature that any coder worth their salt would have slipped in there.

And there it was: The information Kent tasked me to find. The vulnerability I was looking for. Right there for me to squeeze on through. When I left the program, I wanted to build everything right back up again. Not every person breaking in would be working for the government and simply taking a sneak peek.

My job wasn't to steal formulas or funds. There

was little doubt anyone else's agenda would be nefarious. I wouldn't make it easy for them.

A fine line existed when working for the SICB while searching for answers and trying to prevent the unimaginable from happening. Especially when staying true to my moral code.

But my confidence in our unit was unshakable. We were here to do good. Every single person on our team was someone I trusted implicitly.

Did I feel the same about the whole bureau? Not quite so much.

Even before I'd learned the truth about the demise of the former SICB division leader a couple of years back and how the ITU had taken him down, I wasn't naive to corruption and power.

I'd witnessed it first-hand in my last few weeks at the academy.

But not only that.

Being brought up by apathetic parents who did all they could to put distance between me and them meant I'd never see the world around me or the people in it through a rose-tinted lens.

Numbers and letters zipped across the screen, and my heart stuttered. The wall of encryption faded away, revealing full access to NexChem's server.

Heck yes.

A rush of satisfaction kept me company as I navigated through the system and matched the data pulled from the samples provided by Chris.

"Holy shit." The words rushed out of me when I reread the assigned records. Swallowing hard, I took a surreptitious look around before I researched the name.

The employee record appeared, complete with a full overview, personal data, and a photograph.

Shit. Shit. Shit.

Piercing green eyes stared back at me. The shape and the colour looked so familiar. The lips were different, though, as was the nose. With a shock of black hair against olive skin, there was little doubt the vampire was beautiful.

She just wasn't as striking as her sister.

Hearing Lucas's office door open, I flinched.

Self-protection told me to shut the screen down. Instinct told me to stay still and wait for Kent to appear behind me.

Barely a heartbeat later, I felt her presence. The vampire moved with a stealth I was envious of, even with the shit-kicker boots she'd paired with ripped black jeans today.

"That everything?"

Silently I nodded, then angled my chair a little so I

could see Kent more clearly while still being able to monitor the screens.

Her expression was blank. Not even a tic of her jaw.

The lack of visible emotion was more terrifying than her losing her shit.

"Everything's there," I confirmed, falling back on my training to keep my voice steady. "The batch is labelled as destroyed on site. Signed off by Seraphina Kent four weeks ago."

Our gazes connected, and she nodded sharply.

"Good going." Kent folded her arms, narrowing her eyes a little at me.

I spun my chair immediately to give her my full attention.

"Get your service weapon. You can come with me for an early-afternoon trip. Finally get to meet... the golden child of the family." With that, she turned around and headed to her desk, leaving me with a frantically racing pulse and wondering what level of shit I was going to be seeing.

Ivy Kent in action, I suspected.

And her sister, a woman I only knew two things about.

The first was that Kent loathed her.

The second—she used to date Agent Lucas.

Not that I wasn't already moving to get ready, but intrigue made me move faster.

I'd only been out of the office in an official capacity once since working for the unit. And while my two years of training had equipped me for every aspect of life as an agent—including being in the field—I suspected Kent confronting her sister wasn't something I'd be prepared for.

It took twenty minutes to get out of the city and another fifteen minutes to reach our destination. The whole journey, Kent questioned me about the case I was working on with Chris. The plan was to confirm by late this afternoon that everything was in place for tomorrow.

I didn't want to let him or anyone in our unit down. Whatever it took to make sure this case was closed and he returned to base safely, I'd do.

I stared out the window as the gap between buildings stretched further apart. Signs of winter surrounded us, and with no clouds drifting in the sky, days like these never seemed to fully warm up. The southerly winds bringing frigid air didn't help. The early-afternoon sun pressed down on the metal of Kent's car, though, providing a welcome warmth.

Spending so much time in the temperature-controlled office meant it was always a shock to the system when I stepped out of the comfortable twenty-three-degree heat Lucas maintained.

Sure, my early-morning runs always jolted my senses, but the frigid air was also what helped me to get my arse moving and picking up speed.

Kent, angling to look at me as she cut the engine, caught my whole focus. While she usually wore an expression of indifference, there was a fierceness in her gaze that I struggled to comprehend, let alone glance away from.

"Seraphina is a viper."

Surprise had me shooting my brows high.

"She was forty when I was born and had already carved her place in the world," Kent continued, her voice steady, her gaze unflinching. "She manipulates and won't let anyone, or anything, stand in her way."

My brow furrowed. "Yet she's the golden child?"

"Always. Think Cersei Lannister crossed with the skills of Natasha Romanoff. Fuck, throw in the sadistic streak of Ramsay Bolton for good measure."

"Jesus." I huffed out a breath. If this were a conversation I was having with Shaw, I'd be laughing my arse off. This description coming from Kent... not a chance would I dare.

That she was a fan of Marvel as well as *Game of Thrones* threatened to boggle my brain.

"So, bundle all that together, but stick a halo on her head, as no fucker thinks she can do wrong."

"Except for you." There's no challenge in my voice, just unwavering concern and curiosity.

"There's something to be said about the bond between sisters. It just took me fifteen years to see beyond her mask." Kent's blink was slow, and the first inflection of emotion edged into her voice when she said, "She'll already know about you and what you mean to me and Jada."

My training flew out the window at my sharp inhale. But it was a hell of a thing: being cared for and considered family. In just eight months, Kent... *Ivy* had made me feel like I belonged.

Like I mattered.

All those months ago, when she'd jokingly announced she wanted to adopt me, she pretty much did so. Just without the formalities.

Hell, she'd thrown me a graduation party. From all the movies and shows I'd watched over the years, that reeked of something that family did for people they cared for.

"It's why I brought you here."

"O-kay." Puzzled, I waited wide-eyed for an explanation.

"Whatever we're about to walk into is undoubtedly going to be her attempt at a pissing contest. She'll weave her web of lies. She'll also be all over you like bees on honey."

Well, at least she didn't describe me as shit and her sister as a fly. I took it as a win.

"This is me staking my claim."

My brows jerked high, but heck if I didn't want to laugh at the discomfort pouring off Kent. It was the first time I'd witnessed her behave in this way.

"And if you tell anyone I said that, I'll write you out of the will."

"I'm in your will?" The fuck?

In response, Kent rolled her eyes. "You're important to Jada," she said stiffly.

My heart squeezed with affection for this fierce take-no-shit vampire who'd decided she liked me enough to bring me into her somewhat obscure fold. "You're both important to me too."

A twitch of her eye was the only tell she let slip. Yeah, she loved me. Having two vamps as mums who'd unofficially adopted me went beyond anything I'd imagined happening to me.

Gratitude buzzed in my chest.

"Right. You ready?"

With Kent at my side, I suspected I'd be ready for anything. Before I could answer, her cell buzzed.

After reading the message, an honest-to-god wicked smirk split her lips. Her vivid green eyes glistened, elation swirling in their depths.

"My contact came through."

Well, that was a relief. For a moment there, I'd been confused as hell. A contact who wasn't Seraphina made much more sense. And that Kent had a contact at the company where her sister worked wasn't even all that surprising, given what I now knew.

"Let's go, Smythe. After this, we should have what we need so you can reach out to Chris and get the team assembled for tomorrow. Sound good?"

"Damn straight, it does."

It took but a few moments to get through security and make our way down the sterile corridor that would apparently lead us to Seraphina's office. We passed six labs along the way, and I counted nineteen employees in white coats and six security guards. That tally didn't include the single lion shifter who escorted us.

Lions were one of the easier species to spot without supernatural senses. Panthers were right on up there, since they had golden eyes. However, the popularity of species-specific contact lenses could make it tricky.

The sheer size of born lion shifters coupled with the way they moved was one tell—all grace, strength, and an abundance of confidence. All of which could be faked if someone had the will and the patience, however.

What really separated them were the birthmarks all lion shifters were born with.

With no real origin story beyond myth and legend that seemed to change from country to country and generation to generation, no scientific explanation had been provided.

Nature's branding tattooed various shades of golden browns along all lion shifters' necks at birth. While they differed in shape and size, a distinctive shimmer was always present. And as far as I was aware, nothing and nobody had ever been able to replicate it. Even lion shifters who were gifted the gene—which was rare, as the exchange usually resulted in death—received something similar. The same shimmering of golden browns but always in the distinctive pattern of the lion's claws who'd shared their gift in their last breaths.

Hypervigilant, I kept my gun hand relaxed but close to my side, ready to draw should I need to. The ratio of security to visible staff was off, but my quick research had already revealed that the Sydney base employed more than ninety staff. Add in the size of the compound, and there was a lot hidden away from this route clearly intended for unannounced visitors.

Before the shifter could reach out to knock on the closed door, Kent brushed on by, opening the office doorway without an official announcement. Though technically her "Knock, knock, Sera-fang. No doubt you were expecting me" was a greeting of sorts, right?

I clamped down my amusement, my gaze eating up the opulent office space. Like the rest of the areas we'd been led through, it was clinical with its glaring abundance of white. Sharp lines of furniture made the room feel cold, and from the icy glint in Seraphina Kent's stare, it suited her completely.

"Agent, how lovely of you to pay me a visit." A well-aimed arch of her brow followed, and I had to hand it to the vamp—she managed to say a silent "fuck you" in that one movement. It was kind of impressive.

Seraphina's gaze snapped to mine, the ice melting to something more calculated.

"Oh, and you've brought your little pet." She covered her mouth, eyes widening, and a tiny, regretful gasp followed.

Shit, she was good.

"I'm so sorry, I meant Agent Smythe. It's so wonderful to finally meet you. Anyone who receives an invite to my sister's summer solstice celebration is clearly important. I don't know why she's waited for so long to introduce us."

I stared her down, offering her a relaxed "Ms. Kent."

Seemingly unaffected, Seraphina, who'd been standing, manoeuvred around her desk and sat. For a beat, she remained quiet, turning her focus to her sister. Leaning back an inch and settling further into her white leather chair, she steepled her fingers in front of her mouth. "And the reason you're here?" she finally asked.

"Hemagenex."

Relaxed in her chair, Seraphina didn't respond.

"Knowing that you've clearly fucked up so much that you're having to scrounge together extra cash by selling to narc manufacturers, I have to tell you, Sera-fang, fills me with so much warm satisfaction."

Despite desperately wanting to see Kent's expression, I didn't look away from Seraphina.

"What was it? Or *who* was it, I suppose?"

The slightest narrowing of her gaze marked Seraphina's first tell.

Kent continued, "You know, selling mutagenics is a felony. I hear Eosteric Penitentiary is really delightful this time of year."

"Unless you have a warrant or are here to arr—"

Kent cut her off. "I'll get to that."

The vein in Seraphina's right temple appeared, a bright blue against her olive skin. It throbbed once, swelling a second time a few moments later.

"For now, how about we cut through the bullshit, and you give me the details of your buyer? It'll make our parents proud, knowing you cooperated."

Seraphina moved. She was out of her seat before I could blink and was in a chokehold by the time I had my hand on my service weapon, my gun aimed at the shifter who barrelled through the door.

"Sera-fang—hell, sister, you must be wading in shit to react like this. Attacking an SICB agent on top of your charges.... Colour me intrigued."

"You don't have anyt—"

Tightening her hold, Kent shut Seraphina off. "You think I'd be here if I didn't have anything?"

I assumed Kent's mole really had come through.

The lion's finger twitched, so I narrowed my gaze. "Slowly drop your weapon"—I indicated the gun at his hip—"then back away towards the window."

Sensibly, he did so. Once he'd eased away, I collected his discarded Glock, my aim unwavering.

I stowed both away and bound his wrists with my issued cuffs—the hardened metal unbreakable. As I worked, I remained aware of Kent, catching her low words as she secured her sister and shoved her into a chair.

Her tone hard while maintaining an edge of disinterest, Kent ordered, "Speak."

I moved so I could see both the shifter and Kent, curiosity and self-preservation urging me on. In my periphery, I kept half an eye on the open doorway.

Seraphina cast a furtive glance at the shifter. Interesting, for sure.

The lion focussed on Kent's sister; a short nod followed.

I swallowed my surprise. The security guard held power?

"Put me in front of Lucas. I want an immunity agreement."

Kent scoffed. "Not a fucking chance."

A honey-sweet, self-satisfied smile tilted Seraphina's lips. "This is so much bigger than one shipment of Hemagenex."

I eyed Kent, who turned her focus to me. Unasked questions filled her gaze, and I nodded, working hard to keep my heartbeat steady.

Sure, she'd led point on this visit, but the Blood-Rush case was Chris's and mine. Despite not needing my response, since she was my superior, she asked me my thoughts. It was a hell of a thing, her trust and faith.

"Marlow too." Seraphina indicated the shifter.

"You've got to be shitting me. All this over a guy?" Exasperation tinged Kent's words. "Smythe?"

"We've enough room in the back." I shrugged, feigning indifference. What I wanted more than anything was to get this show on the road and the information out of her ASAP. Only then could we shut down the lab and the supply chain.

"Fine by me. Let's go on a family outing."

I let my grin break free and pulled out my phone to shoot off a text to the team.

A secure site existed just ten minutes away. I sent the instructions to my boss, confident Kent knew what she was doing by arranging the meet.

An alert signalled he'd be there not long after we arrived. It would give us enough time to secure the vampire and shifter we had in custody and give me a moment to school myself for when I witnessed Lucas face off with Seraphina.

With both Seraphina and Marlow in cuffs, we led them to the SICB-issued SUV and secured them in the back seat. Once the doors were closed, Kent walked to the rear of the vehicle. I met her there.

"What did Lucas say?" Her voice was low, her eyes trained on the back window as she spoke.

"He'll meet us at the Lichfield building."

"Good plan."

I tried not to peacock at her compliment, but I had no doubt the quick and heavy thump in my heartbeat gave me away.

"Your intel?" I asked.

"Video footage of Sera leaving with an Esky the day the batch went missing."

My brows darted high, and Kent huffed out a humourless laugh. "Weak evidence, I know, but Sera doesn't know that."

"Sneaky." I smirked. "So, is there anything I need to know before Seraphina and Lucas come face to face?"

Kent's lips twitched. "Is that your not-so-subtle way of saying you want to know the dirt?"

Heat hit my cheeks, and I shrugged. "Exactly that. Just wondering how Lucas could wind up with Seraphina."

"The only good thing to come out of that relationship was my connection with Lucas."

Seriously, that was all she was giving me?

It was at times like this that it would be useful to have Callen, the division leader, around. While I didn't know him as well as I did those in our direct unit, I knew he gossiped.

"You can dr—"

My encrypted messenger alert went off, and I froze, my heart stumbling as I reached quickly for my phone to silence it.

Kent zeroed in on my expression and watched my every move.

It was obvious the sound was a notification of some kind.

"You going to get that?" A slow arching of her brow followed.

"It can wait." A tug in my gut called bullshit.

"You sure?"

Fuck. No, I wasn't.

That the hacker reached out to me at this second meant something. They'd never done anything without well-timed intent.

I quickly completed the security checks.

```
SPARKLESORCERER:
Get away from the
vehicle.
```

My heart punched the inside of my chest.

"Smythe?"

A new alert.

SPARKLESORCERER:
Now!!!!

"Fuck. We've gotta move." I barely had time to make eye contact before I darted for the back passenger door closest to me, shouting, "Get them out of the car."

Reacting immediately, Kent yanked the other door open. I followed a split second later, my hand on the lion as I shouted, "Move!"

Confusion registered, but he jolted towards me with startling swiftness, lunging out of the car with his lightning-fast reflexes. Before I could check on Kent, a deafening explosion shook the ground, reverberating through my bones. The world around me quivered, shuddering violently, hurtling me skywards.

In that fleeting moment, a searing wave of scorching heat pressed down on me, accompanied by the violent scream of grinding metal. My consciousness clung to a thin thread, the onslaught of pain weighing me down, before everything dissolved into a void of unfathomable darkness.

CHAPTER 2
ROWAN HART

A fast, heavy thud pounded within my chest. My skin rippled, and I swallowed hard, forcing myself to gasp for air.

I couldn't shift. Couldn't let my tiger break free.

Not now.

Not when he needed me.

His prone form burned my retinas.

Move. Fuck, just move.

Being too late was not an outcome I could accept.

A flick of my keyboard and the camera feed from the building's entrance flooded the screen. It gave a different view of NexChem's car park.

Come on.

The cloying sting of fear clung to my skin, no doubt breathing its sickening scent into every square inch of my warehouse den. It would take a whole lot of burning sage to cleanse my space, but I'd set fire to enough of the damn stuff to make someone a millionaire if he'd just get the fuck up.

Movement caught my attention, but it was the vampire whom I'd reluctantly come to respect over the past few months. Sure, she had talent, but it wasn't her skill at her job that impressed me.

Get up. Get up. Get up.

My finger twitched. I balled up my hand, urging myself to keep calm.

Claws and teeth would not help Agent Smythe.

Flynn.

What would have helped was me spotting the threat as soon as it happened. Instead, I'd been caught up in a maelstrom of horror, realising who the lion was and wondering how the hell he'd stayed under my radar.

How could I have let that happen?

The focus on Marlow Prince, the deep dive into what had gone wrong and how I'd missed it, meant I'd only kept half an eye and ear open on the one man who'd caught my attention eighteen months ago. Flynn.... He couldn't die. I couldn't lose him before I even had the chance to—

The shift of a foot. His leg moved.

A rush of relief surged through me, mingling with the fear still clogging my throat.

Flynn hauled himself up. First to his knees, then to his feet.

He shouted something to the vampire agent.

"Fuck. Stupid shit system," I growled into the empty room. Microphones would have been a big fucking help.

My fingers flew across the screen.

```
SPARKLESORCERER:
Are you hurt?
```

After I hit Send, I tapped into the SICB emergency services and rerouted the closest paramedic in the area to the scene.

Staring at the screen, I waited, hoping Flynn would hear the alert over the noise of the burning car, the crackling of flames and screeching metal, and no doubt the alarm in the building going off. I dragged my unsteady hand through my hair.

Flynn was still talking and checking on Prince. My muscles twitched at their proximity. The lion being within touching distance of Flynn shot ice-cold fear through my veins.

Focussing on steadying my breathing, I shot off another message.

Flynn tugged Prince up. The cat really did have nine lives.

With a tic of my jaw, I willed Flynn to hear the alert.

A grin split my lips, my heart bouncing around in my ribcage when I spotted his phone on the charred ground almost at the same time he did.

When he waved it around and shook his head, he winced, pressing his palm against his forehead. A frustrated hiss escaped me.

I summoned my tiger to the surface, and my eyes shifted. As soon as they did, my vision snapped into focus, zooming in through the grainy footage and landing on the blood pouring down his temple.

"Fuck." I jerked to a stand and pushed back my seat.

My impotence tasted bitter.

What was the point of anything I did if I couldn't save the one person I saw... *something* in?

On cue, my face ached, stung, my silver-lined scar mocking me. It always fucking did when I became agitated. Too much movement of my features always provided me a timely reminder of my ruined face.

"Think, dammit."

Panicking wouldn't get me anywhere. I had better restraint than this.

"Come on, Rowan. Think," I mumbled as the emergency exits opened and employees spilled out of the building.

On the screen, Flynn shouted something to Agent Kent again. She signalled to him, and my stomach tumbled in relief when he tugged out his comms unit and placed it in his ear.

I pulled up the access needed and punched in the code I'd learned by heart so many moons ago.

"*—a unit. Medical assistance required. Check on Chris.*"

At the sound of his voice, I released a shaky exhale. While injured, he could still pull his shit together. It was a hell of a thing.

I continued listening in. The need to sneer dissipated when I heard Agent Shaw's voice, which helped to keep me calm. It also gave me the reprieve to check in on Chris myself. Flynn would be worried.

Sure, this attack was unexpected—I cracked my neck, refusing to let my pissed-off emotions rise to the surface—but I suspected the explosion, while targeted, was unrelated to what Flynn was working on.

Seraphina Kent had more pies than fingers. And it appeared as though the SICB had stepped into something of a hornet's nest.

And Marlow fucking Prince was a piece to the puzzle I never anticipated.

I didn't like being surprised. My jaw cracked, a shooting pain zipping to my ear at the movement.

Whatever it was that I'd missed, I would absolutely get to the heart of it—and discover *how* I'd missed it.

I needed to for my own sanity and pride. To put to rest nightmares that still plagued me. But fuck if Flynn getting hurt didn't rattle me in ways that reminded me just how dangerous this new-found obsession of mine was.

As soon as Flynn signed off, I took another stuttering breath. Through the grainy screen, I watched as he held his side and grimaced. The pain was readable in his expression for barely a moment before he blanked his reaction.

Where else was he hurt? How badly?

All rational thought left my mind as I adjusted my headset. Common sense faded into the background while all my carefully constructed rules disintegrated just like lines of code succumbing to a fatal error.

I hit the comms button.

There was no going back.

"Agent Smythe, provide your health status update." My breathing was too heavy, the edge of my voice too tight to go unnoticed.

As I waited, I saw him tilt his head, pausing from the medical assistance he was providing to Prince.

"Agent Smythe on comms. Can you identify yourself? Over."

The roughness of his tone shouldn't have shot a shiver of awareness through me. It was an octave deeper than usual and not holding a single note of the lightness that tended to be integral to his tone.

Fuck.

This was so, so bad.

I squeezed my eyes shut.

"Come in. Over."

I didn't answer. What I should have done was drop the connection. Step far, far away from Flynn Smythe and his light brown hair that I was convinced would be silky soft to the touch. If that thought didn't scream that I was an idiot, then nothing short of a punch in the nuts would do the trick.

"Come in. Over." The slight wheeze that Flynn didn't quite hold back as he spoke sat like a boulder on my chest.

The line opened again, and I waited, still unsure what my plan was. "*Unicorn?*" The whisper-soft word rippled across my skin like a gentle breeze on a late-spring evening. "Uhm...." The sound was awkward; he was about to backtrack.

I dropped my chin to my chest and released a heavy exhale. "SparkleSorcerer checking in."

I lifted my gaze just in time to see Flynn's head snap up. With the way he was turning his head this way and that, he was going to give himself an injury.

"Stop searching and stay still," I ordered, voice gruffer than I intended.

"You're.... It's you...."

How I wished we were standing before each other so I could drink in his expression in close proximity.

An alert on one of my screens indicated an ambulance was just four minutes out. It provided the wake-up call I needed.

"AgentTech." I stuck with his secure messenger name, a pointless attempt at keeping my distance. Hell, as soon as Vinnie discovered what I'd done, I'd never live this down. "How badly are you hurt?" Each syllable tightened, revealing how close I was to snapping.

"What? How?"

"How badly are you hurt?" I hesitated and rolled my eyes at myself before softening my tone and adding, "Please tell me. Are you going to be okay?"

In just two minutes, the EMT would arrive, and I'd gather the information as it rolled in, but now, to finally be talking to Flynn after all this time.... I just needed to hear him tell me he would be all right.

"I'm okay." He pressed his fingertips to his side. "I think a couple of bruised or broken ribs, but I'm breathing okay."

"And your head? You're bleeding."

This time he peered around, searching. He stopped right on target, his gaze focussed on the entrance camera. The intensity of his stare threatened to unhinge me.

Who was I kidding? I was completely gone on the man—a human. Even worse, from the moment I'd discovered his code in an Astraweave eighteen months ago—when he'd still been a cadet at the SICB Academy—I'd been compelled to learn everything about the person who'd created something so intricate and beautiful.

From the first Astraweave line I'd discovered, I'd been mesmerised.

While I was not-so-low-key obsessed with him— Vinnie called it stalking, but what-the-fuck-ever— Flynn Smythe held me captive and completely at his mercy.

He just didn't know it.

A thready exhale hit my ear before he answered, "It's okay. Nothing major. Just—"

The sounds of the sirens had him pausing and my heart jumping.

"Be safe. I'll be in touch," I said quickly before he could continue.

I cut the connection, placed my headset on the desk, and repositioned my chair.

Reaching out to Flynn like that broke all my rules. Any communication I had with him was dangerous.

But to hear his voice and know he'd be okay....

I cracked my neck from side to side. Staying focussed was imperative.

Only by doing so would I work out who'd put Flynn at risk and how I hadn't seen it coming.

First things first... I double-checked on Chris's status, tapping into the servers leading right to his location. Seeing nothing amiss, I relaxed.

One less thing for Flynn to worry about.

Now, time to follow the exploits of Seraphina Kent and Marlow Prince to discover who wanted them dead and had the balls to blow up an SICB-issued vehicle to do so.

There'd be no hiding from me. Not with this. Not when Flynn had been caught in the crossfire.

WITH NO IDEA HOW LONG I'D BEEN following the murky coding and rabbit warren of data, I blindly reached out, searching for my coffee. The oversized mug was empty. I groaned and rubbed my eyes.

My hands ached, and my fingertips were sore. But it hadn't been a complete waste. The hours of searching had led me to discover the vampire who'd planted the bomb. A hired mercenary.

But from there, I followed the money, leading me to a company that didn't exist, which then led me to coordinates that were a black hole to cameras and tech.

So far.

I wasn't giving up.

Meanwhile, Flynn had received medical attention and had gone to an SICB safe house. Not the tucked-away warehouse that Agent Lucas owned.

The latter was the location where Flynn had spent time with the unit a few months back—when I'd first initiated contact—and I could grudgingly admit that the security and setup were impressive.

Not that it kept me out.

But still, impressive all the same. And definitely more high-tech than the government-owned facility.

None of that had softened my distrust of the bureau, but considering Flynn was an agent, I recognised that I could make exceptions for individuals and possibly the ITU as a collective.

Because there was fuck-all chance I'd be assisting otherwise.

Not that they knew about all the moments I'd intervened or my reasons why.

And there had been many.

I checked the time.

I suspected that a couple of hours back, Seraphina Kent had given up the intel Flynn needed for his case. So that was something. Everything for tomorrow seemed to be in place.

It was important to Flynn, this being the first operation he'd run point on. I didn't need his confirmation to know that. It was obvious in every finger tap that he would catch himself doing and each twitch of his lips when something went according to plan.

Kent, though, was in full-on DEFCON-1-mode, from the look of things. Not that I kept too close an eye on what she was focussed on.

Her sister was in the bureau's infirmary at the safe house after getting caught up in the blast and not fully healing from her injuries. Prince was in cuffs and in a secure unit, having given nothing away beyond what Seraphina had shared.

At some point soon, I'd be blowing his world up. I

just needed more information to go on and to figure out how he was here in the first place.

I suspected that after Chris—the agent who'd made my teeth grind over all the time he'd spent with Flynn while preparing for the op—returned, every available member of the unit would be focussing their efforts on this latest development.

I sure as fuck was.

The warning flash of my movement sensors flickered to life. They were set up a quarter of a kilometre away. The monitor brought up two camera feeds, and I groaned out a sigh.

Vinnie.

When he reached the first security gate, I buzzed him in. I grumbled under my breath while giving him access to the next two access points.

He was the sole person granted admittance to my inner sanctum. And that was only because he'd bullied his way in.

Vinnie said it was because I loved him. While he was technically right, my big brother was still an arsehole.

He just happened to be the only family member I had left in this shitty world. Trust played a part—in that he had mine.

A sure-to-god rarity.

When he finally strolled in, whistling off-key and twirling his keychain around his finger like a dickhead, I reluctantly pulled my gaze from my monitor.

"Is that from The Bombay Temple?" I eyed the outline of the containers inside the plastic bag he carried. The scent of garlic and spices, a combination I had a weakness for, tickled my senses. My stomach grumbled, loud and obnoxious.

"Hey, brother, how's everything? Great, Rowan, thanks for asking." He rolled his eyes as he made his way towards the table. "Did you eat at all today?"

I kept my mouth shut, knowing that other than my egg-and-bacon sandwich that I'd wrestled together this morning, I'd relied on caffeine for sustenance. But even that had dried up. I'd finished inhaling the two-litre thermos I'd made this morning a couple of hours back.

"Right, step away from your mother ship, get your arse to the table, and eat."

Tension stiffened my muscles. No way could I leave, not with so much uncertainty. Then there was Flynn to consider.

"Rowan, life as we know it isn't going to collapse if you step away for half an hour."

"It might," I grumbled, but I got moving. The

sooner I inhaled the bhajis and what I hoped was chicken tikka masala, the sooner I could continue.

Vinnie ignored me, dishing up our food onto the plates he collected from the kitchen space in the far back area of the large warehouse.

At the last second, I swiped my phone and turned up the volume on the channel attached to the comms unit Flynn tended to use.

I received an arched brow for my less-than-subtle efforts, but Vinnie simply grinned at me when I sat at the table opposite him.

"Smells good. Thanks."

Vinnie had always stepped up and looked out for me despite my protests. Since the attack that caused my injuries, he'd been my constant support. Even when I grumbled and told him to rack off—admittedly when I'd been at my lowest, the pain almost too much to live with—he'd shown up.

Constantly.

Unwavering in his care. And fuck if I didn't love him all the more for it.

But for a while there, he'd been close to smothering me. And I understood why, as much as it had infuriated me. The past couple of years, he'd finally eased off.

No longer did he check in three times a day. Hell, he no longer called me every day. It was a win.

And despite my complaining and the occasional glimpse of sadness he wasn't fast enough to smooth over when he looked at me, I was grateful to have him.

I was even more grateful for the curry.

Having demolished half of my meal, barely chewing in my hunger, I finally glanced across at Vinnie, whose gaze was already on me.

I paused, knowing that look. "What?" I put down my fork and took the reprieve to chug water from the glass Vinnie had passed me.

"I heard about the explosion over at NexChem. You know anything about that?"

Of course he had.

As the city's fire chief, Vinnie would have been kept in the loop when it came to an explosion that size.

"Apparently, the SICB was involved. A few injuries." His quirked brow let me know he was onto me. "One name jumped out at me in particular...." He trailed off, losing some of his amused arrogance and switching to concern. "Is he okay?"

A huff of breath punched out of me. How could I be pissed off when Vinnie was worried?

Truth was, Vinnie knew about my fixation. He'd never held back his concern. But he also knew me.

Understood how I'd left the warehouse a grand total of seven times over the past three years.

The hermit status was my choice.

Was it because of the extent of my injuries? Partly. There was little point bullshitting anyone, including myself, about that.

But also, here in the confines of my workspace, in arm's reach of technology that could be used as a key to unlock any information in the world, I could make a difference.

That I'd ended up immersed in all things Flynn along the way was just happenchance. I also knew Vinnie had hopes that this one-sided fixation I had would lead me back to society. To normality.

To some sort of happiness or some other bullshit feeling.

Telling him that it wouldn't happen grew more and more exhausting. It was easier to simply not respond.

That didn't stop me from blurting, "I spoke to him."

Vinnie's eyebrows shot high, and he jolted in his seat, sitting ramrod straight. "No shit? Damn, Row... that's—" He shook his head, struggling for words before continuing, "That's amazing. How was it? What did you say? Are you meeting up? What—"

"Fuck, Vin. Calm your shit. It wasn't me asking him for a date." But fuck, did I want to. What would I give to meet Flynn in the flesh?

The vision of him recoiling from me shut that thought down, and nausea formed deep in my gut.

I wouldn't be able to handle his horror.

Nor his pity.

"But still...." A smile formed, wide-open excitement peering back at me through his flinty ice-green eyes that were the exact same shade as mine. "It's a start, and the other questions still stand."

Knowing he wouldn't let this go without me offering something, I channelled calm disinterest. It would be easy to let the bubble of emotion I always felt deep in my chest when I thought of Flynn escape and shine through my words.

"He's injured but is safe, and he'll heal."

Vinnie flicked out his hands with a "that's it?" gesture.

"Fucking hell." I tilted my head left to right, the crack of my bones easing some of the tension in my shoulders. I ignored the pinch of discomfort as I angled to the left—the scarred skin travelling from my right pec, up my shoulder, and halfway up my neck before jumping to my chin and up to my cheekbone. It was a familiar ache.

Didn't mean it stopped a flare of emotion from trying to break the surface every time the pain reminded me of what I'd been through.

"He figured out it was me without me even saying who I was."

Eager for me to continue, Vinnie sat forwards, chin on his hands as he settled his elbows on the table—our half-eaten meals momentarily forgotten.

When I didn't speak immediately, he asked, "That has to mean something, right?"

"What, that an unknown voice appearing in his ear must be his stalker?"

"Well, if the shoe fits." He bounced his brows, having far too much fun with this development. "And you admitting you're stalking him—" An exaggerated sniff followed as he wiped away a fake tear. "—I'm proud of you, little Row. Acceptance is the right path to something or other. A restraining order, probably."

I flipped him off, and he burst out laughing.

The thing was, he wasn't wrong. Instead, the wrongness of it all sat completely on my shoulders. But it wasn't like I wanted to kidnap the guy.

Far from it.

I wanted to—hell, *needed* to protect him.

Was I going about it in a way that was slightly

psycho? Sure, but I never said I was perfect or even completely hinged.

Vinnie's laughter petered out. When concern morphed his features, I wished he'd continued to laugh his arse off at me.

"Don't you think it's time to either tell him who you are or perhaps let him go?"

Ice-cold fear caught my breath. Neither of those outcomes was acceptable.

At my lack of response, Vinnie's brows dipped further. He didn't need me to vocalise my "Fuck no."

"You know I love you. I'm just worried."

I eyed the fridge, considering grabbing a beer. Maybe vodka would be better.

"Rowan."

I reluctantly made eye contact with him. "Just drop it, yeah?" When Vinnie parted his lips to speak, I quickly said, "Tell me about your date last night instead." I scrunched my nose, adding on, "But not any sordid details, because gross."

An amused snort escaped him, and I relaxed, knowing he was letting me have the out. "All good until that Tim from the printers rocked up with his mum or aunt or something and gave me shit for not calling him back."

Amused and grateful for the distraction, I added a titbit. "You mean *Tom* from *the bowling alley*."

"Fuck, that's it. Tom." My brother snorted again, not looking the least bit guilty. "That explains why he threw my whiskey at me when I called him Tim."

I burst out laughing, quickly controlling the stretch of my lips to stop the pull of my irreparable skin.

"Who fucking wastes a good whiskey like that? And dramatic much?"

My laughter trickled away. "For sure, but if you will leave a trail of broken hearts...," I teased.

"Jesus, now I know you're even more full of shit than usual. Every hookup, I spell it out, letting them know there'll be no callbacks."

His words sobered me up. "We're a pair, huh?" Sadness for my brother going through life this way pierced my chest. Sure, there was a whole pot-and-kettle situation going on here, but seven years ago, Vinnie had been engaged and absolutely up for a forever kind of love.

Six months into their engagement, an explosion at a local distillery had changed all that for Vinnie. Five firefighters had been lost to the blaze. The thought of Vinnie being killed on the job had been too much for

Lee, his ex-fiancé, to deal with, so he broke it off. Since then, Vinnie refused to even consider settling down.

And sure, living a life of freedom without relationship restraints worked well for lots of people. But it was not my brother's MO. Despite how he'd been trying to convince himself otherwise—that he didn't want the whole wedding band and cubs thing—he wasn't built for a solitary life.

He deserved more. Deserved to have the dream he'd once so desperately wanted.

"That we are." Vinnie tapped his water glass to mine, pulling me from my thoughts. "Now finish up before your curry goes stone cold."

An hour later, Vinnie left, having kept me distracted enough to stay at the table with him.

The whole time, my phone and the comms remained inactive. While that should have been reassuring, all it did was put me on edge.

Another couple of hours passed by, and it was creeping close to ten in the evening.

The chilly air had me tugging on a hoodie, and I contemplated finding the crappy electric heater. An incoming alert stopped me. Trapped my breath in my lungs.

The particular secure messaging app I used for exchanges with Flynn was solely for us. Not only was it not available on the market, since I was the creator, but only I could determine when he could access it.

And apparently, I'd forgotten to switch off his access rights when I'd remotely installed the app to his new phone he'd organised a couple of hours ago.

I never forgot.

Shoving away exactly how dangerous it was to mess up like that, I opened the app.

AGENTTECH:
Can we talk?

My gaze danced over his words, my breathing picking up speed at the thought of talking to him again. At hearing his voice in conversation.

```
SPARKLESORCERER:
I don't think that's a
good idea.
```

Already in deep, opening the channels for more spelled disaster. A hyperbole, sure, but every day, I broke the law. Every day, I pushed boundaries. Both could get me landed in prison.

The likelier outcome would be for me to wind up dead.

AGENTTECH:
Please.

Fuck.

AGENTTECH:

I've been able to get
away with not answering
questions today, but as
soon as tomorrow's
mission is over, all
hints of leniency will
be over. The ITU are my
team. My family. I don't
want to keep lying to
them.

Tilting my head back, I froze halfway, remembering the action didn't come without a boatload of pain. I heaved a sigh, returning my attention to the app and Flynn's words.

AGENTTECH:

I'd also like to be able
to say thank you. You
saved us all back there.

You, I thought. My concern had all been for him. *Liar.*

Calling myself out sucked. Since Flynn cared so much for Kent, and her being killed would have hurt him, I grudgingly admitted I wanted her safe too.

The hell was Flynn doing to me?

I'd watched the man from afar for almost a year, never stepping close to his orbit.

It had been safe.

I had been careful.

And then along came that fucker Hornell. Sure, I'd known what the man had been up to. I had been quietly investigating and, every now and then, loudly burning a part of his operation to ashes. I'd never been close enough to take the man down despite the fact that the pain that plagued me daily was the driving force for me to do just that.

I wanted to turn him to cinders. For his world to go up in flames.

And it would. Somehow, some way, I'd make it happen.

When he'd moved against the SICB, I could have happily watched it play out with a smile on my face. My allegiance to the government had at one time been unwavering, a bond forged through years of dedication and sacrifice. I'd given everything to them... until that had no longer been enough, and instead, they'd taken everything from me.

Including the skin from my flesh.

The government's... *Prince's* betrayal had been branded in burns and blood on my skin. The bitter taste of their deceit and their treachery could never be erased.

It powered my reason to get up every day. Pushed me to do better. Be better.

While I didn't always actively fight against the SICB, corruption was like jagged tentacles latching on to as much goodness and honesty as it could. It turned Hornell. Took Prince. Nearly destroyed me.

That had been until clever, talented Flynn was pulled into the investigation linked directly to the man who'd orchestrated my demise.

Hornell.

When that had happened, no way could I have not helped, not worked alongside the bureau I'd promised to allow to disintegrate as I lanced the infected—the corrupt.

Not that I'd given them all the answers.

I refused to bend that far.

As far as I was concerned, all government-led agencies were responsible for so much of my pain. My loss.

And after the attack, they'd wiped their hands of me, burying anything related to Rowan Hart under the proverbial rug.

Each time I felt compelled to help Flynn—more specifically, the SICB, since that was who he worked for—burned me. It sliced a sliver of self-loathing into my skin.

But still, I couldn't stop.

With a shaky hand, I lifted my phone, exiting the app. I opened a different app, worked through the security encryption, and punched in Flynn's digits.

One ring and the call picked up.

Silence, then a shaky "Hello?"

The thundering of my heart filled my ears, but I'd be able to hear Flynn's voice even in the loudest of spaces.

A breathy, whispered "Is that you?" followed.

His words cut through the chaos of my mind like a beacon in the night, a melody during a deafening storm.

Powerless to do anything beyond speak, I closed my eyes, gruffly saying, "It's me."

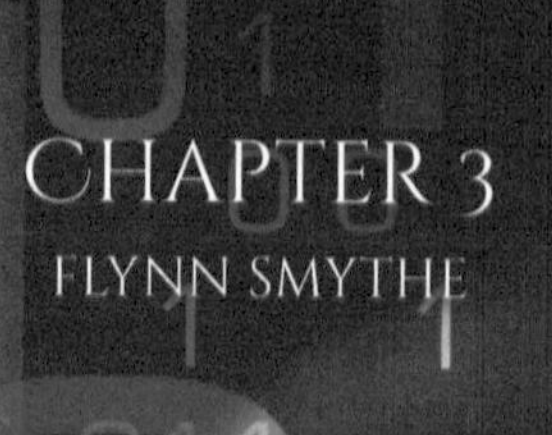

CHAPTER 3
FLYNN SMYTHE

IT WAS A STRUGGLE TO CONTROL MY BODY'S reaction, let alone organise my thoughts.

He called me.

And not just because he was saving my life.

And holy shit, by the way... the unicorn hacker really was a *he*.

From the moment I'd heard his voice through the ringing in my ears and the pain pummelling my body, a zap of awareness had broken through it all. Somehow I'd known the unknown raspy voice was his.

"Hey." My throat thickened, nerves clogging my throat. I quickly cleared it. "You called," I stated, immediately rolling my eyes at myself.

Fortunately, my apartment had no cameras, so he couldn't see how flustered I was.

Although....

I darted my gaze to my computer system. It remained unplugged—just one of many precautions I took with technology.

"I did."

The deep gruffness of his voice was an inexplicable pull, raspy and sexy as hell and oh so ridiculously alluring that I wanted to roll around in the sound. How two simple words had the ability to send vibrations skittering down my spine boggled my tired brain.

"Are you really okay?"

Four more words, and I sank down onto my mattress and closed my eyes, actively ignoring the bolt of pain from my bruised ribs.

"I am. Thanks to you."

"I should have been paying better attention. I should have spotted the device being set.... Prevented him from doing it in the first place."

His voice was gravel, his words threatening to unravel me with their protective growl.

Why the hell was that so hot?

I did not need protection.

If we ignored today and how I nearly got blown up. But I could handle myself. Had trained long and hard to ensure that was the case.

"You saved me and Kent. Even her arsehole sister."

I swallowed hard, trying to push away all the thoughts racing around my mind. But it was hard.

I'd suspected he'd been looking out for me. Of course I did. But his words made it sound like he thought I was his responsibility. I just had no idea why that was the case.

A frustrated grunt filtered through the phone. "And you got what you needed from her."

An absolute statement that made my lips twitch.

This was so, so bad. The effect he had on me. How all reason fled out the window when he consumed my thoughts. And now that I'd heard his voice and had a full-on conversation with him, my reason had grown wings and disappeared into the ether.

The likelihood of me getting it back was slim.

"For this case, yes," I responded, even though he didn't need the confirmation.

"That's good. And you'll then be reassigned. Not work the bullshit Seraphina Kent's caught up in."

"Uhm... no. The whole team will work on that as soon as everyone is back tom—" I clamped my mouth shut. Spilling the ITU's secrets was a sure way to get me fired.

In truth, all that had happened—the exchanges so far—was already grounds for a whirlwind of shit from the SICB.

"Which you know I already suspected, so it's not like you're revealing anything here I couldn't have confirmed with a few clicks."

"How do you do that?" The question was out there before I could stop it. The reverence in my tone, the absolute admiration, shouldn't be etched into every syllable. But there was so much about the enigma of a man on the other end of the call that destroyed every wall I'd painstakingly built up to protect myself.

What made it worse was the lack of self-preservation. And I still didn't know who he was or even his name.

The need, the desire to have those two questions answered were coiled springs just waiting to be released.

Rather than responding with an explanation, he took me by surprise, saying, "You didn't go to Kent's place after work."

Confused, my brow furrowed. "Why would I go to Kent's?"

He didn't respond immediately, giving me time to consider why he'd asked. What he was getting at.

Kent had wanted me to head home with her, it was true. Was that what he meant?

Even when she'd shot me that intense stare of hers

and insisted Jada was worried and didn't want me to be alone, I hadn't buckled.

It would be too easy to rely on them. But after twenty-four years, some habits were harder to break than others. Relying on myself just one of many.

"I'm going to be okay." While I wasn't sure that was what he meant, from the heavy silence, I suspected it was. "I'll be sore for a while, but my brain and fingers are still fully functioning. It just means I'll not do my gruelling runs in the morning."

Maybe there was a positive to the throbbing pain in every limb and muscle of my body after all.

Nothing but soft breaths filtered through the line. He was preparing to drop the call.

The knowledge formed a ball of tightness in my gut. I wasn't ready to say goodbye. "I'm pleased you finally reached out to me."

Heat burned my cheeks, mortification like an oncoming freight train threatening to slam into me. Could I get any lamer?

Pleased you finally reached out to me. Who said shit like that, as though this was a guy I'd been flirting with, and we'd finally reached the point of catching up and organising a date?

"I'll be in touch."

I parted my lips to respond, but the line going dead simply left me gaping.

"Fuck." Wiping a hand over my face, I grunted at the ache in my shoulder. The jolt of pain cleared my head and settled the uncoiling awareness that had been upsetting my stomach since the moment I'd heard his voice.

I still had no idea what to tell the team tomorrow.

I'd been given a free pass with all that had unfolded today. That pass would be taken away as soon as I set foot in the office. Or at least after the BloodRush op was over. Honestly, I still wasn't sure why I'd been let off the hook for the rest of the afternoon.

The fuck was I going to do?

***

DRAGGING MY BUTT OUT OF BED HAD ALMOST buckled my knees. It would have if the thought of falling hadn't made me break into a sweat.

There was only so much a human body could take.

I should have stayed in bed.

Should have disappeared into the welcoming abyss of sleep and kept my head buried in the proverbial sand for a few more hours.

None of my team would have, though. By now,

they'd likely be healed and ready to jump into the next fray. The frustration and joy of being human remained a complex balance.

This morning, frustration tipped the scales.

With two sets of eyes staring me down, it seemed that even my eyeballs ached. But I couldn't close my eyes.

There was no looking the other way, not when Kent and Lucas waited for my response.

The vibration of my phone was less than subtle, not when it was two vampires staring at me.

I should have turned the thing off.

Kent's eyebrow quirked high, and I swallowed hard.

She knew, because of course she did.

"I think you should check that."

Sensible enough not to argue with her or plead ignorance—there was no point after she'd witnessed my reaction to the message I received yesterday—I tugged my new phone out of my pocket.

A glance showed me a message waiting to be read on the secure app. A second glance at Kent told me I needed to stop dithering.

After I passed the security checks, a single message waited for me.

```
UNICODESPARKLES:
Make sure to answer
that.
```

A heavy thud punched against my chest. I jerked my attention up, aware my bosses would hear my speeding pulse. Plus, no doubt my expression said it all.

I was fucked.

The central monitor on the wall of screens in the large war room flickered to life, capturing all our attention. A second later, a notification alerted us of an incoming call.

"Smythe."

I snapped my focus to Kent, wincing at the stern tone. She was going to kick my arse before I was escorted from the building. No doubt about it.

A pang of regret tightened my gut.

She'd never forgive me. And I got it. Betrayal stung, and in our line of work, it could cost someone their life.

"I'm so sorry. He said we need to pick up."

Lucas's head shifted just so, letting me know he'd registered the pronoun.

"Go ahead," he directed, his voice eerily calm.

With a surprisingly steady hand, I connected the incoming call and held my breath, just waiting to hear *his* voice and wondering how long it would be before I was fired.

It didn't matter that the BloodRush case had been carried out successfully and without casualties and that Chris and the other field agents had finally returned to base an hour ago. My win wouldn't save me from the mountain of shit I suspected I'd drown in.

"The lion you brought in, Marlow Prince... Hornell is his custodian."

A wave of astonishment surged through the room at the words shared through the speakers, its electrifying energy gripping me. I reared back, unable to contain my reaction as my gaze shot to Kent.

Just catching her raised eyebrows before they settled, Kent's face once again a mask of indifference, I focussed on Lucas.

Despite the revelation hanging in the air like an unexpected thunderclap, the magnitude of the hacker's words didn't seem to have breached Lucas's calm façade. As always, he exuded serenity—a heck of a talent considering his position. But that was the thing about Agent Lucas: he emanated strength and composure—often in a world of chaos—that I envied.

"You're the creator of the Mirrormat coding." A flick of his gaze to me accompanied Lucas's statement. He didn't wait for confirmation before he continued,

"Can you explain to me the link between Prince and Hornell?"

There was no need to add that we hadn't discovered this titbit.

Meanwhile, I focussed on calming my racing heart and concentrating on the intel. This was big. Huge, in fact.

Any kind of lead on Hornell took all precedence. The involvement of Seraphina and Marlow skyrocketed this information to a whole new level.

I didn't need Kent, who was wound up like a tightly compressed line of code beside me, to tell me that.

"Check the Desert Sandfire file."

Kent's fingers flew across the screen as Lucas said, "I've never—"

"That's because any reference to the black op was erased," the hacker explained.

"But you have the files?" Lucas clarified.

"And now so do you," the unicorn stated, his tone matter-of-fact.

"Got it." A final click from Kent and multiple screens filled with documentation relating to the operation, one I'd never heard of before. But why would I have, since every page on the screen was tagged Top Secret? And apparently had been wiped from the

SICB's database.

"Open the file on Rostrine," the hacker directed, and almost instantly, the document opened.

An image of Marlow Prince appeared on the screen, along with documentation.

"Prince was Hornell's past lieutenant's nephew." The detail spilled out of me as I read, but I continued to scan, shock reverberating through me the more I absorbed. "That can't be right." I shook my head, struggling to process the words in the file.

"Marlow Prince was pronounced dead during Sandfire. There's no mistake."

The certainty in the hacker's tone rang true. And for all the secrecy and the pile of dogshit I knew I was in, there was no need for me to doubt the man.

How my trust could already feel like steel was a concern for another day. Instead, I glanced at Lucas as he continued to scroll through the documentation and asked, "And there are no forgeries? This was confirmed?"

"Check the—"

"Lockwood file," Kent cut in. "Here."

Images of Marlow Prince flooded the screens again. What was left of his uniform was melted to his burned skin. But fire hadn't done the damage.

The fuck?

"So what are we talking here? Cloning, a walking, talking zombie who's shacking up with my sister, or what?"

Those thoughts bounced around in my brain, but there had to be a simpler explanation. "No siblings? Relations who look remarkably similar?"

"No. And the records are accurate."

"How can you be sure?" Lucas asked.

"Because I was with him when he died."

Surprise rippled around the room with crackling energy. What did this mean? Did the unicorn kill him? How was he involved? What—

"Prince was a double agent. His real allegiance was with Hornell."

My heart stuttered when I heard emotion in his tone.

Lucas, his unwavering gaze on the screens, no doubt absorbing as much of the information as possible, said, "The mission was preventing technology from being stolen."

"HelixGen," the unicorn confirmed. "Something the government has been working on for eight years. Genetic modification, gene editing, AI, and nanotech... with the add-on of cloning."

"They can do that?" Horror clung to my question.

"They couldn't three years ago, but it appears there've been some developments."

"And what went wrong?" The more information he read over, the more Lucas's jaw tightened.

"Hornell and Prince happened. The word is, the tech was destroyed in the blast that took out half of the town linked to the facility."

Kent brought up an image on the screen, and fresh horror formed in my chest.

The blast radius was huge. The aerial shot showed a small town, half destroyed by a crater, the other half charred and blackened. Another photo that held the remains of a concrete building caught my attention. Debris littered the red soil. A fire had passed through, but the damage to the concrete confused me.

"What did that?" I asked.

"Xenonite." Gruffness filled his tone, a rumbling sound vibrating through the speakers.

The hairs on my arms stood on end. He was a shifter. The tone, the vibrations told me as much.

"Xenonite?" Lucas shook his head and shot a questioning look at Kent, who shrugged.

"Its properties are unique. It's a highly reactive and corrosive substance. It burns like acid, and when combined with eradion.... Well, you can see the impact it has. The destruction it can cause."

Icy dread coursed through my veins. Was the government responsible for this compound? Why the fuck would they create such a thing?

"How has none of this got out?" Even though I asked, I suspected I knew the answer.

"The government did what it does best. Covers up their fuck-ups and erases them from history." His anger was palpable.

And fuck, did I get it.

It wasn't lost on me that he'd still gathered this non-existent information. But more than that....

There was no controlling my pulse.

Both Kent's and Lucas's gazes darted to me. I stared back wide-eyed before bolting to a terminal and sending my fingers flying over the keyboard.

He'd been there. Was involved. He'd worked for the government.

Though I was aware Lucas carried on talking to the unicorn—his attention never wavering from the screen as he closely watched what I was doing—I tuned everyone out. With my heart in my throat and my ears buzzing with adrenaline, it took every ounce of control I had to filter through the information.

My gaze danced over records. Over images. Over the list of personnel, of agents. Of deaths, of injuries, of—

My breath caught.

Arctic-jade eyes captured me and held me hostage with their intensity.

Intellect shone brightly, and despite the full lips set in a firm line, those eyes told me everything.

Humour. Lightness. A warmth that contradicted the cool colour of the irises. The man—the tiger— almost came to life with the joy radiating from him. How the hell that was possible from a photograph was unfathomable, but I knew it to be true.

Knew it was him.

"Rowan Hart." The whispered words, both reverent and shocked, pushed past my lips.

The room stilled. The voices cut off the instant his name escaped.

"It's you. Rowan Hart." I swallowed thickly, not even wincing at the loud click of my dry throat. "You're the associate deputy director of the Alliance Division." The speed of my pulse accelerated.

Alliance? Who the fuck are they?

The silence continued. One beat. Two. All the way to five before Lucas's steady voice shattered it. "You're with the Alliance?"

Startled, I looked in my boss's direction. For the first time in the months I'd known him, Lucas appeared to struggle with words, to know how to respond.

But one thing was clear: he'd heard of the Alliance Division, something neither Kent nor I was privy to, if I read her expression clearly.

"I was before they wrote me off after Sandfire, then tried to pin the fallout on me rather than Prince and Hornell."

My brain scrambled to understand.

There was a government agency I'd never heard of? Even as the question formed, I cringed.

Of course there was. Our unit was the living, breathing example of how government agencies liked to keep units and task forces off the books.

I parted my lips, ready to fire off questions, but was stopped by Lucas asking, "Hornell was responsible for the catastrophe of Sandfire?" He turned to me, and I froze. "That's why you reached out and supported us last year, because of the link to Hornell?"

Something lingered in Lucas's gaze that I couldn't read.

Rowan's hesitation, the long beat he took before saying, "That is why I chose to assist," helped me understand Lucas's expression.

He thought there was more to it than Hornell.

And from the way he scrutinised me, I suspected he thought I was the reason.

Confusion bubbled to life, mixing with inappropriate amusement.

How? Why?

This had nothing to do with me.

Yes, Rowan had reached out to me and, for whatever reason, continued to maintain loose contact, but...

Why had I been the one person he reached out to? Something I should have questioned a long time ago, but fuck if my techie crush had allowed me to.

"I'd like for us to meet. Somewhere sec—"

"Not going to happen."

Lucas's fingers twitched, the only tell that he was frustrated at being cut off by Rowan.

"We can be somewhere secure. Help each other finally take Hornell down once and for all. That's something you want. Something we all want." As Lucas spoke, he glanced at Kent and nodded. A silent conversation later, she focussed on the keyboard.

"No."

Disappointment twisted my stomach. I could understand it, though. His refusal.

While I knew nothing about the Alliance, based on the documentation I'd read and what Rowan had shared about how he'd been treated, his reticence and outright "no" when it came to having anything to do with a government organisation made sense.

But why, then, after we lost sight of Hornell, had he continued to make contact with me specifically?

"Just me. Meet with me." The words rushed out of me, my eyes wide and breathing heavy.

Lucas's "No" and incredulous look were overshadowed by Kent's "No fucking way."

But I didn't stop. "Yes. Meet me. Somewhere secure. You can even give me a moment's notice so that you know we won't have time to set up surveillance."

I was so getting fired for this. But just the thought of meeting Rowan, having my eyes on him, it was pure need. A desperation that was worrying and dangerous.

What was worse, the urge to meet him face to face had nothing to do with strengthening an alliance. Nothing to do with taking down Hornell.

I couldn't even bullshit myself.

I turned to Lucas and held his gaze. "This could work. The last tip"—I winced—"*every* tip came from Rowan."

I felt Kent's eyes on me, felt her hard stare burning into me, but I didn't dare look. Her disappointment was more than I could handle. Shame bloomed in my chest, warming my neck and my cheeks. But it wasn't enough to stop me from pleading my case.

"Please let me do this. The closest we've ever come is because of Rowan. We need him on this."

Movement out of the corner of my eye drew my attention to Kent.

Fuck.

She stared at me like I'd taken a dagger to her. Like I'd cut her deep. Like I was someone she didn't trust.

Emotion clogged my throat. "I'm sorry I didn't tell you. I know not opening up is unforgiveable. I wasn't trying to betray yo—"

"Stop." Her tone was sharp enough to cut glass. In the blink of an eye, her expression shifted. The hurt erased from her face, and then she looked away, her attention moving to Lucas.

I held my breath, more than aware Rowan remained silent, listening to every one of our exchanges. No doubt he heard the edge of desperation in my request too.

"Hart." Lucas's voice was tight. "You appear to have built some sort of trust with Agent Smythe. Meeting with him could extend that trust so we can support each other with our search for Hornell and finally take him down."

"I can find him myself. I don't need bureau support."

My chest squeezed. If I'd thought Lucas's tone had

been strained, it was nothing compared to Rowan's. Any tighter and it would snap.

"For three years you've had no success by yourself."

"And for years the government just seems to be gifting Hornell all the tech he needs to continue whatever fucked-up plan he's focussed on." Rowan's tone was all bite. "Give me one good reason why I should align myself with a government agency."

"Beyond that it's what you've been doing for the past few months?" Lucas answered smoothly. "I'll give you two."

I held my breath, anticipation pulsing through my veins.

"One, we're clearly not getting results by remaining divided. Logically, joining forces could ensure we get real results by not relying on fragmented tips and hints."

I clamped my mouth shut. If only Lucas knew about the riddles Rowan sent me. And if he discovered just how much I craved them and eagerly awaited the alert on my phone, there'd be no chance I'd be involved.

Honestly, that I remained standing and a part of this surprised the hell out of me.

"And the second?" Rowan asked.

Lucas nodded, his focus on the door. I followed his

gaze, my brow dipping in confusion at the man standing beside Michaels.

The two walked in, Michaels on high alert, and the.... My brain stumbled as I studied him. The shifter's focus was on me.

My skin prickled as I took in his tall form, his confident stride, and the huge-arse grin sent my way. But it was his eyes that had me catching my breath.

Ice green.

"Has just walked through the door. Chief Hart," Lucas welcomed, his hand outstretched to the tiger, "good of you to join us."

"Son of a bitch" filled the room, tearing through the speakers.

If Chief Hart—I glanced at the insignia on his chest—the city's firefighting chief, no less, was surprised by the outburst or the fact that it was his brother's—I assumed—voice through the speaker, he didn't show it. Instead, he shook Lucas's hand, his friendly smile not dropping.

"Agent Lucas. I was going to ask about the invite to join you, but"—he glanced over at me—"I don't expect it'll take much to figure things out. Not with... Agent Smythe, isn't it? Not with you on board."

He stepped towards me, palm held out.

Startled, it took me a beat to react. I reached out

and shook his hand, examining his features and looking at the similarities between him and his brother. I'd only seen that one photograph, but I'd committed Rowan's face to memory.

"Chief Hart?" My training had fizzled away completely.

"Vinnie. Call me Vinnie." He released my hand. "It's good to finally meet you."

Finally? What the fuck is happening?

"For fuck's sake, Vinnie." Rowan sounded pissed.

Nothing but happy amusement poured off Vinnie as he threw me a wink. "You'll have to forgive my brother. He doesn't socialise much."

"I swear to fu—"

"Case in point." He turned his attention to Lucas, his body language shifting. I watched as the smile melted away, tension turning his large shoulders taut. "So, Agent Lucas, let me be crystal clear about something."

Lucas gave a subtle nod, letting Vinnie know he was listening.

"Hurt my brother in any way, bring any attention to him from anyone outside of this cosy unit you have here, and I'll show you the wide variety of ways fire can make a body disappear."

Holy shit.

But he wasn't finished.

"Rowan has been through hell—"

"Vinnie," Rowan cut in. "That's enough."

Vinnie ploughed on as though his brother hadn't spoken. "—all because of our fucked-up government. I will not allow him to be hurt again. It took me a long time to get a semblance of my brother back—"

"Vinnie. Please."

As Vinnie stopped speaking at the broken sound of Rowan's plea, my heart lurched.

What the hell had happened to Rowan?

Flashes of the images on the screen slammed into me. The destruction. The bodies. The burns—and not just by fire.

Dread unfurled in my gut.

Had Rowan been injured?

Prince's body—whatever version of him that was —painted a picture so harrowing, my stomach curdled.

I kept my gaze steady on his brother, respecting his words and his love. Even as I did, fresh shame threatened to overwhelm me, and I cast a look at Kent.

Her eyes were on me. Hard and unflinching.

I'd fucked up. So, so badly.

Would there be a way to get Kent's trust back?

CHAPTER 4

ROWAN HART

I CLOSED MY EYES AND COUNTED TO FIVE. When that didn't help, I continued to ten. The heavy thump of my heartbeat didn't slow or quieten down.

Defeated, I cracked my neck and continued to listen to the conversation between the full ITU, who'd since entered the room, and my interfering brother.

What the fuck had he been thinking?

A spike of heat stabbed at my gut, but I clenched my jaw, keeping my anger at bay.

The thing was, I didn't know who I was most livid with. Lucas, who'd clearly ordered Agent Michaels to bring my brother in; Kent for finding the information about my brother right under my nose; Vinnie for turning this whole thing around and making this absolutely about his mission to make me to get a life; or myself?

My money was on me.

I'd been so caught up in listening to Flynn, distracted enough to intervene—something I'd promised myself never to do—that I allowed myself to get completely swept up in the plan to take down Hornell.

The worst thing was, I'd given up my identity.

I couldn't even bullshit myself that I'd made a mistake.

The contents of the deleted Desert Sandfire file I knew inside and out. Could recite the documents word for word if pressed.

And when Flynn had said my name and figured out who I was with barely a moment to process, something inside me shifted. And since it wasn't like the tiger in me had a separate conscience or a mind of its own, the change was a loosening of the barbed-wire cage fixed in place around my heart.

Again... what the fuck had I been thinking?

"I think I should be there." While I couldn't see my brother, as I didn't have eyes on the space in the ITU facility the team referred to as the war room, I suspected he remained standing, arms folded, legs spread.

Sure, there was a trace of cordiality in his tone, the calm fire chief's voice I knew he pulled out when dealing with an unruly crowd, but the steel behind his suggestion indicated it was so much more than a hint.

"There's not going to be a meeting." Something I'd said several times in a whole manner of different ways, but each time it either fell on deaf ears or my brother piped up, disagreeing.

With the exception of Flynn. Twice he'd spoken up, making it clear we could continue interacting remotely. While it had been his suggestion, one I'd heard while sweat broke out on my brow despite the thrum of excitement that had fizzed to life in my gut, he'd changed his tune not long after meeting Vinnie.

Him standing up for me, backtracking, hell, protecting me, continued to send my mind spinning.

Why would he do that?

He was going to be in a whirlwind of trouble with his unit because of me. *I'd* reached out to him. *I'd* made the need for discretion clear. *I* was the pathetic arsehole who would be responsible for getting him fired.

"If he doesn't want to, we should respect—"

Flynn's words cut off, and I barely held back my groan of frustration. Not seeing what was going on set me on edge.

"There's going to be plenty of time for in-depth conversations about respect, Agent Smythe." Lucas's tone brooked no argument. And as far as I was aware, his pulling out "agent" meant Flynn would not get out of this without punishment.

Guilt sat heavily on my chest, making me wince.

I'd done this. So much for trying to protect the man.

"Sir, I'm sorry for—"

Lucas shut him down. "Now's not the time for this discussion, Agent Smythe."

There'd be no more counting to ten. Each trickle of worry for Flynn that sparked to life made my emotions more difficult to control.

"This is the deal," I gritted out, not giving myself time to pause and think my offer through. "Vinnie will bring Flynn to a location I decide upon. He will be your voice, your liaison. I don't give a shit what his official role will be called, beyond the fact that he will be the only person I see and speak to—"

"I'm not sure that's feasible."

"In that case, Agent Lucas, it's in your best interest to send my brother on his way and forget the two of us ever existed."

Not that I'd be able to do the same.

"But we'll need to discuss strategy, work things out as a team. We'll need open communication at least."

Lucas, for whatever reason, was showing his hand, letting me know just how important it was to take Hornell down. That I felt the same didn't matter. That I knew it made logical sense to work as a unit to finally put down the man responsible for not only my injuries but the death of six good agents was inconsequential.

I wouldn't do any of it without Flynn.

The thought petrified me even as a spark of adrenaline flooded my system.

I chose my words carefully. "That can happen with the proviso that Agent Smythe doesn't receive an official reprimand for receiving my communication."

I was sure as shit that I heard a sound escape Flynn. Not for the first time, I wished I had eyes inside the meeting room. Being blind had already resulted in one near miss, and while I had my ways to infiltrate the impossible, some spaces remained impenetrable.

"That's not something—"

"Then I'll be working alone."

Cutting Agent Lucas off probably wasn't the best way to win him over, but I wasn't there to make friends.

"Agent Lucas." Vinnie sliced through the tense silence, his voice cheery and carefree—completely at odds with the strain I could imagine on the agents' faces. "My brother's the best at what he does. Hell, I don't have a clue about most of the shit he creates, let alone works on, and I suspect it's safer that way. What I also know is that Agent Smythe will be safe with Row, and if you want to... well, to wrap up whatever you have going on here, Rowan is your only safe bet."

A stony silence followed, though my racing pulse filled my ears with a heavy, erratic sound.

When Agent Lucas finally said, "Hornell needs to be brought in, his operations closed down... with no chance of reactivation. If you do your part in making that happen, we have a deal," heat slammed into me.

This was really happening.

"'Brought in' doesn't necessarily mean with a heartbeat, right?" Michaels inquired, beating me to saying something similar.

Hearing Lucas's sigh, I smirked. Michaels could be a loose cannon. I grudgingly respected that.

"A heartbeat is preferable but not essential," Lucas responded, the strain in his voice impossible to ignore. "Okay, let's make this happen."

With unsteady fingers, I shot Vinnie a message.

None of this was how I envisioned taking Hornell out. It absolutely wasn't how I'd intended to meet Flynn. A cold sweat broke out on my forehead.

The reality was, I never intended to meet Flynn. Already I could visualise his reaction to me.

I swallowed hard, fresh nausea swirling in my gut as a familiar chill crept down my spine.

The only way I could get through this and remain intact was to be indifferent. Stay impartial. It didn't matter that I'd done a shit job of that so far.

Readying myself as I shot off instructions to Vinnie, I pulled forth tendrils of barbed wire, hardened by fear and the need to survive, curling them around my heart. They settled against my scars, armed and ready to protect.

Fortifying my expectations, I layered them with caution and a healthy dose of reality, bracing for inevitable disappointment. Anything less was unfair to Flynn.

I'd dragged him into this. Not only that, but I knew—deny it all I liked, I fucking *knew*—we'd started to build something dangerous in our communication.

The photograph he saw, the person he would believe me to be, that man had died in betrayal and fire. My scars ran too deep, the wounds too raw for me to ever be *Agent* Rowan Hart again.

It didn't matter how much I wanted to know Flynn; after this assignment, I would need to let him go.

"You're not Batman."

Not for the first time, I wiped my hand over my face, wondering why my parents hadn't had him adopted.

"Ooh... I am vengeance. I need to stay in the shadows. Grr... argh."

"You can leave any time you want, Vinnie."

Admittedly, his ridiculous commentary distracted me from pacing, but Flynn and I were meeting in approximately five minutes, and pacing helped me not to come out of my skin.

"As if you'd still be here if I wasn't involved."

I didn't need to look to know he rolled his eyes at me. He was also right.

We were at one of my safe houses. My brother only knew about two of the four of them. Not that it mattered, because as soon as this was over and Hornell was in the ground, I'd let this place go.

I couldn't keep this facility once it was compromised.

Flicking my gaze to the wall of monitors, I stopped in my tracks. Flynn's SICB-issued SUV would be pulling up in the front in three minutes.

"Just breathe."

Hating that I needed a reminder, I did just that, even as I backed up towards the far wall. In the shadows.

Fuck my brother for being right.

"Flynn—"

"Smythe," I corrected on instinct, not pulling my attention away from the screen.

"Smythe," Vinnie said, all signs of humour long gone. "You chose him for a reason. So keep trusting your gut."

"'Cause that worked out so well for me th—"

"Rowan, knock it the fuck off."

I gritted my teeth.

"Stop with this shit, get your arse over here, and give the guy some credit. A bat cave sounds all cool and shit, but not for you."

The shift in his tone grabbed my attention.

A flare of guilt bubbled to life in my chest. Vinnie put up with a lot of shit from me, and while he joked about the whole bat cave thing and me hiding in the shadows, that was exactly what I'd done.

"If you won't do it for you, do it for me."

I stared at him, somehow not flinching at the pleading look in his eyes that matched his tone. "Fuck."

"And yes, I suppose for a little bit of vengeance,

since this dickwad you're after needs to pay, but mainly for me because you love me and I'm the best brother ever."

I parted my lips, but the perimeter alarm sounded, announcing Flynn's arrival.

"Now, play nice. I'll let him in."

Wide-eyed, I watched Vinnie's retreating back. Panic kicked up my pulse, and the muscle beneath my eye spasmed. The pinch of my skin reminded me exactly why we were here.

This couldn't be about my fascination with Flynn. This was about closure. It had to be.

I stepped out of the shadows clinging to the back wall and moved to the bank of monitors and computers. The stark light pressed down on me, threatening to steal my breath—and my resolve.

Locking my legs, I stood firm, picking up my digital pad as soon as I heard voices—needing something in my hands to help stop the trembling.

"...off the beaten track," my brother said, and I barely held back my groan when I finally caught on. "Totally worth it for the hot pants."

"That sounds... interesting."

That voice.

How could I not be drawn to the sweet hint of amusement wrapped up in warmth? I closed my eyes for the barest of seconds, needing a moment to centre myself.

"It makes for the best night out. But anyhow, Agent Smythe," Vinnie said, and I heard the smile in his tone, "let me finally introduce you to my brother, Rowan Hart."

A scuffle of feet and I opened my eyes.

Warm brown eyes connected with mine. The instant they did, a flush took over Flynn's skin, and his cheeks lifted, his gaze brightening. I couldn't pull away, not even for a second, to confirm his smile was as incredible in real life as it was when I observed through a screen.

With unwavering focus, Flynn stepped forwards, leaving Vinnie's side. "Agent Hart."

"Row," I croaked, mortified by the break in my voice. "Call me Row."

He stopped before me, his gaze intent, small creases forming at the corners of his eyes. "Row."

Jesus. I wanted to wrap myself up in the sound of my name from his lips. Instead, I stood mutely before him, unable to look away. Light hazel flecks shimmered like golden threads woven into a tapestry.

How had I not noticed them before?

Countless hours—more than I was willing to admit —had been dedicated to studying his profile. While not a single second had been wasted, the photographs and the video footage didn't do the man justice.

"And now the formalities are out of the way."

I startled at the sound of Vinnie's voice, flinching when I realised I was holding Flynn's hand and stood there staring at him like an idiot.

When the hell had we touched?

Releasing his hand, I stepped back, mortified, my face blazing as I looked at Vinnie. Whatever he saw in my expression had his brows dipping, but it also got him moving.

He stepped up to Flynn's side, who I actively avoided looking at, keeping my damaged face away from him.

"How about I make coffee and you guys make a start? I suspect there's a lot to discuss about the case."

"Uhm… yes, absolutely, the case." Flynn cleared his throat.

Rather than looking at him, I angled towards my workstation. "I've set you up here." I directed him to the ergonomic chair to my left, a couple of metres from where my main console awaited me.

"Great, thanks." At Flynn's tentative tone, I held back my wince.

I'd made this awkward as fuck. Who the hell got so

transfixed by a guy's eyes that they lost sight of their actions, let alone the whole purpose of the meeting in the first place?

"So, coffee?" Vinnie clapped his hands, but no attempt at enthusiasm would be able to cut through my weirdness.

"I've already set out the Colombian blend and the hazelnut creamer."

Flynn froze at my words. His hand, outstretched towards the chair, hovered in the air. Instinctively, I glanced at him, wide-eyed as our gazes collided.

And then it happened.

His gaze drifted, reaching my damaged skin, lingering on my cheek, travelling a little lower to the ravaged remnants of unhealed wounds that no amount of shifter healing or medical intervention had been able to fix.

Throat thick with emotion, I waited for the moment. For the point where the gravity of the damage reflected in his expression.

The repulsion. If not that, then the distress. Though, more than likely, it would be pity.

But his gaze kept moving, hovering over my lips for a beat longer before it swept along my unmarred complexion on the left of my face. Once again, our gazes connected, and I held my breath, searching. Waiting.

And then he smiled, the action accentuating his strong jawline and the subtle dimples appearing right next to his lips. Genuine warmth lit his eyes, the hazel flecks capturing me so completely that, without a doubt, I knew I was royally fucked.

And from the sound of Vinnie's not-so-discreet chuckle as he walked away, he knew it too.

"Nice setup you have here."

Right. Work.

I latched on to the bone Flynn gifted me by ignoring the fact that I'd had his favourite coffee beans and creamer delivered. "Thanks. It should be enough for us to work together to follow some leads I've already been working on."

"Leads, huh?" He angled my way as he sat, looking so at home in the space that I mentally shook myself. "Plural, and since yesterday."

The teasing tone almost had me stumbling.

Fuck me dead.

This wasn't how it was supposed to go. It certainly wasn't how I'd intended to react.

Each taut length of the barbed wire around my heart already showed signs of rusting. Before long, it would turn brittle and snap, leaving me vulnerable.

The hell had happened to being indifferent?

"Right, so," I started and took the seat beside him, the couple of metres between us doing nothing to mute his fresh, masculine scent. Talk about distracting. "Based on the intel from Seraphina Kent, I found a link to Barrow Corp."

I pulled up the file I'd sourced.

"That's one of the labs the bureau took down last year. Not our division, though."

I bobbed my head, casting Flynn a quick glance. His focus remained on the screen between us, his eyes darting left to right as he read the information. "Before your time."

At my words, he stilled and darted his gaze at me. Unasked questions practically poured out of him. Most of which I suspected had jack shit to do with information on the screen. That meant I'd be staying far, far away from them.

I jerked my focus back to the information before us. "They're now operating under Kitsuma Corp."

This time when Flynn angled his chair to stare fully at me, I gave him my complete attention. Not a chance he or anyone in the ITU would have heard of the corporation. The reason I knew? Because they'd flown completely under the radar until approximately seven hours ago when I tracked them down.

"What do we know about them, and have you hacked their system yet?" A spark of excitement illuminated his features. The quickening of his breath preceded the slight widening of his eyes. But it was the barely perceptible grin tugging at the corners of his lips that held me spellbound.

"They're operating from New Zealand. The lab in Perth—"

"The one you gave me the intel on?" he asked, his gaze searching mine.

"Yeah." I fought hard not to shuffle under his scrutiny. "I found a link to them."

Flynn's brows shot high. "You're only just finding it now?"

Pressing my lips together, I arched my brow. It took less than two seconds for a flush to turn Flynn's cheeks red and for him to widen his eyes.

"Shit, I didn't mean.... I'm not saying...." He slammed his mouth closed, flustered and looking close to passing out. Before I could intervene, Flynn sat up straight. "I'm sorry. The truth is"—his flush deepened—"you're, well, you're the unicorn hacker."

Somehow, I held back the twitch of my lips even as embarrassment rolled off him.

"You're incredible. You created the Mirrormat

coding. You, well, you're the genius unicorn who knows how to get... everything."

"Please tell me you just referred to my brother as a magical unicorn."

We snapped our attention to Vinnie, who stood holding two coffee mugs and wore the most ridiculous big grin I'd ever seen.

"And I'm already regretting it and wishing I could turn back time," Flynn mumbled, the deep red in his cheeks too damn sexy for words. "I don't suppose that's something you can do yet?"

My pulse spiked when, despite his obvious mortification, his eye contact remained steady. "What, time travel?" Amusement coloured my words, and the fuck-face known as my brother all but snapped his neck with how quickly he jerked his head in my direction.

I pointedly ignored Vinnie.

"Time travel could save us a lot of problems. The first one would be everyone in this room forgetting the last four minutes."

"That sounds like a tragedy." My words spilled out, light and barely sounding like my own. The smirk accompanying them felt almost foreign.

When Flynn gulped hard, making an audible click that was loud to my sensitive hearing, I looked away. We needed to get back on track.

"I'm guessing this hazelnut creamer is yours, since Row takes his black."

I stared hard at the screen, refusing to glance at Flynn when he accepted his doctored coffee with a thanks. So what that I'd been doing a decent thing and ordered in the creamer I knew he liked. It was the right thing to do, since I'd dragged him into this partnership.

"So, if you're both good here...." Vinnie trailed off.

I bobbed my head and made eye contact with him, reading the multitude of unspoken questions in his gaze that he absolutely would be asking me once he had the opportunity. "Thanks, Vinnie. You know the protocol."

Rather than roll his eyes at me like he was prone to do, Vinnie nodded. "Absolutely." Sure, he liked to tease me about my security measures, but he still followed them to a T. "Agent Smythe—"

"Flynn or Smythe is good," he responded with a friendly smile.

Vinnie's gaze darted to me, and I held back from narrowing my gaze at him.

"Smythe," he opted on. *Sensible man.* "Good meeting you properly. You have my number, so you be sure to reach out if Row forgets to feed you while he's got you locked away."

I shot daggers at Vinnie, willing him to disappear.

While it was true that I regularly forgot to stop to eat when buried in a task, it didn't mean I couldn't look out for Flynn and do something simple like make sure he was fed while he was here.

Flynn chuckled. "I'm sure I'll be just fine. And good to meet with you too. I'm confident I'll see you around."

"You know it." Vinnie shook his hand, then headed to me. "Don't get up. I know whatever you're working on is important." He followed up with a kiss on the top of my head and a squeeze of my shoulder. "I'm on shift tonight for twenty-four hours."

"I know." As the chief, he never needed to pull twenty-four-hour shifts. Usually he was relegated to the office, pushing paperwork around the desk. But every month, he insisted on picking up two twenty-four-hour shifts, alternating between the ten fire and rescue stations he was responsible for.

Because of course he was that guy and liked to be in the thick of the action and have boots on the ground.

"Stay safe," I called out to his retreating back.

He flicked me a glance from over his shoulder and bobbed his head, not offering a smartarse remark. He knew better when it came to the reality of his job and his safety.

When the door closed behind him, the lock signalled, and the security sensors flashed and indicated where the movement was, monitoring his exit from the property and the perimeter.

"That's an impressive setup you have." Flynn studied the system and then leaned forwards a little. "Is that...?"

"Yes, and if you tell him, we're going to have some serious issues." I offered a half-smile to take the sting out of my words despite meaning every one.

That Agent Lucas had designed the next-gen security tech wasn't something I wanted to advertise. The vampire's skill set was seriously impressive. But... "I added a few changes, built in the ID software, and adapted the movement sensors a little."

Try as I might not to side-eye him, I couldn't resist.

Wide-eyed, Flynn turned his focus on me. Under his scrutiny, I held my breath, trying not to preen or shift uncomfortably at his attention.

I'd been showing off, clearly wanting a reaction from him, but unused to being under anyone's attention—beyond Vinnie's—it was hard not to crumble under the weight of his assessing gaze. Regardless of how impressed he appeared to be.

"That's...." He cleared his throat. "Your secret's

safe with me." He glanced away, turning his attention back to the data I shared.

"So Kitsuma," I began once Flynn had taken his first sip of coffee. *Work. This has to be about work.* "Here's everything I have."

I guided him through the information I'd tracked down. "They're a chemical distribution company and, on the surface, clean as a whistle. Licences, regulatory compliance, permits, everything. They legit supply chemicals to various industries. It's an operational cover for some seriously shady shit. Their servers were a bitch to hack. There's a maze of encrypted files still to work through."

I danced my cursor across the screen, indicating which files Flynn should take a look at.

"Sounds like a fun afternoon."

Hearing Flynn's genuine enthusiasm, I side-eyed him, struggling to pull my attention away from his quirked lips and the eager way he leaned towards the screens.

I'd already known he lived for this shit. But seeing it up close and personal threatened to push my interest in him into even more dangerous territory.

"It looks like a maze in here." He flicked his attention to me, and I froze, caught red-handed. Rather than call me out, he grinned. "Looks like off-the-grid

communication. Have you been using Mirrormat—"
He cut off when I shook my head.

"I deleted the coding."

His brows jerked so high, it was a struggle not to snort at the shock on his expression.

"You did what?"

I shifted in my seat, uncomfortable under his confused gaze. Only Vinnie ever looked at me dead-on. "When I pulled the coding from the ITU servers last year, it was a reminder of how dangerous it was in the wrong hands. I destroyed it."

It had gutted me too.

Developing Mirrormat took me months. It had been beautiful in its intricacy and devastatingly efficient at breaking through every firewall known to man and AI. The power, though—its potential could devastate industries. Hell, nuclear codes could have been pulled with a few strokes of the keys.

No one should have the ability to do such a thing. Even me.

And in the hands of a government I didn't trust? Fuck that.

Lips parting, Flynn slowly shook his head. When I didn't pull away from his unwavering, shocked gaze, he expelled a heavy breath and bobbed his head.

He got it.

The knowledge loosened some of the tight razor-sharp wire in my chest a little more.

"Yet you sent it to the ITU. Allowed my team to use it."

"I sent it to you." I clamped my mouth shut, already having said too much. Much more than I'd intended to reveal. Looking away, I cleared my throat. "The company has been careful," I continued, relieved when Flynn turned back to the screens. "Barely a slip to reveal the labs they're covering up with the chemical distribution aspect."

"It makes sense to go with chemical distribution. Means they can get movement in and out without attracting curious gazes. Even if it came to someone taking a cursory glance with thermo detectors, the needs of the facilities would explain it all."

"Exactly."

"So what are they doing? The same as Perth?" This time, he glanced at me, and our gazes connected.

"I'm not sure yet." I hated not knowing. "But whatever it is, Marlow Prince knows." Just saying his name aloud grated on my nerves and made my skin prickle. "I need to talk to him."

"In person?" he asked slowly, carefully, and I understood why. He'd read the file I'd sent him.

"If you want me to rip his throat out."

If he was surprised by my words, he didn't show it. "So a call, then? You want him on video, just to hear you?" The calm tone matched his steady gaze.

I nodded, not trusting my voice.

Sure, Flynn had read a redacted file from the government, but there was so much more to the events that had blown my world apart.

"Okay. Just tell me when, and I'll get it done."

I held back my smirk, wondering how he could bring forth my desire to grin when talking about Prince. His quiet confidence was endearing, especially as I was certain he would be overthinking and second-guessing his position in his unit.

A situation I'd led him into.

Could he have said no? Of course he could. But somehow, from the moment I'd discovered his existence from that damn program he'd created that had captured my interest, I'd known he never would.

And fuck if that wasn't a dangerous, heady combination.

CHAPTER 5

FLYNN SMYTHE

Nerves twisted my gut as I cleared the security checks and entered the hallway to our office. That I felt this way despite the building being a safe haven didn't do anything to dull my anxiety.

Kent and Lucas were expecting me. We'd still yet to discuss anything beyond Hornell and Rowan. A save on my behalf, sure, but I had to explain. Had to beg for forgiveness.

And when Kent had looked at me two days ago in the war room after Rowan had reached out and saved my arse from being fired.... I heaved out a sigh at the memory of her damning gaze filled with hurt and a whole lot of anger; it was impossible to shake off.

The door opening stopped me in my tracks. Shaw appeared, his gaze assessing, his smile tentative as the door closed behind him, cutting us off from the main office space.

"You didn't get squirrelled away into a dungeon and held captive by the unicorn, then?"

A strained huff of laughter drifted out of me. The hell would I do without my friend? "No kidnapping."

"And what's he like, this Hart guy? 'Cause I've got to say, from his photo, well, he doesn't look like any nerd genius I know." Shaw's brow shot high. "Yourself being the exception."

"Fuck off," I grumbled with zero heat.

But he wasn't wrong. Just the thought of Rowan —his glacier-hued eyes, high cheekbones, and thick ebony hair—was enough to have my pulse spiking. Not the best thing when in the company of a panther.

Rowan was magnificent. Beautiful, in fact.

And his scars... the patchwork of partially healed injuries did nothing to distract from his keen intelligence or his intensity. When I'd first stepped into the room, he'd taken my breath away; I was hypnotised by his penetrating stare.

It had taken me many beats of my racing heart to break free from his gaze and get my first look at his face. The intricate web of lines told me what I'd already suspected: he'd survived the unimaginable. And fuck if each scar hadn't drawn me in, captivating me.

I knew the official report of the events, but Rowan's story, from his own lips, from his rough, gravelly voice that accelerated my breathing—that was the one I wanted to hear.

"Holy shit, you were hot for him before, but—"

"Shaw," I gritted out, all too aware of the camera pointed down on us.

He clamped his mouth shut and arched a brow at me.

That I didn't deny my being "hot" for him had been noted and filed away for another time.

Was I surprised Shaw knew I had a hard-on for the unicorn hacker even before I discovered Rowan's real identity? It aggrieved me to admit it, but no. Shaw was a hell of an agent. He was also my friend. Of course he figured it out. Not a chance my less-than-subtle panting over Rowan's mad skills would have gone unnoticed.

He stepped a little closer, leaning into my space. "And you've really been chatting to him all this time?"

I angled away to look at his expression. His voice didn't give anything away, but if I expected to find hurt, maybe anger, I would have been oh so wrong. The arsehole appeared amused. Impressed, even.

When I didn't say anything, since there was no need to confirm, as everyone in the unit knew, his mouth split into a gleeful, self-assured grin. "Drinks tomorrow night, just the two of us, and you're going to tell me every sordid detail."

"There's nothing sordid." Fuck my blushing cheeks.

"Yet. But you want there to be." He bounced his eyebrows up and down before schooling his features. "Everyone's in the war room, waiting for you."

My stomach bottomed out even as I bobbed my head.

"Hey, don't sweat it. No one's armed." He threw his beefy arm around me, and I sighed.

At least Shaw was in my corner. Not sure I deserved him, but I was grateful all the same.

"Let's go." There was no point putting off the inevitable.

After spending ten hours with Rowan yesterday, I left reluctantly. Knowing I had this early-morning briefing, Rowan urged me to leave after one jaw-cracking yawn too many. Talk about embarrassing.

Since meeting the man, it seemed all my training had flown out the window. Not only was I unable to control my reactions around Rowan, but it was well-established that I'd deceived those closest to me. And it wasn't even for him. Not really.

This was all on me.

The decision to not share—with my team, my friends, hell, Kent, who was the closest thing to family I had—well, that choice was all mine.

Rowan never forced my hand. Not once.

Sure, he'd since forced Lucas's, made an agreement that frankly still made my mind spin out when I considered Rowan's demand that I was his point of contact, effectively saving me from being fired, or worse.

Deceiving the bureau was a big fat no-no. That my arse wasn't in custody was a miracle.

Rowan's leverage—his skill and knowledge about Prince and by extension Hornell—was invaluable. Something he readily dangled like a carrot on a stick in front of Lucas.

But there would be consequences for my part. Of that I had no doubt.

And they started now.

All heads turned in my direction when I entered the war room. With Shaw still at my side, I stepped towards the large table, stopping a metre shy, my steady gaze on my boss. In my periphery, I saw Kent, but I held back from looking, too chickenshit to see her expression.

"Agent Smythe." Pulling out my title told me all I needed to know. Lucas was on his guard. Gone was the camaraderie. The realisation smacked me in the chest and would have taken my breath away if I hadn't already released it.

"Agent Lucas," I greeted, my face stoic. "I wanted to s—"

"I received your report from yesterday's briefing with Rowan Hart."

I slammed my mouth shut and straightened my spine. There'd be another time for an apology. An offer of an explanation my whole team deserved. Now was not it.

"Yes, sir. I outlined everything, along with Row's —" At the arched brow from Michaels, sitting to Lucas's right, I quickly corrected, "Rowan Hart's request."

Fuck, this was painful. The formality. The edge in the atmosphere sharp enough to cut glass... or at least my balls with the way it was going.

"With only you in the room to oversee."

I didn't flinch, waiting for him to continue, as that absolutely wasn't a question.

"What else can you tell us about Hart? Why's he doing this?" The first flicker of emotion, albeit confusion, appeared in Lucas's tone.

I latched on to it, relieved for anything beyond the

neutral distance he'd maintained since this whole thing blew open.

Jesus, was that just forty-eight hours ago?

"Hart hasn't disclosed anything beyond the file or the conversation in this room," I stated. "At the moment, I don't suspect anything beyond the history they shared with Desert Sandfire. Hart's injuries—"

"Injuries?" Kent's question snapped my attention to her, and fuck if my stomach didn't bottom out.

I hadn't disclosed his injuries in the report. *Fuck.*

Tension buzzed around the room, and I swallowed hard. How the hell could I have messed up so bad? Again?

"Camomile tea."

Every single head jerked towards Callen Broadwater, the division leader who'd obviously only paid us a special visit because this case was about Hornell. However, that didn't explain the request for camomile or the shit-eating grin spread on his face as he glanced around the room.

"That's something people have, right, to keep calm and break the tension. Maybe to stop diarrhoea as well." He shrugged, though nothing about his expression suggested he wanted a response.

"Callen." Lucas's tired groan eased something tight

in my chest, just as it snapped the band of tension holding us in its grasp.

"No? Okay, perfect. No tea, as tea tastes like shit." He leaned back in his chair as he peered around the room at each member of our unit, only stopping when his gaze landed on me. "Smythe, why don't you take a seat? Let's talk this out before you head on in and chat to the zombie locked up in cell C."

Bobbing my head, I gratefully sat next to Shaw. As soon as my arse touched the padding, my friend reached out and squeezed my shoulder. I sagged at his show of support, knowing full well my reaction would be clocked by everyone.

I figured they deserved to see just how much this ate at me. Just as I wanted them to hear me when I apologised and believe I meant every word.

I should have done so much differently.

"Much better." Callen winked at me, something that should have felt oh so wrong and out of the ordinary considering his position, but after being on a mission with the man before I was recruited, I understood this was him.

It didn't mean he wasn't a badass or incredible at his job.

"So," he continued. "Injuries."

"I don't have any details about when or where they

happened, but considering Hart's photo in the file and that it was the last time he worked for the government, and add in the details of Desert Sandfire, it's safe to say Hart's injuries were a result of the same explosion."

I visualised Rowan, knowing I was doing my job and explaining what I knew. It felt wrong, though. Like I was betraying him. And considering I'd done a whole lot worse to my team, I swallowed the emotion down.

"There's damage to his face," I continued, my voice steady. "On his neck. I don't know how far it goes."

"Fuck. He didn't heal?" Chris asked.

I shook my head. "No. Based on some lack of movement on his face, there's some nerve damage."

"And the Alliance hung him out to dry." A sneer appeared on Chris's face.

The Alliance. Despite hearing about the division, I'd barely spared them a second thought, my focus being absolutely on Rowan and whether I'd have a job when all this was over. Not sure if I'd be shut down or not, I still asked, "The Alliance? Do we know more?"

The team looked at Callen, but his focus zeroed in on Lucas. I followed his line of sight, prepared to be fobbed off.

A beat passed before Lucas stared at me, his gaze

roaming my expression. "Needless to say, this stays in this room."

Surprise had me side-eyeing Shaw, who sat up a little straighter, clearly just as eager for the information as I was. Lucas hadn't shared anything with the team as a whole.

"The Alliance is not part of SICB."

"No shit?" Michaels said, followed by "Huh. I was convinced they were like a secret handshake type of unit for the bureau." He did a weird thing with his fingers. "Obviously not as badass as us, but still, all covert chem heads or some shit."

Beside me, Shaw's lips twitched. I might have joined him if I wasn't so invested in discovering the truth.

"The Alliance is an internationally run covert agency. Multiple governments have an investment, but there are private investors too."

"Private investors working with the government? Talk about a shitload of red flags." Michaels eyeballed his field partner, Chris. "You... you weren't surprised. How the hell do you know about the existence of the Alliance?"

I angled to look at Chris. Appearing relaxed in his chair, he arched a brow at Michaels. "That's a need-to-know—" The pen smacking him on the forehead cut him off.

"Fuck that shit. How?"

They continued like this, a ridiculous back-and-forth that was completely inappropriate but absolutely expected. The subtle glimmer in Chris's eyes whenever Michaels acted hard done by was enough to have me rolling my eyes and relaxing into their exchange.

Chris's lips curved into a self-satisfied, smug grin that earned another pen thrown in his direction. This one he caught.

"I work with toddlers." Lucas's groan, filled with familiar annoyance and fondness, caught my attention.

This. I'd put all this at risk. This found family I'd been cajoled into meant everything to me. I couldn't lose them. Refused to.

"I've been crushing on the unicorn hacker since the moment I read the coding he sent." The words rushed out of me, frantic and slightly high-pitched. Immediately, the room lapsed into silence. Dryness threatened to trap my words, but I couldn't stop now.

They needed to know how ridiculously pathetic I was. Maybe they'd feel sorry enough for me that they'd forgive me.

"The day I graduated was the first time he reached out

to me directly... privately." Making eye contact with Kent, I somehow held back my wince at the intensity directed at me. "He... obviously, I didn't know it was a *he* at the time —sent fun riddles. Always something about my day. It seemed harmless. I hadn't officially started here yet." I turned my attention to Lucas. "And then when I joined the unit... well, he... Row continued with the riddles, and I quickly figured out they were still related to my day."

"Your workday? What we were doing here?" I had my boss's full attention.

"Yes." I bobbed my head.

"But that's not surprising, right?" Shaw inputted. "The fact that Hart had infiltrated our systems before.... Hell, the guy managed to wipe that coding from existence, when we'd made it only available offline.... We're not surprised, right?"

My heart squeezed with affection. That Shaw had my back shouldn't have been the surprise it was.

The room stayed silent after Shaw's defence. While neither Lucas nor Kent vocalised their thoughts, they didn't need to.

"That was the point when I should have told you. Found a way to stop the leak. But I promise, I never disclosed anything. No investigation or mission infor- mation. Nothing. I didn't even confirm anything. I would never intentionally betray you like that." I focussed on Kent. "Any of you. I'm sorry. I screwed up and handled everything wrong—"

"But you had a hard-on for the brain of the person who created coding that could rule or destroy the world." Michaels whistled, low and slow. "Hell, Smythe, way to crush high. Nice."

My lips parted, my skin flushing. I wasn't quite sure how or even if I should respond to that.

Beside me, Shaw groaned, while Chris, a couple of seats away, did this awkward cough that sounded suspiciously like he was trying to hide his burst of laughter.

Kent's "For fuck's sake" drew my attention. With her head tilted backwards, she stared at the ceiling, no doubt praying to an ancient deity for strength. That or the power to wind back time and make it so she wasn't here.

The thought made me smirk, because heck if it didn't make me think about yesterday and wishing for the same thing when I was with Rowan.

"I should definitely visit the unit more often." Callen chuckled. "You talk so much more shit and get off task in much more entertaining ways than the division office." A grin stretched his lips wide as he glanced around the room, this weirdly proud expression forming.

"Do not encourage any of this." Lucas followed up

with a shake of his head, but the level of pissed off from earlier seemed to have come down a few notches.

Callen snorted. "You're just still pissed that Cruella in the dungeon started talking shit about what a bad lay you were when we refused to let her have some sexy alone time with her zombie lion boyfriend."

I shot a glance at Shaw, who gave a not-so-subtle nod and a smirk that would likely get his arse handed to him if Lucas looked in our direction. Fortunately, the thud let me know that Lucas, my boss, the one person who I thought was truly sane on our team, slammed his head on the desk.

He was the picture of defeat. Exasperation, too, I suspected.

The snicker started small but rippled around the room until everyone, with the exception of Kent, who shook her head and huffed out a pained breath, full-on laughed.

A tentative smile broke free on my lips. These guys were my team. My family.

"I really am sorry I let you all down. I want to earn your trust again."

The laughter petered out, and all eyes focussed on me. When Lucas lifted his head, he studied me and sat up with a sigh. "We're going to treat this investigation as your probation period."

I swallowed hard and nodded. It hurt but was fair.

"You're a team player. One of us. I know that. We all know that."

Movement from Kent dragged my attention off Lucas and to her. She folded her arms, her jaw hard.

"This... thing you have going on with Hart—"

"There's nothing going on," I interrupted Lucas.

"Yet," Michaels supplied unhelpfully. "You and the sexy-brained tiger, side by side, salivating over code and research...." He smirked and glanced around the room. "I give it five days, tops."

"Three," Chris said.

With raised eyebrows, I jerked my head in his direction so fast, I winced at the sharp crunch in my neck.

Uncaring of my possible spinal damage, he continued, "How many months has this guy been messaging him? That's months and months of cyber flirting. Three days."

I slammed my mouth shut, knowing I should intervene, say or do something, but I was dancing on the precipice of shock and relief. Their teasing meant they were giving me a chance.

The heavy weight anchoring my heart shifted and began to lift. A tender hope fluttered within me as I dared to believe we might just be okay. That somehow, someway, they'd find it in themselves to forgive me.

"I give it a week," Shaw inputted, leaning into my side a little.

"I swear I give up." Lucas stared at me, his gaze still assessing. "Smythe, just do the right thing. I want daily reports. No secrets related to the case."

I sobered, as did the team.

"Hornell has done too much damage, and the thought of what he's doing right this second.... Honestly, we need him found and brought in. And from what you've said about Hart and his injuries, I believe he wants the same thing."

"He does." Of that I was certain.

"Okay, let's get through the rest of this meeting. We have thirty minutes before the interview with Prince, and we need this to work. We need a lead and to get ahead of this."

The room settled, our team focussing on the report I'd sent while listening intently as I clarified questions and we discussed the outcome of Seraphina Kent's interview.

There was a mountain of puzzle pieces spread out before us. At the moment, the mess of information was distracting and senseless. But this was what we did. And well.

And even though Kent could barely look at me, we made progress. After this meeting with Prince, I just hoped she would give me the chance to beg for her forgiveness.

She was family. The one I chose.

Not a chance I could let that go without a fight.

As soon as Prince heard Rowan's voice, the transformation in him had been immediate.

Surprise, disbelief, confusion, and thankfully a flicker of guilt. The combination seemed to inspire confession. For the past thirty minutes, I stood by, my horror growing as Prince shared the specifics of his regeneration.

While we now had intel on Hornell that gave us a workable lead for the first time in months, I struggled to get past all Prince had been through.

He was a traitor and had been partially responsible for the deaths of hundreds as well as the irreparable damage to Rowan—all of which he'd pay for as soon as official charges were brought against him. But the genetic printing combined with the medical procedures conducted while he'd been awake and in a partial shift... the advancement was as ingenious as it was harrowing.

In truth, the creation of his new heart with modified DNA strands had the potential to change lives for the better. But it was the brutality of the procedures, as well as the lack of research and the experimental nature of it with apparently devastating consequences, that made my gut bottom out.

Rowan's voice remained tight as it drifted from the speakers. "So what you're saying is, you're a ticking time bomb, and you don't give a shit who goes down in your desperate bid for a life that wasn't meant to be yours."

I held back my wince. Rowan didn't mince his words in throwing out the truth of Prince's actions.

"Fuck you, Hart. I didn't ask to be dragged out of the wreckage."

"That you fucking caused." Anger crackled in Rowan's words.

I needed to intervene. Sure, we'd made progress, but with the venom that chased each question and response Rowan threw out there, we were going around in circles.

"When's your next treatment?" I asked.

Prince's gaze snapped to me. Steadfast defiance rolled off the man, but still he kept giving us the information we wanted, bargaining his way around every piece he shared. With the team's input drifting in and out of my earpiece that had been set to a frequency impossible for Prince to pick up on, I'd been negotiating the hell out of every sliver of detail.

The end goal here was Hornell's capture. The team would do anything we could to make that happen.

Including bargaining with the piece-of-shit zombie psychopath sitting before me.

"Four days."

If he didn't receive the temporal gene regulator, he'd be toast. Again.

"Where?" I pushed.

"I already told you. Fuck if I know. Hornell changes the location every three weeks. It's the only time we meet in person. And I only get the location once the job that you and Seraphina's bitch of a sister destroyed is done. So clearly that's not going to happen now."

"What do you call a dead man walking who's strapped to a chair?" Michaels's voice trickled into my ear. He barely waited a second before saying, "A real *sit*uation." A self-satisfied snort followed.

"There are days I wish you were still a grumpy jackass constantly going AWOL," Kent grumbled.

I held back my lip twitch. The team could be the epitome of inappropriate, and damn if I didn't appreciate them the more for it. Before Shaw pulled me into the fold, the only joy I got was in training and disappearing into coding. I hadn't had any friends in the academy, and definitely none before that.

And my folks—I couldn't recall one time they'd cracked a joke, let alone wrapped me up in a hug or offered a kind word.

Rowan's gruff, as-delicious-as-warm-chocolate voice caressed my ear. "Hornell had eyes on him the whole time. The car explosion wasn't happenchance." Agreed for sure. "We need to release him and create a plausible trail. Make the information easy to access. It's the only way to get the coordinates."

With the tense silence that followed, I suspected neither Callen nor Lucas would be happy about that, but Rowan was right. Prince and Seraphina needed to be available. Needed to "complete" their task. Or at least for it to look like they had.

Between me and Rowan, we could leave the digital footprints necessary for that to be believable.

"We need to meet. Smythe, get him back in the cell and head to the war room. Looks like the fucker gets to walk, but under our direction and without the opportunity of ever escaping. The man likes playing double agent. Let's see how much he wants to live."

And that was what worried me. With Hornell holding Prince's literal life in his hands, the lion would run at the first opportunity. Double-crossing us would absolutely happen.

Rather than a step ahead, we needed to be at least twenty big-arse strides in front of him to pull this off.

Let's just see how much magic Rowan can create.

I silently ignored Prince's grumbles as I set about securing him in his cell. As I headed to the war room, Rowan's voice filled my ear.

"How long before he double-crosses us?"

I flicked my gaze up at one of the security cameras, knowing without confirmation that Rowan had cut off the team from comms. "Is that a trick question? Who's to say he already hasn't?"

I meant it as a joke, but I stopped in my tracks. The jump in my pulse thumped loudly in my ears. *What if he's already playing us?*

"Fuck, let me check for signals."

"Re-establish connection with my team." Half a beat later, I turned and sprinted towards the staircase, bypassing the lift to return to the sublevel secure unit. "Lucas, check cells two and four."

Kent answered, "There's nothing amiss. Prince and Seraphina are contained."

I continued to run, needing to see with my own eyes. Our detainees had been moved yesterday to our main base of operations while I'd been with Rowan. The location was secure and a well-guarded secret.

"Rowan, do you have anything?" I grabbed onto the handrail, using the grip to spin myself towards the next set of stairs.

"Thirty seconds."

The thundering of my heart urged me forwards.

Something wasn't right.

Two steps from the first secure door, I reached out, lunging forwards to press my finger to the scanner.

"Fuck, move. Get away from the door and down."

Reacting immediately to Rowan's order, I spun and dove in the opposite direction of the door. Hitting the floor with a thud, my breath whooshed out of me, my bruised ribs protesting at the hard hit, but there was no time to gasp for breath.

The roar of an explosion boomed in my ears, shook the ground, and sent the door sailing over my head. Debris flew out, slicing into my skin. I covered my head and edged closer to the wall just as a second tremble and loud bang shook the building.

The fuck was happening? The second rumble wasn't from the sublevel.

Nothing but static filled my earpiece, so whatever had happened, the comms were down. I pushed up to stand, wincing at the sting on my face and the flashing lights in the corridor. The piercing shrill of the fire alarm echoed around the sound of collapsing walls, possibly the ceiling of the once-secure area.

The vibration in my pocket caught my attention. I scrambled for my phone, answering the call immediately.

"You're alive." The rough, tense voice wrapped around me. "You need to get out of there. The building—"

"The second explosion—where did it hit?"

"The ceiling is going to collapse above you if you don't—"

"Rowan." I punched the word out, fear clogging my throat. "Where the fuck did it hit?"

"The server room."

White-hot dread caught my breath, sending my heart racing. It thudded against my ribcage as if trying to escape the smoke and chaos filling my lungs and my vision. The deafening growl of the explosion pulsated in the air, holding my feet hostage, keeping me in its icy grip.

The war room, situated directly above the server room, would have taken the direct hit. My team—my family. A tsunami of dread threatened to crush me and keep me frozen. But I needed to move. Needed to get to them.

Aware Rowan's voice still filled my ear from the phone I held with a trembling hand, I gasped, "Call for help."

Phone in hand, I sprinted back the way I'd come, jumping over plaster and chunks of debris, bolting up the staircase, ignoring the pain accompanying each step I took.

They needed to be okay.

Images of my unit played like a reel—their camaraderie, their ball-busting jokes. Their devotion. Clenching my jaw, I pushed back the paralysing fear and quickened my pace.

They were safe. The alternative was unimaginable.

Reaching the ground floor, I winced at the billowing smoke obscuring my vision. Security personnel and the on-site medical team called out to one another. To me. Two people were trapped under a chunk of ceiling, but they were alive.

My team would be too.

Finally reaching the main office, I stopped in my tracks, eyes widening at the chaos.

"Kent," I hollered, a sob in my throat.

Her frantic gaze hit mine, a softening there I didn't know I'd see again.

I bolted, slamming into her, wrapping my arms around her slim frame. "You're okay. I thought—"

"You're okay?" Her strong grip moved to my arms, and she eased me away, her searching gaze assessing. "It looks deep." She reached for the medkit already open on an upturned desk and tugged out the spray sealant I knew hurt like a beast.

A wince later, the cut on my head was sealed, and I glanced around, my heart still in my throat.

"Your ribs. They okay?"

I turned back at the concern in Kent's voice. "They hurt, but I don't think they're broken." If they were, given the speed I ran here, I suspected I'd have punctured a lung by now and would be dead on the ground.

The twitch of her eyebrow was the only warning before Kent dragged me into her hold.

"You're a fucking idiot, but I love you."

Emotion slammed into me, as fierce as her hold. Hugging her back, I held on tight. "I thought you'd been killed."

Her snort as she pulled away was all incredulous sass, as was her arched brow as I saw her shake off feelings I knew she rarely shared. "It'll take more than a weak-arse bomb to bring me down." She gathered herself, dropping her hand from my arm. "Chris was injured in the blast and is being a punk about a tiny fucking cut. Michaels has a scratch on his face and is crying about not being pretty anymore. Lucas, Shaw, and Callen are fine. We need to go pull everyone's heads out of their arses, since—"

The mention of injuries shot a punch of adrenaline through me.

The cells were hit.

Her sister.

"The first explosion—"

Kent frowned. "First?"

She didn't know? How could they not have felt or heard?

"In the subbasement. The cells."

Understanding immediately, she stiffened. "Lucas," she hollered.

Movement caught my attention, and Lucas appeared. Blood stained his shirt and his cheeks. His gaze was on me in an instant, relief crossing his features.

"The cells were hit." Kent's voice remained steady.

"Fuck. Just go. I'll send Shaw."

We moved without further instruction, dodging timber and plasterboard, ignoring the EMTs who had since appeared on the scene, and speeding down the stairwell.

Kent arrived at the open doorway while I'd just reached the cracked door seven metres away from where it belonged. How I'd dodged the flying door and not been killed was a freaking miracle.

"Sera." Pain laced Kent's tone.

I was two metres away, and the only sound coming from the area after she spoke was crackling fire and the creaks of the building. I stepped into the entrance area of the holding cells. The fifteen-metre corridor contained remnants of walls and the cells' structures.

A fire, miraculously small, flickered in an empty cell to my right, burning the only flammable item in the room: the mattress. The drag of metal, the thud of a movement, and I picked my way through the wreckage, making my journey clumsy and difficult.

Times like these, a fast-healing body would come in—

I jerked to a stop, my breath rushing out when I saw Kent on the floor, her sister in her arms. Beyond Kent wiping away blood coating Seraphina's forehead, there wasn't a flicker of movement. Of breath. Of life coming from Seraphina.

Fuck.

I shifted my foot, dragging rubble, the sound slicing through the air.

"Go check on Prince."

At Kent's wooden instruction, I paused. I couldn't

leave her, right? No way could I let her handle this by herself.

"Now, Smythe."

"But—"

"Flynn, please."

Our gazes caught. I tracked the tear slowly trickling down her cheek, swallowed hard, and nodded. "Okay," I whispered, backing away.

Stepping out of the cell, I tugged my phone out, wincing at the mountain of missed calls from Rowan. He'd saved me again. Guilt stirred in my chest as I ignored his name. Right now, as well as discovering if the lion lived or not, I focussed on Kent—whether she wanted me to or not.

I dashed off a text to Jada, letting her know there'd been an explosion, that Ivy was unharmed, but she needed Jada here.

The phone vibrated in response as I climbed over the smashed cell door. Acrid smoke clung to the air, the walls scorched from the blast. Twisted metal littered the debris-scattered floor, the burst water pipe spraying out from the left side of the cell soaking everything.

The distinct sound of tumbling concrete hitting the ground reached me. I zeroed in, spotting the barest of movements in the far-right corner. Prince, pinned beneath the fallen rubble, gasped for breath. The action stopped abruptly as blood spilled from his mouth.

"Prince, you hear me?" Scrambling my way over to him, I found the lion on his back, rebar puncturing his chest. Part of the ceiling had collapsed. The unlucky son of a bitch had been speared right where he'd lain.

A fresh gurgle of blood oozed out of his mouth as he weakly reached for the metal pole. He couldn't get a hold, which I suspected was a good thing. Its positioning, just off-centre to the left on his chest, was a bad one. I'd racked up enough hours doing medical field training at the academy to know it was directly at the heart, likely lacerating one of the major arteries.

How the hell he remained conscious, albeit barely, didn't make sense.

But from the pool of blood dripping from the bent metal frame of the single cot, it wouldn't be for much longer. There'd be no coming back from this.

Fuck it all to hell.

"Prince." I peered down at him. "You hear me, Prince?"

When his eyelids fluttered open, his unfocussed gaze struggled to settle on me.

"Prince." I touched his shoulder, squeezing lightly.

The man was a murderer. It didn't make watching him die any easier.

"Horn-ell," he panted, wheezing heavily.

At the name, I froze, willing Prince to do one good thing in his life and give us something that would finally take the former captain down.

"Chip."

Chip? I shook my head. "Chip? What chip?"

He moved his arm with a gasp and a grunt, the movement slow and awkward. His bloody palm fell on his neck. "Chip," he repeated, lifting and dropping his arm back to the right of his Adam's apple. "Kn-ows—" A cough racked through him, and I held him down, trying desperately to keep him still.

"There's a chip in your neck?" I clarified. "What does Hornell know? What does it do?"

"Code." His head lolled to the side, his half-mast eyes drooping. His shallow breaths, barely moving his chest, slowed further.

Fuck, fuck, fuck.

A gasp of breath and his eyes sprang open. My own followed suit.

Feeling useless, knowing he was likely taking his last few breaths, I searched frantically for a solution.

What the hell should I do?

Taking me by surprise, I jolted when his hand

latched on to my forearm with surprising strength. Before me, his hand morphed, forming claws, fur sprouting over his shifting hand.

Understanding took my breath away.

What he was offering could only be gifted and not forced.

For a wolf, it was a bite; a tiger, a claw deep into the skin over the heart. For a lion.... I swallowed hard. For a lion, claws in the neck, right over the carotid artery.

And like all shifters, the rare gift of the gene and their memories could only be passed on willingly in death.

The difference with lions was the carotid artery—the destruction of it with the wrong nick would cause death. It was no surprise that so few humans gifted the lion shifter gene survived.

"Do you know his plans? How to stop him for good? What we need to do to take him down?" My voice trembled, barely audible through the splashing water.

Parting his bloodied lips, he croaked, "Yes."

Fuck it all to hell.

"Okay." With a shaky hand, I lifted his palm to my neck as I lowered myself. I kept my eyes open, fear trying to slam them shut, but energy buzzed through my body, pulling everything into sharp focus.

In the distance, I heard a shout. Shaw.

"Do it."

They were going to fucking kill me.

Well, I thought, as pain sliced through me, *that's if I'm still alive after this.*

Bright, searing agony surged through me as Prince's lethal claws tore into my neck. I gasped as each laceration sliced through me, shooting shock waves throughout my body.

What the fuck had I done?

Fear scrambled my brain, but fuck if determination wasn't so much brighter.

I had to survive this. We had to stop Hornell. He needed to pay... for the lost lives, for his monstrous acts... for Rowan.

The moment the claws retracted from my flesh, Prince's arm fell limp, his last breath stuttering out of him. The release of my neck sent me backwards, head reeling. I clutched my ravaged skin as thick, warm blood spurted through my fingers.

"What the fuck?" The shout was strangled and distant.

Another gush of blood stole past my fingers, and I sighed at the gentle touch under my head, having fallen flat onto my back.

"Fuck, Smythe, what did you do?" Shaw pushed

my hand aside as something soft and warm pressed against my neck, sending out a fresh shard of pain.

Fog clouded my brain, a welcome buffer from the torment winding its way through my body.

"No, no, no." Cool hands pressed against my cheeks. "Flynn, I swear if you don't survive this, I'll drag you out of Hades just to kick your arse." A soft mumble followed, Kent issuing orders. "I need you to fight."

Something pressed against me, and the world around me spun. Lights flickered and I jostled, my back hitting something soft. I parted my lips, unspoken words burning in my throat. Blackness pushed against me, dulling my thoughts until I was no longer sure what I wanted to say.

Fight.

The ground beneath me shifted, blue sky filling my vision before my eyes rolled into the back of my head.

Fight.

A quiet voice in the shadows.... Too quiet to latch on to, to make sense of.

A screech, a bang, darkness behind my lids as my body burned.

Fight.

"Flynn."

A gentle caress, the nudge of recognition, but prying my eyes open proved impossible.

"Flynn. You chose this, accepted the gift."

A firm hand against my scorching skin and my body jolted. Writhed.

"Don't fight this. Accept the change."

The gruff voice ignited a spark deep in the inky darkness. A flicker of recognition.

"If anyone can do this, it's you." A different voice, soft and calm.

Jada was here.

I clung to her words, her gentle assurance, a guiding light in the otherwise impenetrable darkness.

"Fly-nn." The broken word, a crack of emotion from Kent. Ivy. The woman I chose as family.

Once more, I heard my name. This time it was spoken with the rough emotion of a pained soul who I'd only just started to recognise.

A flash of pain and my limbs tightened. Arching my back, I stretched my neck taut, the pressure on it finally easing. I gasped, exhaustion a heavy blanket. It was oppressive, too warm, but I struggled to fight it.

I was too hot. The threat of burning up pushed me towards unconsciousness. "Ivy." The strangled word scratched my throat just as a cool hand arrived on my forehead.

The sounds around me started to fade, the flickering lights behind my closed eyelids darkening. Disorientation swept over me as my racing pulse eased, no longer deafening me with its ferocity.

A swirling tunnel closed in on me, my panic receding as the fire in my veins lessened.

Amidst it all, reassuring words echoed like a lifeline. "We've got you." Ivy's words, a soothing balm to my tortured soul, beckoned me to let go.

I could do that.

The voices of my team, my family, and the scratchy gruffness of the man who shouldn't be here were all I needed. The anchor to stop me floating away forever.

I was safe and would survive this.

Letting go, I drifted away, their lingering words a promise I would return to.

CHAPTER 6

ROWAN HART

I WAS A WALKING, GROWLING, PACING CLICHÉ.

Three thousand square metres, and I'd walked every millimetre at least fifty times.

"Here."

Despite my scowl and the snarl in the hollow of my throat, I paused, eyeing the steaming coffee. It wasn't Jada's fault I couldn't keep my shit together. "Thanks," I mumbled, taking the mug from her.

It smelt good, strong enough to cut through the anxiety clawing at me.

Almost fourteen hours had passed since we'd returned to my secure base. My home. The location only Vinnie and I'd known about before now.

That had all changed when I'd discovered the signal pulsing from the ITU's base of operations, sending data wirelessly to the source that was undoubtedly Hornell. That was a few moments before I discovered the trap—the explosion that almost killed Flynn. A-fucking-gain.

With the whole unit compromised, the accessed data making every single member vulnerable, I'd reacted, thinking nothing beyond needing to get to their obliterated base—to get to Flynn.

And when I had, discovering he'd opened up to Prince, accepting the lion gene it was only possible to gift to a human the moment before the shifter's death, I'd lost my shit, issuing orders like they were mine to give.

Callen Blackheath, the wolf who was a pain-in-the-arse division leader of the battered and bruised unit, alongside Lucas, the team boss, had been close to trying to take me down. Close being the operative word.

They could have tried but would have failed.

It had been Kent who'd stopped them, who'd listened intently when I'd explained that moving Flynn to a government facility, to a hospital, hell, even to one of their houses, would be a mistake of epic proportions.

Maybe it had been my desperation that had convinced her. Though I suspected the appearance of her wife, Jada, with her intent, questioning gaze as I interacted with Flynn—the man who in some fucked-up, weird way they'd unofficially adopted as their kid despite him already being in his twenties—was what had done it. Jada had given her a hard stare, silently communicating with Kent.

The truth was, none of the team were safe. Not their homes. Nor their official files.

Which led me to grudgingly accept the coffee from Jada, who was in my home, along with Kent and an unconscious Flynn, who I'd tucked up in my bed.

Where the rest of the unit was, I had no idea. Nor did I care, but Flynn would when he woke up.

"His temperature's come down," Jada said kindly, her unwavering stare pressing against me uncomfortably. "It won't be long."

The bob of my head felt stiff, the intensity of her gaze foreign. "Yeah, okay." I looked away, viscerally aware of her head tilting as she studied me.

"Maybe you should get some rest."

My attention snapped back to her, the automatic desire to tell her to fuck off on the tip of my tongue. At the open concern directed my way, I swallowed my words down. "I'm fine."

I so wasn't fine. Hell, I couldn't even settle in front of my hub of computers, even though studying the signal I'd recorded and trying to find Hornell should have been my priority. Flynn had changed all that. Whether from his brilliant mind all those months ago, the sweet, innocent exchanges we'd had, or the way he'd smiled at me, drinking me in, gaze unwavering, not dimming in horror when he saw my scars, I didn't know; I suspected it was a combination.

But *he* was now my priority, and I refused to regret it.

"Okay. In that case, I'll go check on Flynn, and Ivy's asking for you." With a gentle smile, she turned away, leaving me to wonder at how easily I'd buckled when they refused to let me hide Flynn away without them.

It was less than eighty hours after talking to him for the first time, however many hours after meeting him face to face, and I was questioning my sanity.

That and the power he had over me.

At my computer bank, Kent was right where I'd grudgingly left her. Rather than spending the past fourteen hours pacing and worrying, she'd been deep into researching and tracking. Something I should have been doing.

Considering we looked the same age though she had a hundred years on me, I brushed off my incompetence as simply her ability to get her shit together much more effectively than I ever would.

Not that it was a surprise.

Hadn't I hidden away since being cast aside by the Alliance, my injuries a reminder every damn time I spotted my reflection that how skilled I was didn't mean a thing?

I couldn't ever imagine Kent doing such a thing— crawling away to lick her wounds. Nor Flynn for that matter.

Hell, the fact that he'd accepted the gene exchange, knowing it could give him access to invaluable intel on Hornell, made it crystal clear he was a better man than I was. Could ever pretend to be.

"Come look at this," Kent ordered as if she owned my self-designed and hand-built station.

Only the recollection of her grudging admiration that she wasn't quick enough to conceal when she'd first taken in my workspace stopped me from grousing at her.

Taking the seat next to her, I stared at the bank of monitors. We'd done this a couple of times now, and I'd even been drawn in and spent a couple of hours buried in research and coding before I felt compelled to pace.

"The chip from Prince's neck." She indicated the

layers of code, navigating through it. She stopped before I asked her to. I immediately spotted what she'd discovered.

"A capture device and a locator." All grinding my teeth did was cause a zip of pain along my damaged jaw to my ear, but that the scanners located at the ITU's base of operations hadn't picked up on this when Prince had been brought in pissed me the fuck off.

Whoever designed this was talented. Enough so that they knew what they needed to use to bypass government-issued scanners.

"Have you found a signature?"

Kent shook her head and glanced at me. "Not yet, but not a chance the person who designed this wouldn't leave something behind."

I agreed with her. It took real skill to create this kind of technology. From the look of it, not only did it tap into local servers within a certain radius, but the device was also able to pull files, all while sending a homing beacon.

The camera logs Kent pulled a couple of hours back already showed the glitch in the coding of the video footage of the ITU government building. To the naked eye, even the trained eye, nothing would have been amiss. It was how someone had got inside and planted the two explosive devices.

"If you weren't sitting right here next to me and I didn't believe your worry for Smythe was real, I would have accused you of programming something like this."

We made eye contact, and a humourless snort huffed out of me. "I'm flattered," I deadpanned. "And you're also right. The skill is impressive." My lips curved, the damaged side tugging uncomfortably. Kent's eye contact remained steady as I said, "That means they will have definitely left a calling card. It also means we'll find them."

Talent like this took guts. There was also a strand of the coding that was flamboyant in its design.

The fucker had been showing off.

While I truly thought the skill was impressive, that they nearly got Flynn killed meant they'd be in for a world of shit when I discovered them. No way could I let whoever the arsehole was create shit like this and share it with scumbags like Hornell.

"I'm assuming you have contacts in the ShadowNet?"

In answer, I arched a brow. "Is a government agent asking me if I have access to the illegal ShadowNet?" As if I'd ever admit to having connection to the underground network of hackers and coders.

Obviously, I did. It was a place I'd picked up a few

jobs over the years and a whole wealth of interesting information too.

"Find out who's making noise and showing the fuck off." Her tone left no room for argument.

"Ivy." Jada's voice reached us from three rooms away.

We reacted immediately, jumping out of our seats and bolting in the direction of my bedroom.

With each step closer, the pounding of my heart increased.

He'll be okay.

No panic or fear had strained Jada's voice.

Positive thinking didn't do a thing for calming my racing pulse. Was it possible to have a heart attack from worry? If not that, then maybe the pulsing organ inside my chest would simply give up the fight and either burst free or stop altogether.

Fuck, when had I become so dramatic?

If Vinnie could see me now and hear my spiralling thoughts, he'd laugh his arse off all the way to the local glee club, where he'd swiftly enrol me in whatever shitty musical was being rehearsed.

And why the hell was I clogging my brain with thoughts of musicals? I was losing my mind.

Kent stopped two steps into my room, and I

followed suit. But I couldn't look at the bed. Couldn't see for myself what condition Flynn was in.

What if—

Kent grinned, the action so at odds with everything I knew about her, I struggled to process her expression and what it meant.

The steady beat of a pulse. Half a second slower than any human's.

I closed my eyes, zeroing in on the sound, the glorious rhythm that didn't belong to the vampires in the room.

Flynn.

Relief, so swift it threatened to buckle my knees, swept through me.

He'd survived the change.

Hesitating a step from the open doorway, I considered backing away. The hell had I been thinking, demanding they come here? Why had I insisted that this was the safest place for Flynn?

Had it been true? Undoubtedly. But still, what right did I have?

Uncertainty had me easing back. Obviously Flynn was alive. He'd be happy to see Kent and Jada. Me? As soon as he realised where he was, he'd be wondering what my damage was.

I should just—

"Rowan."

The hypnotic gravel in Flynn's voice froze my feet. Peering into the room, I watched as Jada angled my way, a relieved and welcoming smile directed at me.

I willed my pulse to behave, trying not to overthink my reaction. Because of course I knew why I behaved like a fucknugget. Not once had I been drawn to a person as viscerally, as powerfully as I was to Flynn.

When he'd been unconscious in my bed, the image had simultaneously torn down those impenetrable vines of barbed wire around my heart while filling me with selfish dread that I'd never get the chance to know him better.

And now....

I stepped into my bedroom, focussing for a beat on the familiar exposed brick walls, knowing I needed to stop being a princess and look at Flynn. When my gaze drifted to his, finally making eye contact, relief with the power and speed of a tidal wave rolled into me.

Bright-eyed and smiling, he held my attention completely.

"This room smells of you."

Holy fuck.

Heat burned my skin, my cheeks blazing, somehow growing even warmer when Flynn's eyes widened in an almost comical "what the fuck did I just say?" expression and his face glowed red.

I parted my lips despite not knowing how to respond.

Thank the gods for Jada as she stepped closer to Flynn and stroked a few long strands away from his forehead. "What do you need, Flynn? Some more rest? Maybe you're hungry?" Affection coloured her tone. Nothing but genuine warmth and concern rolled off her as she peered down at him.

While I knew a lot about Jada on paper, before today, I'd never heard her voice or got an actual sense of who she was. The truth was, I hadn't quite understood the dynamic she and Kent had with Flynn.

That had all changed. When Jada had been at Flynn's side as they'd wheeled him out of the damaged building on a gurney, devastation had shrouded her like a heavy blanket. But despite that, every word she'd whispered had been full of hope, a determination that he'd get through this and be one of the few who successfully made the transition.

And since then, I'd witnessed her steel, her kindness.

For as much as she loved her wife—it was there with every touch and unspoken word—her love for

Flynn was different. Pure. And absolutely that of a doting parent.

And who the hell was I to question that?

"Jada, babe, let him breathe." Kent stepped to her side and wrapped an arm around her waist. Her gaze didn't stray from Flynn, who'd since focussed on the two women, the colour in his cheeks returning to their natural shade of pale peach.

Flynn's smile was immediate, soft, and warm. "Food would be good. I'm tired and sore, but I could go for something to eat."

Doing a mental checklist of the contents of my fridge, I owed Vinnie one. When he'd stopped by with my takeout a few days back, he'd shoved some staples in the fridge. And since he knew me so well, he'd brought items that wouldn't go off immediately.

"I made breakfast burritos. Do you think you can manage eating at the table, or...?" Jada trailed off, raking her gaze over Flynn. I did the same, struggling not to ogle the expanse of skin on display. But it was either stare at his pecs and his dusty pink nipples or zero in on the four golden claw marks on the left of his neck.

They were smooth and mesmerizingly beautiful, and so rare that I'd only ever seen a turned-lion-shifter's markings once before. They truly were remarkable, especially because the fact that they'd healed like this meant that not only had Flynn survived but he would live what I hoped would be a long life—likely double compared to his human life.

And wasn't that something incredible.

"Rowan." From the bite in Kent's tone, I figured this wasn't the first time my name had been said.

"Huh, yes?" I dragged my gaze away from Flynn, turning my attention to an unimpressed Kent, who looked even more pissed off at me with her arched brow and studying gaze.

Yeah, the vampire could read me like a damn book.

"Clothes for Flynn," Jada asked, not hiding her amusement as heat spread across my cheeks. "Do you have something he can wear?"

I nodded on autopilot and stepped into my closet.

When we'd all left the scene, there'd been the barest of discussions after I'd disclosed the basic intel I'd gathered about the signal. Not leaving anything to chance, we'd agreed to retreat to off-the-books locations. No packing up of anyone's shit. No grabbing a coffee en route. Everyone needed to disappear until we discovered more.

From what Kent had just discovered, at least we now had more insight.

What we were really waiting on was Flynn to come

through. And fuck, did I hate it. Hated he'd put himself in so much danger. I respected the hell out of his decision, though.

It took a fuckload of guts to accept Prince's soul memories and gift.

Flynn, being smart as fuck, would have known the risks. It was likely he could have died, given the low percentage of known successful transformations and a heap of figures about the likelihood of dying rather than changing.

Grabbing a pair of sweats and a tee, I snapped my jaw closed, grinding my back molars together at the thought. The fucker would have known the odds most definitely were not in his favour.

When I returned to my room, Jada and Kent were gone, likely in the kitchen organising food I hadn't even realised Jada had made. And that it was breakfast food? So much had passed me by and flown under the radar since returning with an unconscious Flynn—apparently the whole night being one of them. I'd been all but useless as he'd lain there comatose, and now....

My lips parted, mouth agape.

Naked. Flynn fucking Smythe was naked next to my bed, his gaze already on me and not at all looking fazed about it.

Flustered, I stayed rooted to the spot, my cheeks

burning as I raked my gaze over him. It was impossible to pull away, impossible to keep my eyes fixed on his face, not when so much delicious unmarred skin was on display.

"Are those for me?"

At the gravel of his gruff voice, my attention snapped to his. *And holy fuck...* molten lava swirled in his eyes. The once familiar warm brown of his irises shimmered into an intense and mesmerising shade of amber. Flecks of gold sparkled in the depths, a gleam in them hinting at the dormant power and primal instincts awakening in him.

As we stared, each taking our fill, his eyes glowed brighter. A wildness flickered there as he took a step towards me, the predator in him rising to the forefront.

He was magnificent. Beautiful in his confident stride, undeniably hypnotic when his muscles bunched, then became taut as he flexed.

Frozen, I forced myself to exhale before inhaling a slow, steady breath.

At the shift in the air around us from filling my lungs, Flynn paused, a smile, wide and bright, stretching his lips.

This was still Flynn, just changed from the new power humming in his veins. As shifters, we didn't have separate identities, an animal consciousness. Primal instinct, however, was as real as it was ancient, embedded deep within our core, guiding our actions and reactions with an undeniable force.

Flynn's instincts told me a whole lot. It had been years since I'd witnessed a gift transfer. Truth was, I'd only observed two, and both were from the sidelines.

His hard cock, standing proudly and pointing at me, let me know more than anything the direction of Flynn's rapture.

Fuck, fight, or shift.

Sure, he'd said he was hungry, but the instinct for something more primal, more visceral would need to be sated.

While I kept my pulse steady as he stalked towards me, my dick had other ideas. The twinge behind my zipper was bad on so many levels, though not an ounce of surprise existed.

Flynn as a nameless, faceless brain behind code had caught my interest. During the two following hours when I'd cyberstalked the shit out of him, he'd become my obsession.

And the only person since I'd almost died who'd made me hard.

So, given the fact that he was within reaching distance, naked and staring at me with unabated lust...

it definitely wasn't a shock that I was down to sate this ever-growing longing I had for the man.

Fuck if doing the right thing wasn't the only thing keeping me rooted.

Plus, his adopted mums, or whatever their unofficial relationship status was, were a couple of rooms over. Kent was not a vampire I wanted to get in a fight with.

Three years out of the field meant I was not the tiger I once was.

Taking another step towards me, Flynn searched my gaze, not shying away from studying my whole face. Before I could tense, his soft "You are incredible" left me spiralling. He reached for me so slowly that I knew, despite the urgency and primitive need pulsing through his veins, he was giving me time to stop him.

When I didn't, Flynn tilted his head. The action curved his neck, drawing my gaze to the fresh markings tattooed on his previously blemish-free skin.

The touch on my face left me gasping. The caress of the tender skin shot sparks of warmth to my chest. The swipe of his finger over my lips, an added brush over the marred side, and my eyelids slipped closed.

No one had touched my face in years. Even back then, not with so much tenderness or reverence.

After undergoing hours of surgery, days and weeks

of grafting and being prodded and poked, the very thought of anyone touching my skin still twisted my stomach.

Anyone except Flynn.

The ghost of his breath danced across my cheek, and I startled, my eyelids bursting wide open at the press of his lips against the ugly scars ruining my face.

Fast breaths punched out of me. I fisted my hands at my side, no idea what to say, what to do.

His lips left my cheek for the barest of moments before returning an inch over.

"You are remarkable."

My lips parted, instinct pushing me to call bullshit, to tell him he'd lost his mind, but the shift of his head, the appearance of his intense amber eyes sent my thoughts speeding towards the abyss.

"You," Flynn started, the word zipping fresh heat and interest to my groin, "are the most amazing person I've ever known."

Then he slid his lips against mine, capturing my breath and swallowing it down. My groan was stolen by the glide of his tongue against my bottom lip before he pressed gentle kisses to my mouth, not sinking deep.

I held back my frustrated moan, just wishing he'd kiss the shit out of me, but the fluttering kisses, testing and teasing, continued.

With the taste of him finally on my tongue, I wanted more. Wanted to chase his mouth, savour it. Drink him down and disappear in the kiss and welcome the head-spinning joy I just knew would come with it.

"What are you waiting for?" The raspy question burst free as I pulled away enough to make eye contact.

A smirk played on his lips, almost enough to piss me off, but the heat in his gaze and the flush of his cheeks stopped me.

He wanted this. Wanted me.

Fuck, Flynn wanted me, yet I was being a fucking bitch and whining rather than taking what he clearly offered.

Screw that.

My lips crashed against his like a tempestuous storm, igniting an inferno of need. A bite of pain erupted within me, my sensitive flesh shocked by the contact. I embraced it, revelled in the contact, in the touch, having longed for this moment more than I knew was natural.

The taste of longing, all heat and sweet nectar, lingered in the air as our breaths melded. Feverishly and urgently, we kissed, our mouths parting, tongues swiping as I pressed my fingers against the smooth skin of his back.

Flynn's touch turned into a wildfire, searing and consuming, as if we were both starved for the intimacy our bodies demanded. His one hand cupped my injured cheek, while his other clung to my back.

But there was no way I'd be letting go.

A low purr, all hunger and distinctively lion, tore from deep within his chest. And still we kissed, the touch primal, an instinctive dance of tongues and teeth fuelled by this insatiable hunger clawing at us.

The world around us ceased to exist as we drew close each other. I dipped my finger down, touching the crack of his arse before tugging him nearer to me. The pressure bit against my oversensitive dick. It was worth it to have Flynn arch against me, his cock rubbing my covered groin.

"Fuck, I want you." The words, barely discernible, were grunted next to my mouth.

How I wanted that to happen. Wanted him.

I lost his mouth, the complaint on my lips halting when he traced hot, wet kisses down my throat. My skin came alive, the touches a balm to my sensitive neck.

"Clothes off."

Our eyes connected at his order. Desperation peered back at me, and I nodded, knowing he needed this. I stripped as he clawed at the material to get me naked sooner.

"Door," I somehow managed to splutter, my brain nudging at me.

Flynn's hesitation was all I needed to take three big strides to the door, then close and lock it. Heat covered my back, and his dick nestled between my thighs.

Fuck.

I shivered at the contact, at the position. Bare, pressed against the door, and fully exposed. But fuck, it felt right.

Searing kisses smoothed along the back of my neck as his hips worked, encouraging me to spread my legs a little. The head of his cock brushed against my balls. Light flashed behind my closed eyes, and my knees damn near buckled at the sensation.

It'd been over three years since another man had touched me. Three years since lips had been pressed against mine, let alone another cock being anywhere near my naked skin.

No way would I last if he kept this up.

"Lube and bed." Rather than sounding like the demand I'd intended, my words were all needy breaths.

I'd give Flynn anything he wanted. Whether in rapture or forever, he could take it all.

In a flurry of movement, we were on my mattress,

his scent strong here from being wrapped up in my sheets. His back hit the mattress, and I landed on top, blindly searching for the lube I kept in my bedside table.

"What do you need?" The strained question passed my lips, but there was nothing cavalier or even honourable in the words.

That lust controlling him should have had me backing off. His body wasn't completely his own, not with the gene shifting still being in the final stages. But undoubtedly, he needed this. It was only in the loss of control—the fuck, the fight, or the shift—that his lion could fully form and meld.

The adrenaline, the release would let down the body's guard to allow the exchange to be complete. It sounded like I was being magnanimous as fuck, but I'd never been good at bullshitting myself.

I wanted Flynn in any way I could have him. And since this was realistically the only time I'd be close to him like this—when his choices were narrowed down to only me—like the sad fuck I was, I'd take it and reap the consequences of loss as soon as it was over.

"You. I need inside you." Gravel coated each word as he flipped me over and hovered above me.

A ripple of anticipation moved through me, and I bobbed my head. The last time I had a dick inside me,

I'd been a cadet, handpicked by the Alliance to join the international agency. That was so long ago, I barely remembered the sensation.

It seemed leaving myself open and vulnerable to any request Flynn made was my new MO.

I shoved the thought aside, an easy task when his lips danced across the column of my neck. Sighing into the touch, I barely got myself together enough to push down on the trigger to release the lube.

The sound caught Flynn's attention, his gaze drifting to my hand. His heated stare snapped to mine, a slow, teasing smirk lifting his lips. My lungs seized at the playful look, and I committed it to memory.

With a slow movement that was at odds with the speed of his pounding heart, Flynn's palm touched mine, and he stole the slick before lazily trailing his hand down my stomach. As soon as he encircled my cock, a shock of pleasure jolted me. I arched my back, a needy groan wrenching past my lips.

Subtlety had flown right out the fucking window. I didn't have the chance to be embarrassed, not when Flynn reacted immediately and jacked me off as he captured my mouth. My head spun, over-whelmed with sensation, feral for each kiss and tug of my cock.

"No," I gasped against his lips when I lost his hand.

I wanted it back. Needed to fuck into his tight grip.

He pulled his head back, peering down at me, his golden eyes swirling with so much intensity, I slammed my mouth shut. "I can get you off with my hand or my cock."

Well, when he put it like that....

"More lube," I instructed, the click of my tight swallow sounding loud.

Slow went out the window, too, when he added more slick to his fingers and immediately circled my entrance before sliding a finger deep inside. The intrusion ached, burned....

"More," I grunted.

Two, then three fingers pressed inside me, moving and stretching, brushing against my channel, opening me up. Our kisses didn't let up, all passion and heat, fast and dirty, and fuck, how I needed him inside me.

"Do you need—"

The shake of my head cut Flynn off. "I'm ready."

"Fuck."

The growled word tore out of him as a new desperation took control of his movements. I rode the wave with him and let him take the lead as he spun me around and positioned me on my knees.

I dropped my head onto my arm, panting heavily.

Exposed and vulnerable, I shivered, feeling a nudge against my hole.

"Do it," I whispered, sensing his last thread of hesitation.

"Fuck." His shuddery breath bathed my back in heat as he pushed into me. Firm hands squeezed my hips, holding me in place as he inched deeper. The slow progress left my panting breaths choppy, the steady push taking me by surprise.

From the way Flynn's body vibrated, it was clear he was barely hanging on.

"I'm a motherfucking tiger. I won't. Break." The last word punched out of me as he bottomed out. Finally. But there was no chance to get my composure. I was too full, too close to spinning out, already on the edge of shooting my load at how perfect he felt deep inside me.

And then he was moving, frantic, punishing in his grip, his powerful strokes. And I was here for all of it.

Unable to keep my arms up, let alone look back at him, I breathed into the mattress, grunting and groaning, choking out my pleasure with every frenzied snap of his hips. Blunt nails sharpened against my hips, stinging, making my soul sing and my cock throb.

"So. Fucking. Tight."

Not able to agree with a nod or words, I simply

braced myself and accepted his perfect intrusion. This was everything I'd been missing. I wanted—no, I fucking *needed* it to last. Was desperate to hold on to this feeling, the sensation of sweet, shy, smart-as-fuck Flynn completely owning me.

"Fuck." Garbled words followed as he pegged my prostate. Limbs shaking, my whole body vibrated, so close to giving in to this feeling. The release I so desperately craved.

White blinded my vision, my balls tightening.

No, no, no.

I wasn't ready.

"Nngh." Flynn's hips stuttered as I clamped around his dick.

His teeth latched on to my shoulder, and I was gone, floating in the abyss as lightning blasted through me, landing in my balls and shooting out of my cock. Prying my eyes open, I gasped, staring down at my untouched cock. Thick jets of cum pulsed out of me, each release causing a shuddery wave of bliss.

"Fuck, fuck, fuck, Rowan."

I sighed at the sound of my name and Flynn's desperate cry as he emptied deep inside me. A fresh shudder raked my body, welcoming his release, his scent.

I'd be carrying it for days. It was sad as fuck, but I'd make sure of it.

A deep groan followed, and Flynn leaned against my back. His heat pressed against me, and I closed my eyes, allowing a satisfied smile to form that he'd never see.

If only we could stay like this. In this bubble of need and desire... in this loss of control. There was little doubt in my mind that if it hadn't been for Flynn's change, we would never have reached this point.

While I'd dreamed it, fantasised about it long before the past three days, such desires belonged in the realm of fantasies for a reason.

My smile slipped at Flynn's tensing body.

And in less than thirty seconds, I suspected the need to lock my flighty fancies down would be the only thing protecting me.

"Shit.... Oh fuck... you're bleeding. I hurt you, Rowan—oh fuck...."

Panic, the fastest bucket of ice-cold water imaginable, rolled off Flynn. His voice pleading, shaking. And all while his softening cock remained buried snuggly up my arse.

What I wouldn't have given to have those thirty

seconds of postcoital bliss back rather than the five-second wake-up call.

I forced my head up and my arms under me, wincing at the movement. I hoped I'd be feeling him for days. He'd gone to town on my arse, so maybe I'd be lucky and my healing would be slow. "I'm okay." I angled a little, catching sight of my blood covering the bedsheets.

Not a chance a cold wash would be getting that stain out.

"No, you're not. Fuck." Hysteria stripped his tone bare. He moved, and I clamped my lips together, refusing to whine at the loss of him when he pulled out. "Rowan, I'm... fuck, I'm so sorry. You're injured—"

"Motherfucking tiger, remember?" I couldn't help but remind him, but I kept my tone soft, a lightness to it my heart didn't feel. "I'll heal."

When he clambered off the bed, all clumsy limbs, I sat up, then stood. Clothes. I needed to cover up, hating the vulnerability of my injured torso being on display. In the throes of passion, pretending I was whole had been easy.

Now, when Flynn—the one person who I thought I could maybe one day have a genuine connection with

—was freaking the fuck out, reality stood front and centre.

I snagged a pair of sweatpants and pulled them on, fighting the wince when the fabric brushed what I was sure were deep claw gouges on my hips. Finally covered, I braced myself to meet his gaze.

And fuck, how I wished I hadn't. I should have just smiled, said thanks, and hightailed it to the bathroom.

What a fuckwit I was.

CHAPTER 7
FLYNN SMYTHE

For the first time in hours, the haze in my brain cleared and the reckless drive to sate my desire faded.

Who the hell was I kidding? Faded? Any semblance of need tore out of me the moment I spotted the blood. It further disintegrated when the damage I'd caused stared me in the face.

I'd bitten him. Clawed at his hips.

I could barely meet Rowan's gaze. How could I when I'd given him little choice but to get hot and dirty with me. Fuck, I'd all but pounced on him.

Rational thoughts about him having the power to say no tried feebly to breach my crumbling thoughts, but I couldn't allow it. Honestly, in this moment, as I stared in horror at the mess I'd caused—fresh wounds on his previously unblemished side—I struggled to process what I'd done. How I'd behaved.

How the fuck could he even look at me?

A sound from far off outside the locked bedroom door startled me. Goose bumps prickled my skin at the realisation that the noise wasn't directly outside the room, yet the sound reached me despite the distance.

"Fuck. Kent and Jada." Whatever blood was left in my face drained immediately.

A fresh tidal wave of mortification slammed into me.

Not only had I injured Rowan, a man who I barely knew but respected immensely and who'd already battled with pain and healing, but I'd done it all within hearing distance of two vampires. Specifically, my unofficial adopted family.

Nausea turned my stomach and kept an unwelcome grip on it.

"I'm gonna be sick."

I finally met Rowan's startled gaze. He swiftly moved and ushered me to a door I seriously hoped was a bathroom. Darting past him, I prayed he wouldn't follow. His sympathy right now would likely kill me. That and the pity. I wrenched open the door, relieved to see a toilet.

Fuck, I thought as I dropped to my knees, *maybe he'll only feel regret. But what if it's hatred?*

I heaved, clutching at the white porcelain, arguably feeling the most pathetic I ever had.

"Do you want—"

"No," I snapped, unable to handle even a semblance of any emotion from Rowan—too afraid of what exactly the feeling directed my way would be. "Please leave." I swallowed back another threat. "I shouldn't.... We shouldn't.... I'm sorry, but please leave."

I whispered the last three words to his retreating back. Alone, I exhaled, then pulled in a shuddery breath.

Maybe I could just lock myself away in this bathroom. Hiding away sounded all levels of inviting.

I'd screwed up phenomenally. And that wasn't even including the very real consequences of allowing myself to be clawed and becoming a lion shifter.

I cut that thought off immediately. My brain could only handle so much.

Another exhale and inhale, and I latched on to the coppery scent of blood. My attention snapped to my hands, bloody and human.

How could I have not felt them shift?

"Fuck." I clambered to my feet and clung to the sink before washing my hands.

So much blood.

I shook my head, dislodging the memory.

Rowan's pants and groans. His desperate, needy cry.

My breath hitched, the memory coming to life in sharp focus.

The way he'd felt. His tight channel. The bliss coursing through me. How he'd clenched, drawing every last drop of cum from my body like I was made to live inside him. Buried deep.

The hell was I doing hiding away?

The need to get out there and talk to Rowan got me moving. I was better than this. More importantly, so was he.

But first, I needed to shower, remove the evidence of his blood. I just wished it wouldn't remove his scent from my skin in the process.

With renewed urgency, I got my arse into gear, washed myself down, and dressed in the clean pair of sweatpants and the soft tee I found on the dresser. Taking a deep breath, I left his room, following the scent of.... I inhaled. Burritos. My stomach rumbled, not that the sound was needed to alert everyone of my presence.

Well, not quite everyone.

Only Jada and Kent were in the partitioned kitchen-diner.

As Jada stepped towards me, Kent's assessing gaze roamed over me, her narrowed eyes softening slightly when they caught on my shimmering clawed scar.

And wasn't that a mindfuck?

I'd barely been able to pull my focus away when I'd first stared at myself in the bathroom mirror. Though between the claw marks tattooed into my skin and the dramatic shift in my eye colour, I remained unsure which spurred my pulse to pump harder.

Jada wrapped me up in her arms, no small feat considering she was a few inches shorter than me. Her hug was restrained but nowhere near as gentle as she'd previously hugged me.

"I'm so relieved you're okay." She pressed a kiss to my cheek and pulled away, cupping my jaw with her dark hands. The intensity of her stare let me know that while happiness had bolstered her mood, she was still pissed off.

"What else was I meant to do?" I said quickly, trying to cut her off before she had the chance to lay into me. "He was dying, and he has so many answers."

As soon as the words passed my lips, a flash of memory, one that wasn't my own, had me gasping.

"What did you see?" Kent was before me now, Jada having stepped away.

Movement in the open space to the far right caught my attention. Rowan.

Freshly cleaned and dressed, his damaged skin hidden behind black sweatpants and a T-shirt, he stared at me, his expression closed off.

I'd done that. Was responsible for this reaction.

"Red mist." I shook my head. That wasn't right. "Dust. Dirt."

It was definitely rich red soil.

"It was everywhere."

"A duststorm?" Kent asked.

I closed my eyes, trying to draw the memory back, but I knew it didn't work like that.

Passing on the shifter gene in death didn't bring with it hard-and-fast rules, especially when it came to memories. With the exception that those shared were completely random. Moments of Prince when he was five could be just as possible as anything related to Hornell. Though fresher memories were more likely.

It was a risk I'd taken. Not that I'd thought beyond the five seconds allowed to accept the exchange. Now there was no going back.

I shook my head, unable to recall the memory. "I don't know."

A flash of a document on a laptop screen. Wide-eyed, I stared at Rowan, who'd stepped more fully into his kitchen area, gaze unwavering as he waited patiently.

Realising what the paperwork was, I turned to Kent. "Stonnington Place?"

Arching her brow slowly, Kent answered, "Melbourne. My...." Her jaw clenched, and Jada reached out to her, moving close to her side. "Seraphina's place."

Guilt pressed down on me. With all that had transpired, I'd not asked about her sister. My actions had put Kent's whole focus on me.

Fuck, had she even told her parents?

"Ivy," I whispered, unable to hold back my wince. "I'm so—"

"Don't."

I pressed my lips together, trying not to let her sharpness bowl me over. This wasn't about me. It couldn't be.

"What did you see?"

Rowan's voice was closer than expected, but his question effectively cut through the unfamiliar tension between me and Kent.

I parted my lips to say it was nothing exciting, just an electricity bill, but paused, eyes widening when I shared, "We need to get into their safe. There's a thumb drive and paperwork. I know the combination."

Urgency had me adding, "We need to get it now."

Kent nodded, understanding my unspoken "Before anyone from Hornell's team gets there first." We'd already wasted hours as I'd changed and healed.

It could likely be too late.

"I'll organise a flight," Kent said, walking away.

I made to follow but was stopped by Jada.

"You need to eat. Sit your butt down."

I knew better than to challenge her.

"You, too, Rowan. I know full well you haven't eaten. The two of you won't be any use to the team unless you have energy. And you," she said to me, "are you really okay?" Concern bled through her question, her expression filling with compassion.

For a split second, I consider fobbing her off, but I owed Jada more respect than that. "I'm not in pain." As soon as my fever broke, the aches and pain stopped. Obviously, in its place came the flame of desire so damn flammable, I had all but consumed Rowan.

Something I absolutely could not think about right this second. Guilt vs. a hard-on forming was a battle without a clear winner.

"I'm hungry." Famished, in fact. Jada was a kick-arse cook, and in this, she made sense. I needed to eat.

She waited patiently while my ears tuned in to Kent on the secure line a good twenty metres and likely two walls away.

"My brain feels fried, and I keep getting blasts of sensations, which I suppose are memories, but they're not all clear cut and like videos playing in my brain." Since my ability to explain myself was usually so much more efficient than the shit job I was currently doing, I had little doubt both Jada and Rowan believed my mind wasn't fully functioning quite yet.

I exhaled a slow and steady breath, the sound loud in my ears despite how soft I knew it to be. With so many changes going on physically, as well as Prince's memories surfacing, it would take time to process everything. That was a problem, as time wasn't some-thing we—

"Fuck," I blurted. Thinking about time had trig-gered something. I searched the room for a clock of some kind, finally settling on the oven.

"What is it? You've thought of something." Rowan was fully at my side, offering a whole load of distraction. Citrus and jasmine, a weird combination that somehow worked, drifted off him. But... time.... What had come to me?

"Here." Jada shoved a wrapped burrito in my hand and passed me a spoon. "Eat and think."

My lips twitched, my heart softening at Jada's mothering. "Mmm... this smells *egg*-ceptionally good." I snorted at my lameness, but as I followed up with a cheesy smile and a "Thanks," hearing Rowan's gruff chuckle was totally worth the pink in my cheeks.

"You, too, Rowan." She passed Rowan his foil-wrapped breakfast and urged us to sit.

I did so, both happy and relieved that Rowan sat close enough beside me that I could feel his heat, and this way, I wouldn't have to be staring him in the eyes.

"So... what was the 'fuck' about?"

The mouthful of food I'd shovelled into my mouth caught in my throat at his words. I coughed, half choking.

What the fuckety fuck?

I clutched the glass of water Jada handed me, her gaze bouncing between me and Rowan. A vampire's hearing was better than a shifter's; she absolutely knew what we'd got up to. Fuck knew what she'd thought when he left his room all bloodied up.

And now, this awkward foot-in-mouth weirdness going on between me and Rowan—she was eating this shit up. Amused and mildly curious, I suspected.

As I spluttered, Jada snorted as she left the room,

leaving me to die an undignified death. But at least with her gone, I didn't have an audience.

"Ah, shit, I meant, you said 'fuck' like you'd thought of something. Not like...." Thankfully, he trailed off.

Meanwhile, I managed to control my breathing, no longer close to passing out. Though, honestly, avoiding this whole fuckfest of awkwardness by being unconscious might have been great right about now.

"It's okay," I managed, my voice five octaves hoarser than usual. "I knew what you meant."

A soft hum passed his lips, drawing my attention. Surprised by the amusement dancing in his gaze, which was fixed on me, I stared back.

Was he wondering who he'd opened his home to?

I hadn't had the chance to see the place, since I'd been out of it, but this definitely wasn't the same base of operations we'd met in, what, two or three days ago? Shit, was that all it was? It felt like months earlier. So much had happened in such a short period of time.

The last thing I wanted to lose was his smile, but I had to say my piece. There was never a good time for awkward-as-fuck conversations, so now was as good as any.

"About the... fuck." My voice cracked. I was so not cut out for this. There was a reason I didn't do one-night stands. Just like I didn't hop into bed with guys without a genuine connection. Though Rowan and I definitely had that. A screwed-up, possibly irregular connection, but strength formed the bond.

"Alrighty, then. So we're just going ahead and talking about what happened?"

Envy trickled through me at his steady voice and the lack of heat touching his cheeks.

Calm.... I should totally try to emanate that, but try as I might, staring into Rowan's crystal-mint eyes and seeing his expression that hovered somewhere between curiosity and guarded, all I could think about was that next time, I wanted Rowan on his back so I didn't miss a single expression as I ploughed into him.

I'd missed out on how he looked when he'd made his soft sighs and loud grunts.

Not that I would have truly appreciated them at the time. The post-bite frenzy was off-the-scales intense. Primal need and raw desire had driven me, all but demanding I take what I both wanted and needed.

It just so happened that Rowan fit the requirements to perfection.

"Yeah, so I'm—"

"You've already said you're sorry. And there's no need."

I searched his expression, seeing nothing but calm,

maybe even dogged determination there. "Okay," I said slowly, "but I lost control."

"Which is totally normal."

I nodded, pretty sure he was correct. Hell, he was a tiger, albeit a born tiger, but he likely knew a lot more than me about these things. "And you've healed?" I dropped my gaze, trying not to spend too long eye-fucking his broad chest and instead concentrating on his waist.

"What do your senses tell you?"

My brow jumping high in surprise, I stumbled a little. This was real. I'd survived the change. In the recesses of my mind, I knew this was rare for lions. Who knew why I had, but I was hella grateful that I was still breathing.

I inhaled, attuning to the nuances in the air, trying to differentiate between the heavy fragrances of the spicy meal, Rowan's home, and him. The delicate scent stirred, rolling over me like a gentle wave, acti-vating my instincts. Man, distinct and intriguing, carrying with it the subtle fragrance of vanilla.

My newly formed instincts recognised the soothing aroma, a unique blend that beckoned me closer. I held true, the struggle visceral as I forced myself to stay seated and not spin in my seat and climb onto his lap.

There was only so much humiliation I could take.

And throwing myself at Rowan for a second time would be my undoing.

Drawing in more air, I held the scent, tasting it on my tongue. The heady vanilla intertwined with a layer of citrus, somehow rich and spicy. Reminiscent of forests and wetlands, the earthy undertones mingled with sweetness.

Fuck, he smelt amazing.

Blood. I mentally slapped myself when I zoned in and realised he was studying me intently, a quirked brow and an amused expression aimed my way.

Not a hint of blood remained.

He'd healed.

"You're okay."

He bobbed his head. "I'm more than okay."

My dick twinged at his tone, so much deeper than usual. Was he remembering how it felt? Recalling how deeply I'd slid into him? How I'd pounded into him until the scent of our cum filled the air?

My breathing turning ragged, I felt an instinctive, undeniable pull, an inexplicable yearning to do... something. Maybe to lick the column of his neck? Maybe sink back into him?

"Whatever you're thinking, if you don't want me to drag you back to my room, I'd suggest you stop."

Gravel and sin roughened his words, the sound shooting straight to my balls.

Fuck, he wanted that? Would do that?

The click of my swallow was audible and would have been embarrassing if not for the drop of his gaze to where my Adam's apple bobbed.

"Before the two of you get any not-so-bright ideas, Jada and I are heading out."

Kent's appearance, which I was sure I should have heard coming, jolted me into a non-sexy level of awareness.

The job. Right.

That was the priority. Not me getting caught up in Rowan's sinful gaze that spoke of promised dirty deeds.

Snapping my attention to Kent, I aimed for a confident nod. From the narrowing of her eyes, she wasn't buying my bullshit.

"Do I need to split you up?" She looked between us, her attention assessing and intimidating—at least I would have been intimidated a year ago. But this was Kent, and with Jada standing a little behind her to her right, a shit-eating smirk directed my way, I didn't fear for my life.

But Rowan's? I wasn't quite sure.

"Ivy, they're fine, and they need to be here. Plus,

Flynn will need to shift soon. I don't think that's wise on a plane."

The slam of my heart against my ribcage caught everyone's attention.

I was going to have to change. To shift.

Holy shitballs.

A subtle ripple in the air warned me of his presence. Rowan knelt beside where I sat, his warm, firm touch on the back of my neck steadying in a way that should have scared me.

"I need you to take five slow, deep breaths for me."

Right. I needed to breathe.

Counting my breaths, I mulled over what lay ahead.

I was a lion. Irrevocably changed.

I jolted upright, wide-eyed and staring at Kent, whose muscles tensed, alert at my behaviour.

"Prince had panic attacks when he was brought back." My brows dipped. "Seraphina used to help him through it." I felt it, gut deep. While I had more questions than answers, and I suspected most would never be shared, one thing I knew for sure was that Seraphina and Prince loved each other.

"It's weird, knowing how he felt about her." Jada stepped closer to Kent as I spoke. "Prince was trying to get out—away from Hornell." Certainty was woven through my words. "Those documents in his safe—we need to get our hands on them now. He was collecting information, storing it away. Deliberately had hard copies, knowing that with his genetic makeup, Hornell would know."

Sickness curled my gut as Kent said, "The chip," reaching the same conclusion I did. "Hornell was able to monitor everything through the chip."

"Yeah, it could pull audio and visual as well as provide the remote data suck."

"We need to keep working through the coding of the chip." Rowan was all business as he stood, removing his warm hand from my neck.

I held my body tight, refusing to let anyone in the room know how much I missed his touch.

"We're heading out. You eat and work on that." Kent's voice gave no room for argument.

My brain caught up to the "we" part. "Jada, you're going?"

Arching a brow at me, she bobbed her head. "You're safe here, and if Hornell hasn't got to the property in Melbourne already, not a chance I'm not providing backup."

Fear for Jada sat heavily in my chest. Just because she was a vampire didn't mean she—

"I've haven't told you all my stories yet, Flynn. Ask

me about my thirty-five years in the special forces another time. I wasn't always a doctor."

Aware my jaw had dropped, I not so subtly slammed it shut.

"This safe," Rowan cut in, drawing our attention. "How did Prince manage to pilfer information without Hornell being on his case?"

I shrugged, not having the answer to that. "No idea. I just know that Prince was confident that Hornell was in the dark." If only memory transferal worked differently. How incredible would it be to search through memories at will? Instead, relying on trickles here and there meant we had no real control over what information I could access.

But this was a start. It was something I hoped would finally put us a step ahead. We were all frustrated at cleaning up the mess and destruction Hornell left behind.

After a brief discussion of logistics and orders issued by Kent before she left, I sat a metre or so away from Rowan and a much larger, much more impressive version of the setup I'd used when I'd first met him at the other, smaller warehouse.

The high-tech lab sprawled around me, an imposing collection of glowing screens, sleek interfaces, and humming machinery. The sound, familiar and reassuring, helped ease my heart that kept trying to break free and race frantically.

Sure, I was side by side with the man who'd been the faceless star of so many fantasies over the past month, and honestly, my dreams didn't do justice to the reality of being deep inside him, but the computer lab was my domain. Just as it was his.

My fingers danced over the keys of my workstation, tapping out a rhythm in harmony with the soft whirring of processors. Yet it was Rowan's area that I struggled to look away from.

Seated beside the man, I was privy to witnessing first-hand the genius at work. Rows of monitors stretched across the walls, each displaying lines of code flickering in mesmerising patterns. The room was a blend of dim ambient lighting sources, casting an ethereal glow over the metallic surfaces, and the occasional flash of neon from the equipment.

It bathed the tiger, pulling into stark focus the angle of his jaw, the cut of his cheekbone. Was it just a couple of hours ago that I'd dragged my tongue over the back of his neck and bitten on the skin between his neck and shoulder?

Everything about Rowan commanded my attention. He navigated the labyrinthine networks with an effortless grace, his hands blurring as he manipulated the holographic interfaces, piecing together the puzzle that would grant us full access to the chip discovered inside Prince.

While I'd been recovering, Kent had already made an impressive start. Before even bringing it back to his domain, though, Rowan had cut off wireless access, ensuring Hornell could not receive any more data. We were currently working our way through the code that would lead us to the central hub where the pulled data was stored.

We were so close that the air between us buzzed with anticipation. The room felt alive with the rhythmic pulses of data flowing and practically breathing through the network cables.

Rowan punched in some coding, effortlessly working his way through data streams while I manipulated firewalls and kept half an eye on him. Fuck, he was magnificent.

And yes, I was staring again, my fingers frozen. Not for the first time, I'd grabbed his attention, a quizzical look on his handsome face. I immediately dropped my gaze, realising I'd been caught ogling.

"We need to find time for you to shift and run."

My gaze snapped away from his hands. Looking straight at me, Rowan arched a brow.

"I do?"

There was admittedly an itchiness in my skin, and clearly my concentration was for shit. Was it the need to transform causing these issues? My shoulders relaxed a little. If that was the reason, perhaps I wasn't being such a lusty dickhead after all.

"You do. It'll help you concentrate. We have time before Kent and Jada arrive in Melbourne. I have a plot of bushland not far from here. We can go there."

I nodded immediately; the more he spoke, the more it made sense.

I was going to change into a motherfucking lion.

Holy shitballs.

CHAPTER 8
ROWAN HART

Forty acres wasn't a lot of space when in shifter form, but after several loops and speeding through the bushland of the acreage I owned, the size didn't matter. All that did was Flynn's happy roars, the chuff of contentment when he'd successfully launched across the five-metre-wide creek that meandered through the land.

But with the sun finally rising, the minutes ticked by, and it was time to be heading back.

It had been a risk, leaving my den, but essential, and seeing Flynn content and magnificent in his lion form was worth all the potential of being attacked.

Having shifted back and dressed, I stood in the untamed bushland, admiring Flynn as he bounded towards me. Seeing a lion grinning, his tongue hanging out, was a first. Warmth suffused my chest, the sensation alien and impossible to squash.

Fuck, he looked adorable. And how the hell a huge-arse lion, likely twenty kilos heavier than me when I was in tiger form, could appear cute-as-fuck was beyond me.

I had it bad.

Me swooning over the tongue-lolling shifter simply proved it.

When he'd first shifted, his body shimmering and contorting in mere moments, he'd stolen my breath. Sure, Flynn had seemed bewildered by his new-found shape, his muscles tense and his movements shaky, but after his first few tentative steps, the change within him had been almost immediate.

Bold and brash, almost cocky, it was as though the melding of his genes had awakened something inside him. But more than anything, he exuded an undeniable sense of belonging in the wild terrain.

Magnificent didn't do him justice.

His golden mane billowed in the gentle breeze as he bounded closer, the soft padding of feet over fallen eucalyptus leaves barely making a sound. Tranquillity all but radiated from him as he stopped before me, satisfaction and contentment blazing from his gaze.

"We have to go." Stopping his fun went against the

grain, but we needed to do this. We needed to be back on comms by the time Kent, Jada, Michaels, and Shaw landed. "Remember, all you need to do is—" I slammed my lips shut as Flynn shifted, his human form appearing in the blink of an eye. "That. All you have to do is that, apparently."

The man was a natural. He was born to shift.

He was also butt-naked.

With the expanse of his perfect skin on display, it was a test of my willpower to not eye-fuck him, let alone step into his space and drop down to my knees to swallow his half-hard cock, because *that* I had noticed.

"I best, uhm... dress."

My gaze snapped to his face to see amusement and heated cheeks.

"My clothes?"

Shit. Not even realising I'd been strangling the fabric of his borrowed sweats and tee, I quickly passed them over, already trying to think of something... *anything* that would get my hard-on to behave.

That I'd never given Flynn undies had escaped me, not having paid attention until he'd stripped in the cool morning air earlier and his cock springing free from the sweatpants had almost made me swallow my tongue. I didn't know how we'd get home intact. Or more specifically without me saying something inappropriate like I wouldn't mind bending against a tree so he could fuck me.

"What's the time?"

Flynn's question jolted me to awareness. A check of my watch and I clutched my car keys. "We really need to get moving. They'll be on the tarmac in twenty-five."

I didn't need to add that we still had the chip to decrypt as well as intel to chase up.

Tugging on the sweatpants, Flynn nodded. "Let's go." Barefoot, he headed towards my vehicle, not even bothering with the T-shirt.

"Do you not want to dress first?"

He peered over at me, a question in his gaze before a soft smile formed. Yeah, I'd been salivating over him. "Am I distracting you?"

As soon as the words were spoken, his eyebrows shot high. He was surprised by his own question, the boldness of it, the not-so-subtle flirting tone. I kind of was, too, but that didn't mean I wasn't a fan.

"Maybe," I offered, not flat-out rejecting being called out. "And as much as I appreciate...." I trailed off, settling on a general wave in his direction, ignoring how lame my awkwardness was. Fuck, my flirting skills needed work. Something I never thought I'd be worried about. But Flynn had me questioning everything. Every guard I'd put in place. Every determined thought I'd had that I'd be alone... unloved.

"Appreciate...?" he encouraged, as I'd lost the ability to communicate.

"You... your skin.... Fuck, everything about you."

His surprise was back, but it was all directed at me.

"Yeah?" The sweetness of uncertainty was a fuck of a thing. I liked it a lot.

"Most definitely," I continued, "*but* we really have to get our arses moving."

When he hesitated, my stomach flipped, anticipation a jolt of lightning. Finally, he bobbed his head, and I started breathing again.

We really were in a time crunch.

The thought jarred a memory of our unfinished conversation. As soon as we settled in my car and I was driving us towards my place, complete with the usual mixing up of the route to shake possible tails, I asked, "Earlier, it sounded like you'd thought of something when we were eating."

"Shit, yeah." He stopped speaking and closed his eyes.

I couldn't imagine how surreal this whole thing was for him. When he'd mentioned Prince and Seraphina, their feelings, that had been odd enough.

Who knew what other sorts of traces of memory, of emotions he'd experience?

"Something about a date or time." He glanced my way, his nose scrunched in concentration. A headshake followed. "I don't know, beyond that it felt important."

And that was the thing—whatever memory came to him could potentially be a game-changer. Of course, it could also mean nothing and never fully form. The memories wouldn't come to him indefinitely. They had their own time limit—usually disappearing for good in a few short weeks.

We had so many slivers of information, yet none really helped form a whole picture.

"When we interviewed Prince," I started, turning left at the quiet T-junction, "he said every three weeks for the injection, right?"

"Yeah."

"And based on Hornell being behind the attack"— something we hadn't confirmed, but we all 100 percent believed—"are we in agreement that was two-pronged? Taking out Prince and Seraphina being one, and then compromising the ITU's task force, not only the building and the team but also the data?"

"Definitely." Flynn angled to look at me, twisting a

little to do so. "Lucas was looking into the data storage, seeing if anything was compromised."

I nodded, knowing that. "When he has answers, that should tell us if Hornell was looking to see what the team has on him or if he's searching for information."

"Shit, okay, so you're thinking it wasn't just about shutting us down and Prince up?"

"No." I felt the truth of the words. No way would Hornell go to such lengths just to mess with the ITU. "There's a possibility that your team was getting closer to discovering him."

"We weren't, not really."

"That you know of," I corrected.

"But you don't think that's what it was about?"

I didn't. "We need to think about what his long-term goal is. Go over what information your team may have that he would like access to that's significant enough for him to infiltrate and attack."

"We really need to know what's in those documents and trace the chip." Determination threaded through Flynn's words.

And I couldn't agree more.

It didn't take long to get back to my warehouse space. We were inside at our workstations, a comfortable quiet between us, when the secure phone rang.

Flynn answered, putting the call on speakerphone while I focussed on the surveillance camera feeds located at Melbourne Airport that I'd previously pulled up. I spotted the team of four immediately, Kent with her phone to her ear as they headed towards a waiting SUV.

I'd already watched the SUV being dropped off by a Melbourne agent, and no one had tampered with the waiting vehicle.

Checking the surrounding area, focussing on different angles, I searched for any tails and for anything out of place. Not seeing anything, I let Flynn continue holding the conversation while I checked on the drone positioned above Seraphina's home.

No movement. No telltale signs of entry.

"The house is clear," I said, receiving an affirmative from Kent.

It would take thirty minutes for them to arrive in Toorak, maybe less if they put the SICB sirens to good use. Sometimes stealth was required—nine years in the Alliance taught me that. Other times, it was all about the speed and the race to the finish.

"Do you want comms on and open?" Flynn asked.

The team entered the vehicle, and the start of the engine filtered through the line, along with Kent's

"Yeah. I'll sign off, and we'll get them switched on. How are you getting on with the chip?"

Flynn winced at my side. "Uhm... I needed to shift." A thread of guilt was woven through his words. I didn't like it.

"And he rocked it." The defence fell out of my mouth, and Flynn shot a surprised look at me. I shrugged, trying not to let on I was just as surprised.

"I bet you did, Flynn." Warmth coloured Jada's voice. "We're so proud of you."

There was a shuffle, and I was sure I heard a grunt followed by what I thought was Michaels snorting a laugh.

"We are." Kent's voice came across stilted. I smirked, hearing how much it pained her. "Reach out when you have something."

The line went dead, and I sneaked a look at Flynn, whose cheeks blazed.

"She's good with the whole compliments thing, huh?" My lips twitched.

A startled blink, and then he erupted in laughter that filled the space like the sun erupting through storm clouds, radiating warmth and light. The sound, a melodic burst of happiness, caressed my skin. It was infectious, a beautiful shock that illuminated his whole being.

Where have you been all my life?

Mesmerised, I struggled to keep my eyes on the screen before me. As his laughter continued, he replied, "You could say that. Kent shows her warmth by not kicking your arse and by not giving you the shit assignments."

Like this, Flynn was a sight to behold. His features softened, his eyes crinkling at the corners, emitting pure, unadulterated joy.

I could get used to this. Being in his presence. Getting wrapped up in his smiles and laughter.

"You're lucky," I offered, a genuine smile pulling at my lips. While I was aware of the lack of movement to part of my face—I always was—in this moment, I didn't care. All I cared about was appreciating Flynn's happiness. After what he'd been through the past few days, he deserved the grace of uncomplicated laughter.

While his chuckle petered out, he didn't lose his smile. "I am."

Wings took flight that I hadn't needed to explain myself.

"By the time I was twelve, I figured out who my parents were and why they didn't love me."

The matter-of-fact tone hurt my heart, but I simply shifted my head, letting him know I was listening. That I pretended to be busy on the computer, too busy to switch on the comms unit to give him three more minutes to share, would remain my secret.

"My obsession with joining the SICB from a young age didn't help, and my fixation on computers pushed home how different we were. They were cold to each other, so it figured they'd be cold towards me. They only wanted a child to carry the family name, continue in the family business."

My research had shown me most of this. Or at least who his parents were. Both were defence lawyers in their family-owned law firm. Their clientele raised more than my eyebrows when I first read through their history. Red flags had gone crazy.

It was no wonder they were pissed off that their only child wanted to join the very bureau they regularly fought against to get high-powered criminals off whatever charges were brought against them.

They had a worrying success rate.

It made sense that the checks I'd found the SICB had carried out on Flynn were incredibly thorough and so much more detailed than the arguably already comprehensive checks on most academy candidates.

"They paid for the best education, though, and since I took law electives, they grudgingly allowed me to pursue my specialty at university. They didn't come to any open days, even at primary school. My master's degree didn't get acknowledged." Another chuckle followed, and I glanced his way. Warmth shone in his eyes. "Did you know Ivy and Jada threw me a party when I graduated from the academy? That was after they almost brought the house down with how loud they cheered during the ceremony."

I nodded, not willing to lie. I didn't add that I'd watched the ceremony through the live feed.

"It was the best day I've ever had."

Unable to delay the inevitable, knowing we were short on time, I stood, ready to move over to the wall where the comms centre lived. "Best days are important. You be sure to hold on to them." I kept my gaze on the unit, aware he stared at me.

"Have you had many?" Caution quietened his voice.

As I fiddled with the unit, I powered it up and peered over at him. "Today." I kept my gaze steady. "I think today counts as one." Swinging my head away, I stared hard at the black comms unit like it was the most fascinating thing in the world, my heart beating fast.

I heard his chair moving on the concrete floor. Flynn's cautious footsteps were completely at odds with the quickening of my pulse.

"Are you going to let me respond to that, or are you going to avoid me?"

Fuck it all to hell.

When did he get so confident? Not that I didn't think it was a good look on him, but I was so out of my comfort zone.

With the comms unit light on green, I ensured our mics were on mute before slowly turning to face him. Despite him calling me out, pink painted his cheeks, and the wariness in his gaze was easy to spot.

My admiration for Flynn grew. That he was putting himself out there like this when he clearly struggled to do so was a hell of a thing. It was also sexy as fuck.

When we made eye contact, a stuttering breath left him. His nerves gripped my heart, tearing away those pointless barbed-wire defences I'd erected. Biting steel had no defence against Flynn's honest response. And he was letting me see it all.

Sure, he was a computer specialist, but he could handle himself. Had been trained at the academy for all the skills needed to not only survive as an agent but excel.

"Yesterday, I was turned into a lion shifter. It's a mindfuck."

No doubt it was.

"And then there's you," he started, and my heart bounced around in my chest like it was a damn ping-pong ball. "This incredible magical unicorn"—his lips twitched—"who I didn't dare dream I'd ever get the chance to meet, but I did, and you're *you*, all mysterious and defensive and a little bit grumpy and sarcastic, and then you go and do whatever you can to save me, and even come out of hiding for me—"

"You remember that?" I asked, startled. He'd been so out of it, balancing between life and death, I hadn't for a second believed he'd recall me being there.

"I heard your voice. You sounded pissed."

I snorted, the sound cutting through some of the tension between us. "I thought you were going to die."

Flynn's whole posture, along with his expression, softened. "And you came out anyway, and I get the feeling you don't leave this place often, let alone see anyone besides your brother."

"You get the feeling, or...?"

"So, Vinnie may have let that slip." His lips twitched again. "But still, you came for me. You seem to always be there, saving my arse. Why is that?"

Fear kept my mouth clamped shut. Telling someone you stalked them wasn't the best conversation starter, but this connection between us was something.

Since I'd already admitted to him that today was one of my best days, it would be a dick move to stop now. Nobody forced me to admit that to him in the first place. That I had told him meant bullshitting myself was no longer an option.

For years I'd locked myself in my tower of surveillance and computer software. I'd already started to let him in eighteen months ago. He deserved to know that.

"Come in, Smythe. Kent checking in. Over." The comms unit light blinked with Kent's voice.

"Fuck." Flynn took a step in my direction, stopping close enough that his heated breath brushed my skin. "This isn't over." He reached over me, leaning in even closer.

My breath caught as he grasped a headpiece, my nose so close that with a slight shift, I could graze it along his neck. And fuck it, I did. I couldn't hold back if my life depended on it.

Flynn froze, and he stopped leaning back, keeping his neck in position. What he did do was place the headset on, and with a steady voice that belied the vibration of his skin, he said, "Message received. All okay? Over."

Slowly, I reached for Flynn's waist, finding purchase. On contact, he shuddered, and I squeezed lightly, going all in and pressing my mouth to his neck, the skin warm and covered in goose bumps.

"We're five minutes out. How are the feeds looking? Over."

I exhaled quietly, letting my forehead drift to Flynn's shoulder. Work beckoned.

He angled back, making eye contact, the flush on his cheeks deep. "Just checking now. Over." A press of the mic put it on mute, but rather than moving immediately, he leaned into me, pausing when his lips were a whisper away from mine. "Will you answer my questions later?"

"Yes."

He pressed his answering smile to my lips, barely a caress before he pulled away. "Despite everything, today's one of my favourite days too."

And then he was gone, back at the workstation and talking to Kent while I stood there, mouth agape.

The world as I knew it seemed to be arse up, backwards, and inside out.

As I stared at Flynn, who shot me a wink before he focussed on the video footage and worked the drone, a smile curved my lips.

This was madness. The one-eighty, the warp speed, the absolute conviction that there was nowhere I'd rather be.

I was here for it all.

"THAT'S THE LAST OF THEM," KENT DECLARED a moment before the final scan appeared on our screen.

The collection of the files had gone off without a hitch, the key code Flynn had provided worked, and with the paperwork we'd glanced over while waiting for Kent to finish uploading them, the information was damning.

We just needed it to prove fruitful too.

Kent and the team with her were in a secure location in Melbourne, not wanting to race back to Sydney until they knew there were no more leads in Victoria.

"Kent, you all focus on the paperwork you have, and see what you can find," Lucas, who'd joined the briefing call, instructed. "Smythe, what's the status with the chip?"

"We're close to following the signal," he explained. "We managed to decode the encryption of some files that were... trapped?"

I nodded. "Yeah, it seems like when we severed the transmission, rather than some information deleting, it got caught in the device, which is strange, as a chip like this isn't really equipped with storage capability."

"Any idea who made it?" Lucas asked.

"Not yet." Which was frustrating. "But we don't think Hornell would have known about it." It was something Flynn and I had discussed while waiting for Kent's team to make their way to the safe house.

"Interesting." Lucas's tone turned thoughtful. "So potentially, the chip has backdoor access created by the designer and hidden from any schematics they may have shared with Hornell."

"That's what we think, yes." It still felt odd, talking things out like this—explaining and justifying actions and thoughts. For years it had been how I'd worked, and falling back into the repartee was easier than I'd anticipated.

I was unsure how I felt about that yet.

"Okay, then definitely keep following the lead. Check out the storage, see what's there, and get a signature. We need to track the creator down," Lucas instructed. "I've made some progress with the databanks I secured from the ITU facility."

That had my attention.

Flynn and I glanced at each other, our discussion from earlier popping into my head.

"I was able to locate what information was accessed."

A grumbling came across the line. It could have

been any member of the team, rightly pissed off that Hornell had been successful in not only killing two people but locating and damaging their unit base *while* infiltrating the databank.

It reminded me to triple-check that everything of mine was locked down. No way would I be put in the same position, especially with Flynn here.

He'd been through enough.

"Kitsuma Corp."

My brows shot high. That was the corporation I'd found that had had ties to the Perth lab. Honestly, with everything going on, it had fallen off my radar.

"Kitsuma Corp." Flynn's voice was practically a whisper, but with everyone on the line having acute hearing, I suspected every member heard it. Flynn turned his head quickly, wide-eyed and focussed on me.

"What is it?" I asked.

"Hornell owns Kitsuma Corp. He needs to locate the specimens taken from the Perth lab after we shut them down. One of the samples they haven't been able to duplicate."

He closed his eyes, grimacing and rubbing his temple. When he opened his eyes again, they were bright, holding a wonder that tightened my stomach and made wings flutter around in my chest.

"He needs to find the SICB storage where we kept it for processing and evidence. Fuck." Some of the enthusiasm dimmed, morphing into horror instead. "He has to get the sample by the day after tomorrow. I just have no idea why. Lucas?"

"I'm already looking into it."

The wait was intense until Michaels said, "So, Smythe, which way did you go?"

"What? Which way did I go for what?"

"You know, the whole fuck, fight, or—ow. Fuck, that hurt, Kent." Low grumblings followed. "I was only asking, and you won't tell us shit-all."

"You," Shaw corrected. "There's no 'us' in this conversation."

Michaels scoffed. "As if you're not desperate to get your boy on the line and get all the juicy details from him."

I glanced at Flynn. While his cheeks flamed, he bit down on his bottom lip as though struggling to contain his amusement.

Quirking my brow at him, I smiled when his lips twitched.

"Okay." Lucas prevented the conversation from being picked up. "The facility where the equipment and organic samples were moved to is a location in Melbourne."

"Organic?" Kent asked.

"Looks like the focus was on gene studies," Lucas explained. "Most of the equipment was science lab stuff, like microscopes, but there was also a storage unit in Perth filled with tech. It says on the inventory computers: wafer-handling equipment, chemical delivery systems, SEMs and AFMs, and a bunch of other metrology tools."

The list filtered through my brain as I tried to work out why the huge range of equipment. I'd been the one to provide Flynn with the lead months ago, but I'd thought they were only focussing on chemical creation and the impact on organic matter. The rest of the equipment—

"Was there etching equipment?" I asked. At Lucas's affirmative, I glanced at Flynn. His brow furrowed low. "They were programming chips there."

"That could be what they're after."

I agreed with Flynn. Though a piece of equipment wasn't specifically a "sample," it had the ability to recreate chips. It all depended on how we interpreted the word.

"Is the storage for the machinery in the same location?" Kent asked.

"No. It's right here in Sydney."

"How do you want us to proceed?" Tension

thrummed through Kent's question. I understood it—she wanted back here—but there was the possibility of us being wrong and whatever Hornell hunted for being locked away in Melbourne.

Plus, we still had all the files to check.

Flynn had previously indicated they were important, just like Prince, before he'd died, had indicated that he had the information to help us locate Hornell and take him down for good.

With so many moving pieces, I grudgingly appreciated that having a team working on this had its benefits.

"I'll reach out to Callen, ask him to join Chris and organise a small team to check out the Sydney location. Kent, you stay in Melbourne and take a look at the storage facility. I'll make the necessary calls to let them know to expect you and put both storage facilities on high alert. I'll start working on the documents found in the safe, and Smythe and Hart, we need the chip decoded. Questions?"

Since no one had any, Lucas said, "Okay. Let's touch base in two hours. See what we have then, unless anything urgent emerges."

After ending the call, I cracked my neck and yawned, wincing at the discomfort. Noticing Flynn's attention was on me, I glanced in his direction. "All good?"

He bobbed his head, looking alert as his gaze roamed my face. "Did you get any sleep last night?"

Surprised that was the direction of his thoughts, I shook my head, answering honestly, "Nobody could rest until we knew you were okay. I kind of wore a path in the floor from my pacing. I think I pissed Kent off."

A smirk formed. "She gets pissed off easily, so don't give yourself too much credit."

I chuckled. "Way to wound a guy."

"You want coffee?"

"I would kill for a coffee."

He stood. "I'll go make us some and then get to work on the chip."

"Great, thanks."

I watched him leave, my gaze automatically eating him up and trailing over him. He still wore my sweatpants and one of my tees; both suited him despite the clothing being nothing special. It was possible that the idea of him wearing my clothes was what I liked a little too much.

When he was out of my line of vision, I turned to my workstation. I would make this chip my bitch and figure out who the designer was. That backdoor meant something—likely that the creator had pilfered data in the past.

Pausing when Flynn returned a few minutes later, I inhaled, my chest expanding a little when I scented the hazelnut creamer.

"Black, right?" He placed it on the upright coaster secured to my desk, something I'd invented so I could safely store my drinks without knocking them over by accident.

"Smells good, thanks."

"Not as good as mine."

His teasing tone caught my attention. There was no doubt he wanted to say something about me buying his favourite brand of coffee and creamer, which of course I'd added to the shopping list Jada had put together. The beep coming from my computer speakers prevented any embarrassing discussion.

"Got them."

"The signature?"

When I nodded, he sat and manoeuvred his chair close to my side.

"That was fast. I was gone, what, four minutes?"

"Kent had already been running the chip through a program I created. It was still working in the background," I admitted.

"So, who is it?"

We leaned forwards as I grabbed the strand of coding and pulled it onto a second screen. Once there, I uploaded it and ran it through the software linked to the ShadowNet. Sure, the dark web thrived on its anonymity, but not so much when used with the tracer software.

Code appeared on the screen.

```
def identify_signature(text, shift): encrypted = "for char in text: if char.isalpha(): decrypted += shifted # Creator's signature (00133816351038)

creator_signature = Hackpaw
```

"That fucker."

"What? Who?"

I shook my head, pissed at myself for not even considering Ethan would be behind the tech and programming and even more fucked off with him that he'd be so fucking dumb to work with someone like Hornell.

"Hackpaw." I ground my teeth together.

"That's the name of the person wh—"

"Has a death wish, apparently."

"So, you know this Hackpaw?"

I peered over at Flynn and my breath caught, having momentarily forgotten just how close he was. He was the best kind of distraction.

"Hackpaw?" he prompted, apparently not having the same difficulties I was. In fairness, I could still taste him, feel him. How he'd driven into me earlier had been all desperate need and power. I was grateful for it.

Too gentle, even though it had been years since I'd been fucked, and I would have fully healed by now and not felt even a trace of how he'd taken me. Thankfully, that wasn't the case.

At his raised brows, I cleared my throat.

Right. Hackpaw. I've got this.

"He's someone I occasionally deal with."

"As in...?" Flynn asked, since I was being suspicious as fuck.

In fairness, Flynn was an SICB agent, and me telling him that since I "left" the Alliance and had resorted to taking on some less-than-honest contracts—though in my defence, said contracts helped to fund my own missions to take down corrupt fuckers in the government—I occasionally outsourced to Hackpaw didn't make me feel exactly comfortable.

"If I'm busy or a job I take on is too big, I'll outsource to him."

"Do I want to know what kind of jobs?" While caution laced his words, amusement danced in his eyes.

"I don't know, do you?"

He pressed his lips together as he took me in, searching my expression. "If I said yes, would you tell me?"

"Yes," I answered without hesitation. The voice in my head calling me a foolish prick wasn't so loud anymore. But fuck me, I trusted Flynn. An SICB agent. A man who worked for the government—a system that screwed people over and destroyed them, and if not that, left them for dead.

"In that case, not right now. Maybe when all this is over."

There was no tempering the thundering in my heart. What he said sounded a lot like a promise. Like something more. Something that would come after.

"Okay. We'll file that discussion away."

"So, Hackpaw?"

"I've known him for years, worked with him when I was in the Alliance. He's based in the UK."

Flynn's eyebrows sprang high. "He *was* or *is* in the Alliance?"

"Neither, but he worked for the UK's cyber unit for years. Quit a year before I was shipped home, hanging on to life by a thread with no treatment, just a threat for me to keep my mouth shut."

It went deeper than that, but I'd spent time coming to grips with how I was treated. I'd also spent too many hours culling the corrupt souls for the Alliance since I'd been erased from their system.

Sometimes becoming a ghost had its advantages.

Realising Flynn hadn't responded, I paid attention to his expression.

Fury lurked in the depths of his golden eyes. I swallowed thickly, pretty sure where his emotions were directed. Sure, I had Vinnie, who'd protect me with his last breath, and in some ways, I had Ethan "Hackpaw" Wilder, who, while I kept him at a distance these days, I thought would have my back.

But this.... Flynn before me, his body all but vibrating with trapped fury, was something miraculous. My dick twinged as he stared at me silently. It throbbed as he stood and tugged me up so we stood nose to nose.

"You deserved better than that." Gravelly words and intense eyes held me captive. "I fucking hate that you went through that, were treated that way."

I couldn't speak, trapped completely under his spell.

Flynn like this, weirdly possessive because of something that happened long before we met, apparently got me going.

The place where he was touching my arm practically sizzled. Heat poured off him, and while our temperatures ran high as shifters, this was something else.

"You're burning up." I pressed my palm to his forehead. "Do you feel okay?"

The intensity in his gaze cleared, a new awareness crossing his face. "I don't know." He shook his head. "I feel like I've got a fever." Sweat beaded his brow, trickling down his temple.

This wasn't right.

Keeping the concern out of my voice, I said, "Let's get you into the shower, cool you down."

Shaking his head, Flynn flicked his gaze at the monitors. "We need to—"

"Cool you down," I finished for him. "I know it's Ethan now. That makes this a whole lot easier." But still he seemed reluctant despite how his T-shirt clung to his skin like he'd been swimming. "Come on."

I gave him no choice as I led him away and back to my room. The bed had been stripped, I suspected courtesy of Jada—something I'd have to thank her for. We bypassed the bed, and I ushered him into my en suite.

With the shower on, I methodically stripped him, my concern growing that his cock wasn't hard despite my mouth being in touching distance as I tugged off his sweats, but it was more to do with the shake of his limbs.

His muscles were tight, his skin still far too hot,

but he was alert and becoming more worried by the second.

"What's happening to me?"

I hated that I didn't know. Failure and I were not friends, so there was no way I wouldn't find out. "Let's just get your temperature down, and we'll figure this out." I met his gaze and received a nod, trust reflected in his golden stare.

Once under the cool spray, he sighed in relief. The sound was an instant comfort to the both of us.

"Can you handle being here by yourself? Thirty seconds, max?" Leaving him by himself wasn't ideal, but I needed answers. That meant I needed my laptop.

"I'll be okay." The bob of his head was sluggish.

Okay my arse. Once my back was turned, he'd be collapsing, likely bashing his head on the way down.

I collected the small stool from the corner of my en suite and placed it in the large shower. Once it was in position, I eased him down, not receiving a word of complaint.

"Good?"

"Yes, thanks."

The way he looked at me, his chin lifted, expression open, I couldn't resist leaning in and pressing my lips against his. I pulled away immediately, a little more reassured that his lips weren't burning. When he offered a slightly dopey smile and shooed me away, I left quickly, ignoring the trail of water from my soaked sweatpants.

Fucking Ethan. The arsehole was the only person I could contact. He was the one who created the damn chip that had been buried in a walking, talking zombie; he'd have to have information about Prince and what the hell Hornell did to him.

We needed more than what Prince had told us before his custodian killed him.

And if whatever was running through Prince's veins that kept him alive was now pulsing through Flynn, I'd bring hellfire down on Hornell and make sure Flynn had what he needed to live.

CHAPTER 9
FLYNN SMYTHE

Who knew radio silence could be so deafening?

I stepped out of the shower, finally cool to the touch after the cold water sluiced down my body, and sat at my workstation, eyeballing Rowan as he paced.

I agreed with Kent on this. It was annoying as hell.

He was on a call—with Ethan, the unscrupulous techie, from the sound of it. I could only hear his half of the conversation, which meant Rowan's phone had built-in tech to prevent supernaturals from listening in.

I tried to zone out, but the more agitated he became, the more challenging it was to work on the chip trace. Though why I was doing that, since the man he was talking to could tell him precisely where the signal was being sent, was beyond me.

But I persevered, tuning in to Rowan as he grumbled a threat—something about a needle and ball sac.

We had another hour before we were due to make contact with the team. We needed answers by then.

"No, we're not going to meet up."

My ears twitched.

"Ethan, fuck no. Not interested."

Turning one-eighty so I could watch Rowan, I frowned at the pink in his cheeks. Why the hell was he flushed? What exactly was Ethan asking him?

I felt an itch under my skin, and I repositioned myself on my chair. Discomfort pressed down on me as I full-on stared. That Rowan had flushed over whatever he "wasn't interested in" felt off. My gums tingled, and still, I stared.

Vaguely aware of Rowan's "Fuck, I've got to go," I stilled as he finally stopped pacing. "Flynn."

That voice, Rowan's voice, a soft caress.... I stood, the movement slow, cautious.

"Flynn, talk to me."

I knew I should, but again, that damn tickling.

Wide-eyed, Rowan lifted his hand, a placating gesture. A tendril of vanilla reached me. I inhaled gladly, the scent settling something in my chest that felt tight.

"Hey, Flynn." Another step and he was before me, in my space. Fresh forest, rich and welcome, wrapped around the vanilla I was becoming addicted to. "You're okay." Strong arms cradled me, and I sagged, my misty thoughts easing.

"What...?" I shook my head, confused and a little frightened. "My gums." I jerked away from Flynn and touched my gums. Blunt teeth. My breathing turned ragged, even Rowan tugging me towards him again not doing the trick of calming me down. "What the fuck is happening?"

"Let's go to the couch." He didn't wait for a response, just led me towards the vast open space he'd somehow made look cosy with the two large uphol-stered couches, a chunky coffee table, and a huge TV mounted to the wall.

Taking everything in was the perfect distraction from my growing worry. It didn't help that Rowan's concern mirrored my own.

I faced him, aware of every centimetre between us, every breath he took.

"You zoned out."

I nodded, having been aware of that.

"What were you thinking?"

I scrunched my brow in concentration, trying to recall all that had happened and what I'd felt.

"I think I started to get protective over you," I admitted. "I don't quite understand why or what triggered it, but it felt like I needed to guard you somehow. And my skin itched, and so did my gums." My fingers returned to my mouth.

"You think you may have had a partial shift?"

"Yeah." The thought terrified me. The only other time that had happened, I'd cut Rowan up, hurting him. While he'd shrugged it off and played it down, of course it had hurt. It didn't help that I'd never heard stories of shifters losing control like that.

There wasn't an animal stuck inside our bodies. A second soul wasn't buried deep, waiting for me to communicate with it. When in lion form, I'd been me but covered in hair with a pretty epic mane and huge paws. It was incredible, the sensation, the agility. Honestly, my physique and abilities were all that should have changed. *Should have* being the operative words.

"What is it you're thinking?" I asked him. Since my overheating, Rowan had been on edge and attached to his laptop and his phone. What he hadn't done was talk anything through with me yet. I probably should have been annoyed by that, but between the heat and the exhaustion that came with it and my weird reaction a few moments ago, I didn't have the energy.

All I wanted was the truth.

"Prince being the one to transfer his gene to you concerns me."

As soon as he spoke, understanding slammed into me with the power of a wrecking ball.

Fuck. "Fuck. Do I have a motherfucking zombie gene?"

Rowan looked so startled by my outburst that I couldn't help but laugh. The sound burst out of me, loud and genuine.

"Holy shit," I said, still laughing and maybe on the cusp of hysteria. "Do not tell the team. Shit, I'll never live it down. They'll make me a brain cake for my birthday next week."

Rowan, who'd chuckled along with me, quietened his laughter. It did the trick of sobering me up. A final, hollower laugh followed before my heart clenched. "You think I have the zombie gene?"

I was dead-set serious.

"I'm worried that whatever was in Prince's body, his blood, that kept him alive, that he needed treatment for every three weeks, is impacting you somehow."

My stomach bottomed out. "So you think I could

die without the meds only Hornell himself can provide?"

He pursed his lips, his skin a shade paler than I'd seen before. "I don't know. All I do know is, you're having side effects to the transferal of the shifter gene."

"Me shifting without meaning to."

He nodded. "Your high temperature, your occasional behaviour shift."

"What? What do you mean?" I didn't have a clue what he was talking about.

"I know we've only just met," he started, and I raised my brows in interest, "but I feel like I know you quite well."

"No argument from me," I admitted, though I was pissed that while I knew Rowan, it was only a fraction of what there was to discover about him. "I feel a bit at a disadvantage here. I want to know you as well as you know me."

His frown smoothed out and his expression softened. "I want that too."

That was a relief. Talk about setting myself up for humiliation.

"And your personality... there've been some changes."

"Like what?" I racked my brains, trying to recall what he meant.

"Like now. The whole predator thing."

"Predator?" I half scoffed, half laughed, and was wholly mortified—because fuck, he was absolutely right. That was how it felt.

"You've behaved quite dominant at times."

The flush in his cheeks didn't help my concentration. "I love it when you blush that way."

"Like that. Have you ever behaved that way before? Said anything like that?"

I heard his words but struggled to compute. I shook my head, trying to rattle my brain and clear the wisps of fog trying to settle.

"These side effects," he continued, and I bobbed my head, letting him know I was paying attention. "They're almost instinctual, like you're tapping into—"

"My lion." My brows shot high. "But I don't have a fucking lion." Panic sent my voice high. Holy shit, was I going to turn into a lion? Like a *lion* lion? Not a shifter with a kick-arse skill? Fuck, I'd have to live in a zoo.

Maybe Shaw could hide me? Michaels would be up for it. He was all about breaking the rules. Maybe—

It was only Rowan's soft voice and firm grip on my arm that helped me breathe regularly. The whirlwind of my thoughts settled.

After another round of deep breaths, I calmed enough to carry on listening.

"I don't think you're going to turn into a lion."

I winced. "Did I say that aloud?"

He pressed his lips together and nodded. "None of what you said is going to happen. It's just some sort of side effect that we'll figure out and get under control."

"But Hornell... the case...."

"One and the same. You are more important."

My chest felt tight. Important? Me?

I would not cry like a damn chimp. Not that I was sure chimps cried, but at least boggling my brain helped to ease the aching warmth that made me want to blubber.

"This is what's going to happen. I'm going to talk to Ethan again and get some answers."

"Did you fuck him?" I slammed my palm over my mouth. Mortified, again, I shook my head. "I'm so sorry. I—"

"No, I didn't, and it's okay. Whatever happens is okay. We deal with it, go with the flow. We just need to make sure you're okay, and that we get answers."

"So you didn't fuck him?"

Jesus fucking Christ. There was no hope for me, and apparently, I had a one-track brain and couldn't think of anything but Rowan and sex.

"No, I didn't." And bravo to Rowan for not even a lip twitch when he dealt with my level of bullshit. "I never have and never will."

Okay, that was good. Something loosened in my chest.

"While I deal with that, you focus on the chip. Though I think Ethan will give us everything we need—"

"And that's not sex."

I buried my face in my hands, wanting the ground to open up and swallow me whole.

"Why can't I stop?" I all but whimpered.

"Instincts."

The teasing in his voice had me snapping up my head to eyeball him. While the worry wasn't completely gone—his body was still tense—his amusement seemed real.

"Instincts, huh?" I bit the inside of my cheeks immediately, rolling my eyes at myself for the blatant flirting tone I used.

"Yeah, definitely instincts." His phone rang. "Now, I need to take this call, get some answers, and then we can see what other instincts you may have that need to be"—he perused my body with his heated gaze, doing a fine job at distracting me from my building anxiety— "released."

A soft kiss to my lips and he was out of my space before I could even lick my bottom lip to chase his taste.

Fuck my horny lion self. How the hell was I going to survive being in the same space as Rowan without biting his neck, pinning him down, and taking what was mine?

With a raging hard-on, apparently.

With great effort, I focussed on the screens before me, deliberately wearing a headset, and let the two teams know I was available to put eyes on the live video feeds of their intended targets.

After our two-hour check-in, the Melbourne storage compound remained secure, and after a comprehensive search, all bio samples were accounted for. Kent had put feelers out to listen to chatter. There was zero surrounding Melbourne.

Chris, Callen, and their team had searched the Sydney facility approximately twenty kilometres away from Rowan's place. All was quiet, but they'd since set up surveillance and settled in for the wait.

I'd been having sporadic discussions with Lucas over the past fifteen minutes, the two of us keeping the line open as we passed material from Prince's safe and additional research to each other over the secure servers.

What I hadn't disclosed yet was information about the unprecedented side effects I was experiencing. I would—my promise to the team true and strong—but I wanted to be armed with more information first. Given the intense conversation Rowan continued to have with Ethan and the way his fingers flew across the keyboard, fresh documents flying in and out, I hoped I wouldn't have to wait much longer.

"Take a look at this."

A moment later, a notification appeared on my screen, alerting me to a new document.

I clicked on it, ran it through the decryption program, and a few seconds later, a document opened.

As I started reading, Lucas spoke. "Activity over in Glenorie has been consistent for four years. Deliveries from a variety of firms, plus there's the work order."

I opened the work order. "Holy shit. A helipad application and approval." The date stamp was thirty months ago. "How has this stayed off our radar?"

"It looks like there are another two in the area, so no red flags were raised. But combined with the types of deliveries the address has been receiving, they've definitely got my attention now."

"Can we get a drone in the sky?" I asked, my heart stumbling a little in anticipation. This could be it. If it was, whatever the outcome of my shift, it would be worth it, since Prince hadn't been bullshitting me.

"Definitely, but my concern is, there are safeguards in place around the compound to signal any breach in airspace."

"Makes sense," I answered. The technology had been around for years, and bypassing such alerts could be tricky. Not impossible, though. "Can we organise a satellite feed first?"

"I've already reached out to the director and asked for authorisation. Once we have it and can take a look, I want you to work on the drone access. That should give us enough time for Kent to return to New South Wales."

"Got it," I said, still flipping through the documents discovered in Seraphina's safe. "The information related to Kitsuma Corp is damning."

"There's enough here to shut them down immediately. We need to wait until we check out the Glenorie property first and see what the outcome is of the storage Callen's checking out."

"Are you sure you don't need me to go search the storage?" While I wasn't certain who was on the team Callen had put together, I suspected, as field agents, they weren't as savvy when it came to tech. Plus, they didn't know for sure what to look for.

None of us did, but I was certain Lucas, Rowan, or I would at least have a better chance of knowing when we saw it.

The allusive "it" would be akin to finding a needle in a haystack.

"You're more valuable to us there. The team is on high alert, waiting for someone or multiples to show. How are you feeling?"

"Tired and hungry and ready for all this to be over with Hornell."

"I hear you, but you know it could still take time. As great as these leads seem to be, the bureau has been chasing Hornell for a long time. There's a reason for that."

While he was right, we didn't have Rowan with us then. Together, we were stronger. Better. I believed that as deeply as I believed in the magical ability of coffee.

"While we're waiting to hear back from the director, I suggest you get some rest while you can. We're in for a late and long night."

Considering I had no idea what time it was, or even if there was daylight still outside, I'd take the chance to sleep and eat. "Will do. I'll keep the comms close by in case you need me."

After we signed off, I stretched. Rowan had

stopped talking and was standing a few metres away, holding two mugs of coffee.

"You *are* a magical unicorn." My grin was wide, my teasing strong.

He snorted and waited for me to reach him before handing over my doctored coffee. "You know," he said, turning and leading me towards the open space of the living area of his large facility, "of all the code names, aliases, and nicknames I've received over the years, I'm not quite sure how I feel about this one sticking."

As I sat on the corduroy sofa, I beamed at him, sinking into the comfortable fabric and inhaling the scent of the hazelnut. "You gave it a good shot with the variety of code names you used in our exchanges."

"You noticed that, huh?" He settled beside me, and I relaxed, enjoying his warmth at my side. I was more than okay with following Lucas's orders to have some downtime, and since the communication with him had not been cloaked with the concealment device, it was clear Rowan was too.

"An A-plus for effort, but nothing beats unicorn hacker."

The half-hearted groan was kind of sweet, something I never expected to think about Rowan. But for all his gruffness and sour expressions, over the past couple of days, I'd seen so much compassion and care and absolute sweetness from him that I knew this was the real him.

"I found a pot of chilli in the fridge."

I smiled, knowing exactly who put that there. Jada was a kick-arse cook and a huge fan of spice. "That sounds amazing." I followed up with a jaw-cracking yawn.

"Then a power nap."

Tilting my head towards Rowan from my position on the sofa, I raked my gaze over him. There was space to my other side, yet he'd sat here, the damaged side of his face directly next to me and on display.

Whether deliberate or an unconscious decision, it was dramatically different from when we first came face to face. How so much could change in such a short amount of time blew my mind.

It also reminded me... "Why did you decide to reach out to me all those months ago when I was still at the academy and helping the ITU?"

He eyed me openly, thoughtfully. There was a slight uplift of his lips, yet the damage on his cheek, running to the corner of one side of his mouth, remained pinned down. The struggle to not lean in and place a kiss there was a challenge, but since I wanted answers, I held back.

When I lifted my gaze back to his, amusement peered back at me.

Yeah, he totally knew what I'd been thinking and how hard it was not to shuffle around and climb onto his lap.

"You really want to know, or is there something else you want to do?"

Arsehole. "Answers first," I said with a lot more conviction than I felt. Because honestly, any chance I had to ride a unicorn, I was here for. And the man before me had a horn others would absolutely be envious of.

His chuckle was low, a gruff caress that tickled my balls.

"The Astraweave."

Ho-ly shit.

Taken aback, I startled. My eyes widened. A surge of emotions rushed through me. I knew exactly what he was referring to. It was one hell of a revelation.

"I discovered it and, honestly, was intrigued. Wanted to know more about the person who created it. You."

"That was... what, almost a couple of years ago?" Plus, there was the whole question about how he got his hands on the elaborate coding I created in the first place.

"When I stumbled—"

My snort cut him off, and I arched an eyebrow at him. "Really? Stumbled?"

His smile was all amusement. With a shrug, he continued, "I happen to stumble my way through a lot of firewalls and into places I shouldn't be. I get bored a lot and like the challenge."

Now *that* I believed.

"You know I was just playing around with the Astraweave coding, right?" Legit, when I'd finished the complex coding, reworking the original and very much putting my own mark on it, it had been a fun challenge. It definitely hadn't been for anybody else's viewing.

"In that case, I'm even more impressed."

Praise, as rare as bug-free codebase in complex software, remained a struggle for me to accept. A thrill zipped through me, though, and heat touched my cheeks.

Impressing Rowan long before we knew each other proved an unexpected high. Fuck yes, I was going to eat that shit up.

"You were?" I asked, not so coyly, something I was viscerally aware I wouldn't have been bold enough to ask even this time last week. Would I have thought it? For sure. And I definitely would have wanted to tease.

Along with the side effects, I wondered whether this was normal for made shifters. This boldness. The boost of confidence that thrummed through my veins.

If it wasn't, I hoped I wouldn't lose it, especially considering the amused delight on Rowan's expression.

His gaze flicked down to my mouth, his frost-kissed eyes filling with desire and a surprising warmth as he darted his tongue out and licked his bottom lip. Just the tip. Just enough to have my heart pounding. "Definitely impressed." The gravel in his voice was all sin and heat.

I darted out my own tongue, more than aware that the movement caught his complete attention. "Just how hungry are you?" I asked.

"For...?"

I huffed out a breath with a blend of amusement and impatience, yearning for more than mere words. I desired his lips to claim mine with an urgent fervour. Yet despite the silent invitation I sought, his gaze devoured me, leaving me burning with anticipation.

"The chilli can wait," I smoothly interjected, shifting my position to straddle his lap, a not-so-subtle move that absolutely accepted the chemistry that crackled between us.

He clasped the back of my head with a firm grip.

"Agreed," he whispered, his lips brushing mine as he spoke.

Our breaths mingled, a charged tension enveloping the space between us. With a magnetic pull, our lips met, collided, igniting a blaze so scorching, I was unsure how I'd survive this. His mouth, a blend of heat and tenderness, melded seamlessly with mine.

I was made for this. This connection. His kisses.

Our kiss continued, slow and savouring, light sweeps of tongues accompanied by gently roaming hands. Breathless, my mind spun, consumed by the perfect intensity and the sparking fire threatening to set us ablaze.

The kiss slowed, turning into gentle pecks. I eased away reluctantly, following his lead, and peered down at Rowan. With his expression wide open for me to read, his smile was bright, his desire as obvious as the thickness of his length I happily sat on.

"I want to taste you."

"You do?" This time I wasn't playing or flirting. My brain was too wired and full of lust for that.

"So fucking much."

Hell, with an offer like that....

I scrambled off him, all limbs and awkwardness as I stripped so quickly, I got my leg trapped in the sweatpants.

"Hey." He chuckled, reaching out to steady me. "Let me."

I didn't have the chance to be mortified, not when his fingers grazed my thighs. He helped me out of the sweats, his face so close to my groin that I went light-headed at the warm breaths skirting over my hardening cock.

By the time I was free, I'd tugged the soft tee that still smelt a little like Rowan over my head. Naked and so ready, I swallowed thickly as he caressed my legs, his gaze on my face.

He traced his thumb over the end of my cock, scooping up the beaded pearl. With slow and deliberate movements, he raised his thumb to his mouth and licked. I shuddered, legs shaking in anticipation.

A smile formed on his lips, all seductive sin. Edging forwards, he paused, hovering tantalisingly close. The teasing promise of his lips, mere millimetres away, sent a shudder through me. There was no way I was speeding this up, no matter how much my cock begged for his mouth. The thrill of the anticipation was a high I'd never experienced before.

"You're so fucking hot," I gasped, my voice strained.

Glancing up, he smirked. His eyes were heated yet

filled with amusement, while his lips were swollen from our passionate kisses.

He wasn't just hot, he was perfect. Just like this.

As if knowing what I was thinking, he rewarded me, running his tongue along my slit. My groan was immediate, loud and echoey in the cavernous room. Another lick and my cock glistened, eliciting a loud moan from me.

Thick and yearning for attention, my cock throbbed against his barely parted lips.

"Suck me."

The plea was desperate, demanding, and his smirk almost buckled my knees.

And my neediness worked. Oh, how it worked.

In barely a blink, he was on me, bypassing my mouth, my chest, my stomach that I'd do anything to have him trace with his tongue. But this was so much better.

Heat and suction. Long licks and playful dips of his tongue.

I gripped his shoulder, holding on for dear life. A tremor ran through my legs as he sucked and caressed, his wet slurps a fucking masterpiece of cocksucking as pure pleasure rippled from my cock to my balls and to every nerve ending in my body.

"Fuck, so good." The words tore free, accompanied by a needy, desperate groan.

A firm grip on my butt and my breath hitched. I peered down, capturing his eyes as my balls drew taut.

"So fucking hot." But while his gaze flashed, the tight squeezing of my butt cheek made it clear that praise wasn't what he was after right at this moment.

And since Rowan was close to pulling every ounce of cum from my shaking body, he could have everything I had to give. Anything he wanted.

Fucking his throat was a request I was all too happy to oblige.

Barely able to think with the heavy thud of my heart echoing in my ears, I started off slow. While his mouth stretched around me so perfectly, I had no idea how much he could or wanted to take. How much feeling he had on the damaged side of his face or how —if at all—it would impact him.

Not that Rowan gave any indication of being impacted. He sucked hard, and my knees trembled, capturing my focus completely.

On him.

On how fucking incredible he felt wrapped around me. On how I wanted to paint his lips and watch as my cock disappeared between them.

When his grip tightened, I picked up my pace,

jerking my hips, eyes half lidded as bliss, white-hot and all light, zipped along my spine.

A half-gasped, half-groaned "Fuck" spilled from me as he angled, opening his throat. His nose pressing against the short thatch of hair on my pubic bone as he peered up at me was my undoing.

I shot down his throat with no warning but a cry to not stop, not ever. Sensation, pure and blinding, pulsed through me as I throbbed in his mouth, spurt after spurt trickling down his swallowing throat.

"Holy... fuck," I gasped, the words desperate, breathy, and filled with awe as I focussed, watching Rowan as he gently, so fucking slowly, eased off me. The stroke of his tongue on my sensitive cock as he did so sent a fresh shock of pleasure through me.

With his mouth free, his lips puffy and looking more perfect than they ever had, I all but stumbled against him, clambering back onto his lap as I stole a kiss and licked up the remnants of my cum from his heated mouth.

"You," I said against his lips, finally pulling away and staring at him in blissed-out wonder. I shook my head. "You're so fucking good."

He smiled, and I dove back in, stealing another kiss from his lips and tangling my tongue with his.

His covered cock nudged against me, grabbing my

attention enough for me to slow our kisses and ease away to stare down at his tented pants.

"Come on me. All over me."

There was no need for further instructions as he manoeuvred so I was under him, his grey sweats tugged down beneath his bare cock and his thick, perfect fingers wrapped around his stiff dick.

I joined him, licking my palm, then nudging his hand out of the way to take over.

I wanted to be covered in his scent, absorb his cum so I carried him with me for days.

"Nnnghh."

My eyes flashed to his as he garbled. Heated eyes stared down at me, and he darted his focus between my face and my hand working him over.

"Give it to me." The order tore from my throat, all gravel and heat. "Fuck my hand and come."

"Fuck, fuck, fuck." The last word triggered the first stripe of cum over my chest. The second landed on my chin. Rowan gasped and groaned as he came undone, his body shaking on top of me.

Another small spurt and I dragged him on top, not giving a damn that he was fully dressed. His face close to mine, I made a show of licking my cream-covered hand, delighting in the taste as much as the look of desire he shot me.

"Delicio—"

He cut my word off, pressing his lips to mine, prying my mouth open to chase my tongue. I took his claim willingly, enveloping him, relaxing into his touch as he kissed me more thoroughly than I'd ever been kissed before.

Both our breaths turning ragged, we slowed the kiss until Rowan angled away and peered down at me. A tender, satisfied smile formed on his bj-swollen lips. He dropped down beside me on the overlarge sofa, angled on his side while I remained flat on my back.

I sighed in exhausted delight, inhaling deeply to appreciate his scent. "That was... fuck yeah."

A loud snort passed Rowan's lips. "Articulate after you've been sucked dry, huh?"

I turned my head, attempting to arch an eyebrow, but the movement required energy I simply didn't have. I considered flipping him off, but that gesture also seemed impossible. I landed on a short and simple "Fuck you, arsehole," though I summoned the willpower to press a kiss to his shoulder.

"It *was* all that. 'Fuck yeah' sounds about right."

I managed a half-hearted bob of my head, happy he was in agreement.

"Shower and food?" he asked a few moments later.

"Urgh... yes, but maybe in five hours." If only we

had that much time to bask in the afterglow of coming our brains out by snoozing for so long.

"I can give you five minutes."

I blinked open my eyes, not even realising I'd snuggled down and closed them. "How do you have so much energy right now?"

A devilish smirk tilted his lips. "Next time, you swallow my load, and you'll be all set."

"Ha." The punch of laughter left me, and hell if my heart, my whole body and soul, didn't feel lighter. As for his offer, I'd definitely be taking him up on it. I just needed us to catch a break first.

CHAPTER 10

ROWAN HART

A whole night and full day passed by.

Restlessness and I weren't friends, and if it wasn't for Flynn helping me keep my pacing to a minimum, I would have lost my mind.

Working within the SICB's confines had so much red tape. I wasn't a fan and didn't exactly miss it.

My brother had called this morning, checking in on me. Having already briefly explained the necessity for staying low—both me and the team—he'd kept his distance. Being the city's fire chief, he'd obviously been called onto the scene of the ITU site—not that most people knew that was the purpose of the secure building, due to the covert nature of the team.

And still we waited.

Waited for movement on the Sydney storage facility.

Waited for the director to approve the satellite, which was fucking ridiculous. I could have hacked into it by now a million times over.

And I also waited for Ethan.

The dickwad had refused to discuss anything online or over the phone, which had raised so many red flags, I was close to coming out of my skin.

The twenty-four hours it took to travel from the UK to Australia was a ballache I hadn't planned for, but we were expecting him any second. Another uncomfortable itch started in the middle of my back that he was coming here, having refused to be picked up.

That was one more person who knew my location. I'd considered moving to one of my secure houses, but I needed all my resources at my fingertips and was reluctant to move Flynn.

He'd had another outbreak of fever, which we'd managed to control. He'd also had two moments of zoning out. While he hadn't been aggressive in the traditional sense of the word, my arse was deliciously sore, and he'd made good on sucking my soul out of my cock.

Hands down, the sex was incredible, but the

desperate, almost uncontrollable instinct that drove him to need the release, the connection, the distraction, worried the both of us. As incredible as it was, and I was sure—hoped, would beg if I had to—that the chemistry between us was real, fear pounded a tattoo in my heart.

My stalkery cybercrush had bloomed out of my control. Hell, it was the size of an aged gum tree with roots spreading far and deep. It would take more than a bulldozer to shake it free.

Not that I wanted to.

Which I was sure was all levels of ridiculous. Self-preservation had flown out the window. Hell, it had been booted into the stratosphere.

What didn't help was that my den was overrun with agents.

After Flynn's last fit of fever, we'd had no choice but to call in reinforcements and fess up.

Lucas, with the help of Jada, had been able to source medical equipment. It meant the team who'd returned from Melbourne were in my compound, and the former empty east wing of the warehouse had since been set up as a medical research lab.

Flynn had taken being prodded and poked with surprisingly good grace—better than my growls of frustration I struggled to contain. Only once had his side effects flared in the past couple of hours, which happened to be when I'd returned to my workstation and been deep in discussion with Lucas about Ethan because, apparently, I was now sharing all my secrets and intel.

But what wouldn't I do to ensure Flynn was safe?

His possessiveness would have been amusing if not for the concern rolling off his team. It punched home just how erratic his behaviour was.

"Here, drink this."

Suspicious, I sniffed at the contents of the mug Flynn passed me. "That doesn't smell like coffee."

"It's camomile."

I scrunched up my nose at the piss-smelling concoction. "I'm good, thanks."

Determinedly, he continued to hold the mug out to me. "You're not good, that's the point. Drink it. It's meant to be calming."

Michaels's snort drifted over to us from the couch, earning him the stink eye from Flynn.

"I can lace yours with cyanide if you want?" Flynn offered, then turned his attention back to me. "Just drink the damn tea and stop driving us all to distraction. Ethan will be here in five minutes."

"You know," Michaels hollered, "I kind of like this sassy version of you, Flynn."

Not taking his attention off me, Flynn's eyes narrowed. "Did he seriously just call me sassy?"

I nodded, more than happy to get Flynn's focus off me drinking the damn tea. "He did."

"Michaels needs to understand that I don't make hollow threats, and my claws are bigger than his."

I bit the inside of my cheeks. Flynn was totally being sassy. Damn right I was here for every word.

"Hey, Smythe, why did the lion get kicked out of the claw salon?" Michaels grinned, not waiting for a response before he said, "Because he refused to *paws* for a manicure. Hold on. I've got another one."

Everyone within hearing distance—so the whole damn team—groaned. It didn't perturb Michaels one bit.

"Why don't lions use smartphones? Because every time they try to type, they always end up roaring instead of using their claws to tap."

"For the love of all that is holy. Shaw, please remove Michaels before he gets himself hurt," Flynn interjected.

"Hey, I've been working on all these lion puns and jokes for days." Michaels kicked up his feet onto my coffee table.

He seriously had a death wish, especially as he

simply smirked at me despite the murderous stare I was sending him.

"This one's for you, Hart. Why did the tiger break up with his lion boyfriend? Because he was just *lion* around all day."

"Michaels, make yourself useful before I send you for another stint at the academy," Lucas threatened, his voice carrying from the makeshift lab they'd set up. He'd been here a while now and sensibly seemed to be avoiding Michaels.

"What, too much? Just because we don't have the official word doesn't mean we don't know what this love den smells like."

Flynn growled, his body tensing to do something I suspected he'd regret. Snagging an arm around his waist, not giving a shit what it looked like to his team —though to be fair, Michaels wasn't wrong about the lingering scent—I tugged Flynn close, his chest pressing to mine.

"You know, we could tell him what we did earlier on the couch he's sitting on."

My words hit their mark. Flynn laughed, his tension melting, while Michaels jumped up, complaining loudly and cursing us before sitting on the chair and kicking his feet back up on the coffee table.

Unable to resist, I pressed my face against the crook of Flynn's neck. I inhaled deeply, regretting that the shower he'd taken this morning had washed away the remnants of our combined scent.

He angled his neck to the side. The sensible thing to do would be to pull away, knowing I was playing with fire. But Flynn being temptation personified, I pressed a small kiss to his neck.

"Bloody hell. Seriously?"

My gaze snapped to Michaels, who then finally left us alone, muttering the whole time about boundaries and being like rabbits in heat. He wasn't wrong.

While Flynn had little control over his need to mate, I technically did. Though, as he rubbed against my covered dick, it was possible my restraint had long fluttered away.

I had zero regrets.

"You know," Flynn whispered, continuing to rub against me, "before we met, I had some hot-and-heavy, dirty-as-fuck dreams about riding your horn."

My lips twitched, but the lust slamming into me had me groaning instead of laughing.

Flynn angled his head so I could see part of his face. "There's a lot we can do in twenty-five minutes."

My dick turned to steel at the thought of sinking into him.

"Not sure twenty-five minutes will be enough for what I want to do to you." But fuck, I could try. This morning, I'd finger-fucked Flynn while we'd given each other head. It would mean he was still a little loose, right?

A sultry smile curved Flynn's mouth, and I had no doubt he knew I was thinking about how tight he'd been around my fingers earlier.

"Sounds like a challenge." He bounced his brows and grinded against me. "Time's a-wasting."

That was all it took for me to nudge him forwards. We hightailed it to my room, heading straight for the shower.

I wanted to fuck him on the bed, make him scream as he called my name, but I didn't think anyone else in the building would appreciate it. At least the extra door and the water would offer a little more sound-proofing.

"Shower and strip." Gravel scratched my voice, need urging me to sink into him.

With a smile, Flynn backed away and turned, stripping off in record time. "So, your *horn*...." A salacious curve of his lips formed as he slowly rubbed his hand up and down his cock.

"You said you wanted to ride it?" I was so on board

with that. At this point, I was even past caring that the whole team referred to me as a damn unicorn.

"Ride it," he said, stepping into the spray. "Be pounded by it. Have you split me open so I forget my own name and pass out from the pleasure."

Fuck. Yes, I want all of that.

"I'll take you any and every way I can, Row."

Standing under the steady stream, Flynn looked at me with sin in his eyes.

I would never have enough of him, and he could absolutely take whatever he wanted.

Spotting the lube that was still in the shower, I stepped into his space and pressed against him. Once we were skin to skin, I eased him back so he was leaning against the tiled wall. He went willingly, heat and promise in his gaze.

"Do you want my tongue first?"

In answer, he slammed his mouth to mine, kissing me passionately and grinding against me while pushing my hand between his legs and past his taint.

With each touch of tongue, he whimpered. That may have had something to do with my finger rubbing his hole oh so lightly. Just enough to have him quivering.

"Yes," he gasped. "I want your tongue."

I smirked, taking one last kiss from him before I knelt before him, ordering, "Turn around."

In the blink of an eye, his arse was before me as he arched over, just so. Without instruction, he parted his cheeks, and my cock throbbed.

Fuck, I'd be lucky to spend a minute buried inside him before I blew.

"You are so fucking hot." I punctuated my words with a kiss to his hole.

A ragged moan escaped him, which quickly turned to a deep groan as I speared my tongue into him. I pushed hard, licking, kissing, caressing, easing him open.

As his ring of muscle loosened, I dove deeper, encouraging Flynn to bend lower to give me better access.

"Fuck, yes, like that." His panted words were guttural as he flexed and rode my tongue. "Hurry, I need you to fuck me. Need that fucking horn up my arse."

I speared him again, my lips twitching a little as I filed his words away for a moment I could tease him about the magic he'd discover when my horn made him come.

Now was not the time.

Not when his soft gasps and needy growl drew my balls up tight.

With one last kiss, I stood.

"Hurry."

The need in his voice punched pride right into my chest. That he wanted me so much, as desperately as I did him, was a high nothing could ever rival.

I slicked my fingers and buried two immediately inside him. "You okay?" I checked. Sure, he was a shifter so would heal fast, but I didn't want him in pain.

"Yes, fuck, yes. But just give me your cock."

My lip ticked up as I continued to push in and out of him, adding a third digit. "Back to wanting my cock and not my horn, huh?" He was so damn tight, I needed to push him close to the edge before burying inside him.

Lasting was going to be an issue.

"Cock, horn—just give it to me."

With smiling lips, I pressed a kiss to his shoulder just as I rubbed against his prostate.

"Oh, fuck." His groan was deep, rolling over my skin like a sinful caress. "Please, Rowan."

He didn't need to ask again.

Without pause, as soon as I pulled my fingers away,

I was inside him with one long thrust that had him singing my name.

Wrapped within his heat, I felt my breath stutter out of me. "You're so good. So beautiful." I followed the praise with a kiss to his neck when I pulled him upright, needing to feel as much of his skin as possible.

He sighed into the touch and reached an arm over his head, clinging to my shoulder.

Flynn angled for a kiss. The position was awkward, but it didn't stop me from taking his mouth in a heated kiss. I pulled out and pushed back into him in time with our tongues touching and sliding against each other.

"Make me yours," he whimpered against my mouth.

My eyes glazed over. I wanted nothing more.

I thrust into him and lost his mouth. He grinned, and then, as I punched my hips more forcefully, I lost his smile to heated eyes and a gaping mouth.

"Yes, like that."

I surged in and out, his channel gripping my cock and shooting need and desire into each cell of my body. Flynn was perfect.

Like this, we fit. Like this, we could make it work.

Always.

The thought of us lasting the course, spending our

days wrapped around each other, him fucking me like this, long and hard, shot tingles to my balls.

Gliding in and out of his tight channel, I shook, feeling the strain of holding back. I was close to exploding. Close to losing control and filling him with my cum, which was a visual that wasn't at all helpful when he clamped around me.

"I'm close," he grunted.

Thank fuck for that. For as much as I never wanted this to end, we were on a time limit, and I wanted Flynn to unravel.

Letting go of his chest, I gripped his hips. He leaned forwards, bracing against the tiled wall. Once I was sure he could support himself, I pounded into him. With long, hard, and fast strokes, I drilled deep, savouring his gasping breaths and needy exhales.

A long, dirty moan followed, his channel contracting around me. I let my groan fly free, wanting him to hear what he did to me.

Renewing my mission, I slammed into him, pounding against his prostate until he clawed at the wall, my name spilling from his lips.

"Fuck, fuck, Row. Fuuuuuck."

I reached for his dick, jerking him off quickly in time with my hips, moving at a punishing rate. Relentlessly, I made him mine, each of his panting breaths spurring me on.

A loud gasp and a moan so deep, the sound tugged at my balls, and he spilled into my hand, clamping around my cock.

"Fuck," I called out, cum pulsing out of me, filling his tight channel. I gasped, wheezed, my whole body shaking as I held on to Flynn by his hip and his softening cock. "What you do to me."

He'd wrecked me. There was already no going back, but now, after finally taking him like this—a position I knew he wasn't usually a fan of—I wanted to be his forever.

A final shudder burst through me, and I held Flynn close as one last shot of cum pulsed into him.

"You were...." He leaned back against me and angled up so we could make eye contact. A deep and scratchy "Fuck, you really do have a magical cock" fell past his lips. I caught his smile with a soft kiss.

Pulling away, I pressed my nose to his neck, one of my favourite places to inhale his scent.

I tugged on his earlobe with my teeth, recalling how much he liked it earlier. Then paused. *Fuck.* "The security alarm's going."

Despite his hitch of breath, he straightened. "He's here?"

"Looks that way."

"Talk about timing," he grumbled.

I chuckled and reluctantly eased out of him. Flynn stepped out of my hold and turned to face me. His pupils were blown, his lips puffy, and he looked truly well-fucked. My heart flipped at the sight, loving that I'd put that blissed-out expression on his face.

"We need to hurry." I followed the admonishment with a barely there kiss.

With a dramatic sigh, he nodded. "I know. But I'm not showering the cum out of my arse."

A surprised laugh burst out of me. "O-kay?"

He arched an eyebrow at me, and immediately I knew why. A possessive Flynn was one I could definitely get on board with.

We quickly dried off and changed, then headed over to the workstations.

The camera feeds revealed a vehicle with the plates Ethan had confirmed with me.

When he reached the first set of security checks, he peered directly at the camera, his deep brown eyes intense and looking less than impressed that I was making him wait. Allowing him access, I continued watching the screen, Flynn at my side.

"He's not what I expected, physically."

I huffed out a laugh at Flynn's observation,

wondering if he thought the same way about me when we first met. "The grizzly look is not something the media associates with computer smarts, right?"

"Or my experience, since I'm one of the biggest geeks going."

And the hottest. I kept that thought to myself, not wanting to give Michaels any more ammo.

It was true, though—yes, Flynn's hotness, but more specifically, bears tended to be stereotyped a lot. They weren't known to work well with others, so it actually made sense to me that they'd be holed up by themselves behind a keyboard and screens. It was more about their sheer size, the physical presence of bears that made it more usual for them to be field agents, or carpenters, or hell, I had absolutely met a few lumberjacks in my time.

Who knew what the ITU would think of Ethan, or he them.

Realisation hit me smack in the face. Fuck. Flynn and his possessiveness.

I hadn't warned him about Ethan, about his determination to fuck me. Honestly, I'd been so caught up in the nerves that Ethan, someone from my past, would finally be seeing me face to face for the first time since my injuries, I hadn't even considered his fixation on me.

Though the scent of my cum on Flynn would make it crystal fucking clear what we were to each other.

Ethan was out of his car and heading towards the caged doors.

Shit. It was not the sort of conversation I wanted to have now, in front of everyone. But it was too late. I just hoped Ethan was in one of his surly moods. I suspected having government agents around him would ensure that, which should hopefully mean everything would be strictly business.

"I'm going to go out to meet him."

Immediately, Flynn tensed beside me. A slow exhale later, he relaxed. "I'll see how Jada's getting on," he mumbled.

I kissed his cheek, aware of but not caring about our audience. "Okay. Remember, you smell like you're mine." I pulled away, catching his surprised expression, pretty sure it matched mine.

That I'd said those words aloud was not the version of myself I was familiar with. I liked it a hell of a lot. And so did Flynn, judging from the heat in his cheeks and the way his pupils flared.

Leaving the unit to it, I headed towards the west entrance. Before I reached the reinforced outer door that would allow yet another person into my inner sanctum, I took a moment to simply stop and breathe.

The days had become a whirlwind of chaos chasing our tails, and I'd been falling pretty fucking hard for Flynn. I struggled to process everything, especially the latter.

All my fears from a few days ago, before that fateful day when I'd opened the lines of communication in a way I'd promised myself I'd never do, seemed inconsequential compared to the new threat. Flynn's life potentially hung in the balance.

It was a clusterfuck: my heart, my head, my goddamn soul at constant odds, while a moment later, everything seemed to align.

The truth was, I didn't want to lose him. Couldn't. And as far as I was concerned, I wouldn't.

I refused to believe someone so incredible could be lost. And this coming from a man so warped about the whole concept of hope. Hope had died in the explosion in the desert. In acid and fire and blood and pain.

But hope, the fickle fucker, flickered to life the moment I'd spotted a seemingly innocuous piece of code. Then it went and flared to a new brightness seven months back when I first reached out to him. I chuckled, deep and low, no doubt sounding and looking insane as I stood here outside a reinforced door.

But fuck it all to hell... hope now blazed like an inferno and had done from the moment Flynn stepped into my safe house, his gaze not straying from mine. That right there was brighter than any fear I might have known.

I unlocked the door, opened it, and was greeted by a growled "Took you long enough."

I craned my neck to take in the behemoth of a man I sort of called friend. "Hello to you, too, dickface."

He stepped through the doorway, blocking out the light of the entrance holding area. A hint of a smile tilted his lips as he stepped closer, closing the door behind him.

"Looking as douchey as ever." His gaze flicked over my face, but he didn't flinch, didn't cringe, just gave me an up-nod by the time his gaze returned to mine. "I'm not feeling especially social, and I'm concerned about the company you're keeping these days."

I snorted, stepping out of his space, and turned away to face the enclosure door that would lead us into the heart of my den. "Fuck you. You're never feeling social. Now get your arse inside and tell me what I need to know."

He grunted, his wary eyes on the closed door ahead

of us. "I could do with a shower and some food. The flight is for shit."

"You can have food, but shower after you've finally told me what the hell is going on and why you wouldn't risk doing so online."

That he wouldn't filled me with unease. While neither of us was infallible, we were some of the best in the business. If we couldn't keep a line secure, shit had really hit the fan.

"As long as you don't try to feed me that Vegemite crap, that's fine."

"That was one time, and you behaved like I'd forced you to swallow sump oil."

"May as well have been."

Throughout our banter, his gaze didn't stray from the door. He didn't smile, didn't relax a muscle. Ethan seriously was a grumpy bastard, but despite how much his being here—and being involved in this shit—pissed me off, he was a good guy.

Most of the time.

Which didn't mean he didn't break the law or sometimes trust the wrong person, and as much as it pained me, I hoped it was the latter that was at play here.

If I found out he had anything to do with Hornell

—and my initial deep dive said he hadn't, directly—then he was a dead man walking.

He just didn't know that yet.

Or hell, maybe he did.

He could be a ballsy arsehole.

"Come on."

His heavy footsteps followed me—a deliberate show if ever I heard it. Despite his six-six stature and his frame that was all bulky muscle and thick skin topped off with an unruly beard, he could be light on his feet when the occasion called for it.

Pushing open the final door that led us fully into the den, I searched for Flynn, zeroing in on him immediately. His gaze was already on me, his tight expression relaxed. I nodded, stepping into the inner sanctum, Ethan hot on my heels.

Even though tension kept Ethan's muscles tight, the man on high alert, his steps didn't falter as he took in the roomful of government agents—including Jada, who'd exited the lab.

Hating the formality bullshit, having thought such instances were long over since being discharged from the Alliance, I considered just getting on with it. The need for answers was urgent.

Taking in Lucas's body language, his rigid shoulders and assessing gaze, I knew this was an occasion that I'd have to suck it up.

"This here is Ethan. Ethan, Agent Lucas runs this team." I stopped at that, not willing to go around the group and play a name game or some such shit. Plus, there was the whole introducing Flynn to Ethan, which I actively wanted to avoid. Obviously, that wouldn't stand, since he was one of the main reasons Ethan had breached my once-impenetrable den walls.

"Ethan." Lucas nodded, having already made an assessment within a split second of the introduction. That much was obvious from the barest of tension lost from his shoulders. "Thank you for coming."

"I wasn't invited. I came because this arsewipe here managed to get involved in a bunch of government bullshit." Barely any inflection marked his tone. Hell, he sounded almost bored.

I knew better.

"Largely due to illegal technology you invented, which puts you smack in the middle of said government bullshit." An eerily charming smile curved Lucas's lips.

Hell, he was good. I could reluctantly admit there was a reason he was the leader of this talented, if not motley, crew of agents.

"But let's just focus on getting you a Vegemite

sandwich, and then you can start explaining to us everything about this chip, its link to genetic modification and cloning, and just what the fuck is happening with one of my agents, since he was turned by the monstrosity I'm assuming you had a hand in creating, shall we?"

Lucas swept his arm out, indicating the two tables pushed together in an open space of the room I tended to use for gaming—something I wouldn't be sharing with the team. My eyes widened, and I pressed my lips together, dragging them in between my teeth to stop myself from snorting out a laugh.

On the table was a Vegemite sandwich.

I peeked at Flynn, and my lips twitched at the amusement in his gaze. I turned my focus on Ethan, not quite sure what to expect. The man really was a grump. But beyond his gruffness, his sarcasm regularly entertained me.

"You Aussie twats really know how to make a guy feel welcome. Fuck you very much. And you," he said, turning towards me, "you just had to go and find arse-holes with your same winning personality, huh?"

I quirked my good eyebrow at him. "I'm not just a pretty face."

"It was never your face I was interested in."

Ah, shit.

Flynn's growl was immediate. Loud and aggressive, it echoed around the makeshift meeting room, catching all our attention.

My gaze snapped to his, but he had Ethan in his line of sight.

Studying him, Ethan had the good sense not to react. He waited a beat, then two before he sniffed the air and sighed. "Easy there, lion boy. I was just teasing. I can scent him on you from here and have no interest in challenging you for him."

Flynn clenched his teeth and finally released the tension in his shoulders. Pink hit his cheeks, and he cleared his throat. "Okay, thanks. I'm just going to pour myself a coffee."

Hating his embarrassment, I left Ethan's side, going directly to Flynn. Once beside him, I took his hand and squeezed, forcing him to make eye contact. As soon as he did, he exhaled, a shy smile forming on his lips. He nodded, answering my silent question asking if he was okay.

When he released my hand and busied himself making a coffee that would give him a moment to calm down, I turned back to Ethan.

Curiosity stared back at me before Ethan seemed to shake away any interest. His gaze then narrowed, and he shook his head. "You owe me for this."

I scoffed and headed over to the table. "And you could have easily said this shit online. As you said, nobody invited your miserable arse here. Now sit, eat, and explain."

He stared at the Vegemite sandwich as if it was going to grow jaws and bite his cock off.

I sighed. "There's still lasagne warming in the oven. Let me get you some."

Seeming mollified, he dumped his rucksack next to one of the chairs and sat, the chair groaning under his weight.

While I organised him a plate, Flynn joined me, standing close enough for me to appreciate his warmth. He side-eyed me, and I offered a small smile, making sure to brush against his arm as I turned back towards the table.

Ethan hadn't missed a thing. His attention narrowed on me, his expression neutral. I didn't react, just dumped the plate before him, along with some utensils, and sat at the end of the table. Michaels swiped the uneaten sandwich and sat next to an already sitting Lucas. And when Flynn took the chair to my right, Shaw, Kent, and Jada joined us.

One big, happy dysfunctional family.

The odds of surviving the dynamics were about as likely as a blindfolded government official navigating a labyrinth while juggling paperwork and hoping to find efficiency at the end. But this was for Flynn, and I'd already established that I'd do anything and everything within my power to make sure he got out of this intact.

"WHAT THE FUCK WERE YOU THINKING?" Wide-eyed, I stared at Ethan like I didn't recognise him.

Beneath his bushy beard, a tinge of pink crept across his otherwise pale features. The shock of anger in his eyes all but sent out an invisible challenge that would likely get us both injured. "Fuck you, Hart. I did what I did, and I'm here, aren't I?"

My back molars groaned in protest. I wanted to lay into him, lecture him for the rest of my days, add a few kidney jabs in there for good measure. When did he get so stupid? What had happened for him to turn into a greedy bastard simply chasing the money? Honestly, I couldn't see any other reason for his decisions, but money had to be it, right?

Lucas's steady voice cut through the building tension of our stare-off. "Do you know what you're looking for if we show you the samples?"

After another moment of glaring, Ethan dragged

his attention away from me, settling on the vampire who somehow was keeping his emotions in check. "Yes. I didn't have anything to do with the genetics side or its creation, but I was sent samples so I could fine-tune the chip's ability to function. The chip runs on biometrics. It's not just any old chip you can shove into a body. Not with that level of sophistication or its capabilities."

"We're not interested in a TED Talk about what a shitbox you are, dickhead." I slammed my lips together at the biting look Lucas sent me.

But fuck the both of them. Lucas for being so cool and calm, and Ethan for doing something so abhorrent, I wondered if I'd ever really known him.

"I'm happy to leave whenever the hell I want," Ethan bit out.

Movement from Kent drew my attention. I'd thought I was pissed off, but if Kent had the ability to kill from a single look, Ethan would be eviscerated.

She was eerily still after her initial movement. But whatever she was up to, I was absolutely on board with it. Surprised as fuck at the shift in my allegiance, I simply eased back in my seat from where I'd pushed forwards, considering launching myself at Ethan should the opportunity arise.

Though, in reality, it sounded like we needed his input on this. It didn't mean I had to like it.

As if sensing the new threat, Ethan angled a look at Kent. His muscles bunched and became immediately taut. For the first time, unease rolled off him, recognising just how precarious his position was, I expected.

"You saying I can't leave whenever I want?" He spoke directly to Kent.

"The only thing I'm interested in hearing from you are answers and solutions. The how or why, I don't care about. You'll take a look at the samples, tell us what you know, and if a solution is necessary, you'll hand it over wrapped in a pretty red fucking bow."

Thick silence descended. I eyed the group, and everyone but Michaels was tense. He appeared to be lapping up the exchange in big-grinned amusement.

"And if I don't?"

Even I winced at his foolish boldness, which quickly morphed as a dagger flew through the air, nipping a chunk of hair off his wild mane and landing in the wall with a soft snick a few metres behind him.

"The next will be three inches to the left," Kent said matter-of-factly.

Jaw muscles rippling, Ethan sensibly seemed to be weighing the odds. Bears weren't known for keeping cool and had moments of going berserk at the slightest irritation. Thankfully for us—and for him—he simply gave a sharp nod and stood. "Lead the way."

We trailed into the space taken over by Jada. The area, prior to me purchasing the warehouse years back, had previously been used for quality checking in what was once a confectionary manufacturing building. While I'd demolished some walls when I'd first taken over the place—more due to safety than style—the older building still had a late-Victorian feel to it.

Intricate mouldings adorning the high ceilings remained in place here, and despite the modern upgrades, some parts of the structure maintained their historical architectural details, like the ornate pillars that stood tall.

This space had transformed in the past twenty hours. What was once likely a bustling area filled with the sweet scent of confections was now a sprawling chamber converted into a temporary lab. State-of-the-art equipment hummed softly, a far cry from the calming, quiet space usually containing only a single yoga mat.

Yeah, I'd totally hidden that away from prying eyes.

The makeshift laboratory was where I hoped we'd uncover answers about Flynn's side effects. Were they serious? Were they permanent? Was he a ticking time bomb?

But he was more than just a project and more than a fixation I'd admired from afar. I was inexplicably drawn to him, the connection and depths of my attraction having grown exponentially over the past few days.

I stood back, scrutinising Ethan's every move.

The samples under the microscopes and whizzing around in the multiple machines belonged to both Flynn and Prince—Lucas having sent Michaels and Shaw to the coroner to collect the samples earlier today.

Flynn appeared at my side, not so subtly pressing against me. Any comfort he wanted was his to take.

Jada spoke softly to Ethan. While I heard every word, I tuned out, concern growing at the increasing heat pouring off Flynn.

Not wanting to draw attention to him, I pressed my hand to the arch of his back, finding his T-shirt soaked through.

Shit.

This wasn't good. The time between symptoms seemed to be shortening.

Reaching for his hand, I latched on. His gaze caught mine. Glazed eyes peered back at me, his pupils like pinpricks.

I eased him out of the area, leading him towards

the kitchen for a drink of water before I would shower him down. By the time we reached the fridge, a shiver racked through him, and beads of sweat trickled down his temples.

"What's going on?"

I was so caught up in concern that I'd barely paid attention to Kent's appearance despite being aware of approaching footsteps.

"Shit, is this like the other times?" Alarm saturated her tone.

"Worse. This has come on faster. He hasn't trembled quite this badly before."

Concern was etched in her expression. "He needs electrolytes."

"In the cupboard to the right of the coffee machine." Why the hell hadn't I thought of that?

She set to work searching for the pack of electrolytes, her movements fast and efficient. "I'll bring this to you."

Shock reverberated through me. She was letting me take care of him? While there was no argument from me, it surprised me all the same.

I turned on my heel, my arm around a sweat-soaked Flynn. "Come on."

He sagged against me—something else that was new. By the time I had manoeuvred him directly into the en suite and stripped him down before positioning him on the stool under the showerhead releasing cold water, my own fear threatened to take hold.

Nothing about this was right. If Ethan didn't get answers and find a way to fix this, I didn't think any agent would be able to hold me back. Though maybe they wouldn't want to.

"Here."

After ensuring Flynn was propped up against the wall, I backed away to the closed door and tugged it open. Kent was there, a glass of cloudy water in her hand.

"Thanks."

She bobbed her head, not concealing her worry from me. Maybe she could see mine. I barely had any control over my emotions at the moment, so it was likely.

"If you need me, just call. He'd be mortified if I came in there and saw him like this, but if you do need me, he can get over himself."

My lips twitched into a semblance of amusement. She really did love him. It was absolutely the main reason I respected her.

"I will do. Can you get him a fresh change of clothes from my closet?"

"Anything else?"

A wave of despair threatened to take a tight hold of my lungs. "Make sure Ethan gets us answers."

"He will." Steel tightened her words as a silent exchange I never imagined possible drifted between us. We'd do whatever it took to care for Flynn—the man she loved like a son, and the man who had stolen my heart.

It took almost twenty minutes for Flynn's tremors to ease and for his temperature to reduce to normal. After dressing him in another pair of sweats and a pale green T-shirt, I tucked him into bed.

"I need to be out there."

How had I not realised how stubborn Flynn could be? It was kind of sweet and a little entertaining, but he was pushing my patience.

"If you try to get out from under those bedsheets again, I'll tie you to the damn bed."

At the flare of heat in his eyes, I spotted my mistake instantly.

"Kinky. We can absolutely try that." He reached for me, sitting up a little. The sheet slipped, pooling around his waist. Thankfully, he still wore both the tee and sweats despite having tried to strip a couple of times.

Apparently, if he couldn't leave the bed, then neither could I.

Staying with him sounded like heaven. I'd be totally on board with it if I didn't have a den full of nosey arseholes. Plus, the whole "what the fuck is wrong with Flynn?" fear was a big cock blocker.

"Please, just sleep."

His eyes narrowed.

"Flynn, please." I wasn't above begging at this point.

"But—"

He tried again, but I cut him off, giving in by shutting him up with a kiss. When I pulled barely more than a centimetre away, I whispered, "I promise, once we get usable information, I will wake you up."

His expression shifted, vulnerability appearing and making him look a few years younger.

My heart squeezed, hating everything that was happening to him. I leaned back a little more so he could fully see my face without going cross-eyed. Wordlessly, I promised him he'd be okay. Let him know that it was all right to be frightened. He had a whole team rooting for him.

"Okay?" I asked softly, sure he'd understood everything I'd wanted to say.

A beat, then two, and my shoulders relaxed at his slow nod. "Okay."

A smile tugged on my lips, and I pressed one final

kiss to his mouth, breathing in his scent as I did so. "Call me if you need me. I'll hear and come running."

"I know."

The absolute faith and conviction threatened to bring me to my knees and then into bed with him. How I deserved a man like Flynn, I didn't know. Really, I wasn't sure I did deserve him. But fuck no would I let him go.

As long as he wanted me, needed me, I was his. Completely. Resolutely. Irrevocably.

Dragging myself away, I closed the door behind me, thinking it would be a good idea to get some sort of soundproofing on the walls of my bedroom. Not that I planned to have my den taken over by SICB agents again, but it would be smart to plan ahead.

Alone in the kitchen, Kent stopped unpacking the dishwasher, which honestly fuddled my brain. Kent being domestic did not compute. She stared at me, a challenge in her arched brow that dared me to mention what I'd caught her doing.

I was too exhausted to be that brave. Perhaps another time I'd give her shit, but now wasn't the moment.

"He didn't want to settle."

While it wasn't a question, since she would have heard every word, I still answered, "No. He's struggling not being in the thick of it." And while he hadn't said anything aloud, he felt guilty for pulling his unit's attention away from the search for Hornell to instead focus on him.

As far as I was concerned, Hornell would get his comeuppance. Whether that was in a week, a month, or a year, I'd ensure it happened. Flynn deserved to be our priority, and from the discussions floating from the medical lab, his whole team felt the same way.

Kent nodded in response, and together, we headed towards the unit.

Ethan had pulled up something on a large monitor. I scrunched my brow, trying to make sense of what I was seeing. Not wanting to interrupt whatever it was the bear was saying, I stood by, listening intently and hoping I could catch up.

"...definitely different." He pressed a button on the microscope, and the image on the screen changed, zooming in on something. "If you look here at the mutation," he continued, and my stomach bottomed out at that word. Nobody wanted the word "mutation" associated with them, right?

"Which bit?" Shaw asked. "The green blobs?"

Relieved he'd asked, since I wondered the same thing at the variously shaped and coloured blobs on the screen, I peered at Ethan for confirmation.

"Yes, the green *blobs*," he said with a sneer of distaste. "This is the mutation from Prince. It matches the signature I was sent a few years back."

"How can you be sure it's the same?" Lucas asked. He stood off to the side with a view of the whole space and all the players.

At the question, a frustrated growl eased past Ethan's lips. His narrowed gaze zeroed in on Lucas. "How can you be sure of matching the real-life version of a target with an image you were sent over your servers?" He didn't wait for a response before biting out, "You fucking memorise it and spend so many hours staring at the damn thing, even years later, there's no chance that image can fade. How the fuck do you think?"

And from the sounds of things, I needed to step in.

Oh how I hated this shit.

"Ethan, can you catch me up?"

The slow turn of his head to stare at me showed just how pissed off he was. Tough shit, though. He needed to suck it up. If I could keep my ego, as well as my distrust, in check, then he could too.

"Put your dick away, get your head out of your arse, and tell me: Do you know what's happening with Flynn? And if so, do we need to do anything, or will it just fix itself?"

A long pause followed before he said, "I don't really know anything about this genetics bullshit, especially this synthesised stuff. The *only* reason I have even a semblance of knowledge is that the chip I was asked to create had to work *with* the specific blood of Prince. To be crystal clear, I didn't know who the blood was from and had never heard his name until we spoke yesterday."

Unsure whether he told the truth or not, I pushed, "I don't care about any of that. The whys or the hows or your pride over the fact that it's a phenomenal piece of technology."

"Thank you."

I groaned. "That wasn't a compliment."

"Sounded like it to me."

Holy shit, I was going to lose my damn mind. Aware that Kent stood a couple of metres away from me, I considered giving her a nod, confident she'd interpret it as firing a dagger his way. A couple in his leg would be super satisfying. As long as he had his hands free and his brain still functioned.

"How about we get back to the genetic marker differences?" Jada, with more patience than a saint, asked. She peered at me. "Ethan was just explaining everything now, but in layman's terms for the team."

"Yep, hurry up and dumb that shit down for me,

Winnie." Michaels threw a piece of popcorn in the air and caught it effortlessly in his mouth, both missing and unconcerned by Ethan's face of thunder.

It wasn't the time to laugh at Michaels winding him up by going through bear names. When I'd been out in the kitchen earlier, I was pretty sure I'd heard both Yogi and Baloo. If he wasn't a shit-hot wolf with some fierce fighting skills, I would have been afraid for him.

Ethan clamped his mouth shut, his eye twitching. I suspected he was counting to ten. Maybe even twenty. After a few beats, he turned his attention back to me. "The kid's blood," he started, and I shot him the stink eye, since the bastard was getting a dig in, "has traces of the same nanogene sequencers."

I parted my lips to ask a question but thought better of it when his cheeks heated and the vein in his temple throbbed.

"Which means at a molecular level, the shifter genes in his system keep trying to grow and spread as a result of the nanobots used in Prince, which I've learned today were to bring him back to life."

I half expected someone to start another rant about a zombie, likely pushing Ethan to his breaking point. Thankfully everyone remained quiet, listening intently.

"Anyway, the blood has been behaving peculiarly, allowing these bursts of side effects that I suppose are more instinctive and intrinsic to a shifter's nature, or rather, the animal's nature."

"But when we shift, whether made or born, our behaviour doesn't change." Shaw leaned forwards, his elbows on his knees. "A panther in a zoo or out in the wild is a totally different species to me, regardless of my form."

"You're right," Jada interjected, "but also remember that shifters are not fully human. Shifters share some traits with the wild mammal, usually when it comes to instinct and movement."

"So, what exactly are you saying?" Shaw asked.

"While nanobots are not present in Smythe's blood"—a collective sigh went around the team, which Ethan ignored—"during the transmission of the shifter gene, the nanogene is targeting his cellular landscape, trying to draw the lion instincts and reactions to the surface while suppressing the human responses."

"So it's trying to turn him into a fucking lion?" Michaels jolted upright in his seat, popcorn forgotten and horror on his expression.

Meanwhile, I could barely hear over the frantic beat of my racing heart. A cold shiver ran down my spine as his words sank in.

Turning into a lion.

Disbelief warred with dread as I struggled to comprehend the gravity of the implications. Flynn had rambled about something similar, and I'd barely been able to contain my amusement as I'd shut him down, knowing it was ridiculous.

As Ethan continued, each word felt like a punch to the jugular, making breathing difficult, while each syllable turned heavy, slowly threatening to crush my chest.

"Yes," Ethan finally answered. "A genetic specialist will know more and be able to break everything down and, I'm sure, figure things out. I'm self-taught, having needed more information when I took on the contract for the chip. The chip itself is *nothing*," he emphasised, "to do with the whole necromancer voodoo shit. It's something used to help monitor as well as transit and track. But some fucker has messed with the chip since it left my hands."

I only half paid attention, too stuck on the horror of Flynn's blood, his genes, or whatever, battling for dominance inside him. Time slowed as I grappled with the terrifying reality unfolding.

The image of Flynn, his laughter, his kindness, his sharp intelligence, flashed vividly before me, a montage of visuals and feelings.

Our exchanges.

My ridiculous riddles.

His absolute faith and conviction in his team. In the cause. In me.

Desperation threatened to bowl me over, unravel me while Ethan continued talking.

How was everyone so calm while my heart was so close to beating out of my chest?

"Despite the high temperature and the lethargy, which, if I had to hazard a guess, is a result of the nano-gene trying to take control, what other symptoms has he experienced?" Ethan asked.

All eyes were on me.

Ah, fuck. The spotlight effectively jolted me into awareness, my fast pulse speeding off for a whole other reason.

Was there a way to diplomatically say that Flynn was super horny and wanted to be constantly fucking me while making sure we practically bathed in each other's cum?

Probably not.

It was probably best I started with his protective urges and go from there. I just hoped Flynn was fast asleep and didn't bear witness to our private life becoming a spectacle.

CHAPTER 11
FLYNN SMYTHE

A WOMBAT HAD CRAWLED INTO THE ROOM and taken a shit in my mouth. It was the only explanation for why I felt like crap... and my mouth tasting like it too.

"You're awake."

I startled at Shaw's voice close to my ear. Angling my head, I widened my eyes in surprise. On the bed beside me, Shaw's legs were stretched out as he sat with a laptop on his thighs and concern in his gaze as he peered down at me.

"What time is it?" A satisfying jaw-cracking yawn followed. I stretched, the black sleeve of the fabric confusing me. I'd changed into a green T-shirt after my shower.

Heat touched my cheeks as I remembered how,

once again, Rowan had taken care of me. The shower was a blur, as was him dressing me, but I remembered enough to know what happened and what I'd been wearing. Partly because the tee, while smelling of detergent, held undertones of a forest after a summer storm.

I'd sniffed long and hard on the neckline of the fabric when Rowan had left me to go and work with Ethan. I'd been a little pissed, a bit frustrated, and a lot jealous, but it probably took me all of five minutes to fall fast asleep.

That didn't explain why Shaw was beside me, staring at me with a furrowed brow, and I was pretty confident he'd changed too.

"Did everyone stay over?" I asked, aware he still hadn't told me the time.

"Uhm...."

I paused from wriggling my toes and fixed my attention fully on him. Worry and nerves shrouded his features. Considering he was my closest friend and spent a lot of his time being loud and confident—even more so with the development of his relationship with Michaels—his fumbling shot a bolt of worry through me.

I sat up, examining the room around me as I asked, "What's wrong? Why are you being weird?"

"It's five thirty," he said by way of answer. Apparently I needed to ask four questions ahead of schedule before he backtracked. But five thirty—hell, I'd slept a lot longer than I'd planned. Rowan had promised to wake me if he had news, though, so I assumed they'd had no success yet, so everyone had got some shuteye.

That didn't explain the odd sleeping arrangements, though.

Nor the silence.

"I can't hear anyone." As I became more alert, trepidation buzzed under my skin. "Please don't tell me something happened with the bear. I know he was all sarc and grump and was pissing everyone off...." My eyes bulged. "Shit, have they had to go to headquarters 'cause Michaels has kicked his arse or something? Shit, it's Kent.... She used her daggers."

With my thoughts spiralling, I hauled my butt out of bed. Feet on the floor, I winced. Pins and needles shot through them, landing in my calves and cramping up the muscles. "Fuck."

"What is it? What?" Shaw scrambled off the bed and was beside me faster than I could even grip the annoying muscles screaming at me.

"Stupid cramp." I fell back, my backside on the mattress as I rubbed the offending muscles. "It's been years since I've had a cramp like this." I glanced at Shaw's worryingly ashen face but chose to ignore it, focussing intently on getting my circulation going. "Please tell me cramps like this are just a short-term side effect of the gene transfer." I pushed humour into my voice despite not feeling it at all.

I knew full well that cramps were not normal, but then again, hardly anything that had happened so far since becoming a shifter had been normal.

The lightness of my tone didn't do a thing to shake the blast of anxiety pouring off Shaw. What that meant was that I needed to rip off the proverbial Band-Aid and get real answers. The silence was deafening. That I was awake and Kent, Jada, and Rowan weren't already at my side made the alarm bells ringing in my brain go berserk.

Not that I needed or expected anyone to dote on me. Though it would have felt really damn nice right about now, but still, where the fuck was everyone?

"It's five thirty."

My hands froze on my calves, and I stared at Shaw, wondering if he was broken.

"O-kay. You already said that. Time for breakfast."

The slowest headshake known to man followed. Shaw's eyes remained wide and worried, though a little more colour had bled into his cheeks. "As in, it's 5:30 p.m. on Thursday."

I tucked my chin to my chest, head jerking back in

confusion. "I have no idea what you mean." Or even what was happening.

"You've been unconscious for almost forty-eight hours, Flynn."

I waited for the punchline, half wondering why he'd first-named me. His expression didn't waver. With no smirk, no bouncing brows, and no deep laughter, he was deadly serious.

My lips parted and closed a handful of times before I croaked, "Two days? I've been asleep for two days?"

He was already nodding. "The team's been losing their minds. Hart lost his shit. We had to call in his brother to stop him from killing Ethan."

Horror burned in my chest. "He only *almost* killed him, right?"

"Well—" This time, a full-on smirk appeared, and I almost blacked out in relief—finally a little normality. "He got in two punches and swiped one of Kent's blades, but Michaels and Lucas were able to subdue him."

My heart beat a frantic tattoo. This was not good. I needed to get to him. Know where he was. "Fuck, did they hurt him? Arrest him?" Nausea swirled in my stomach. If my team had done either.... I couldn't complete that thought, not knowing how I felt.

Before I could spiral and dive deeper into making

up scenarios in my head, Shaw answered, "No. He's fine. He's out with Kent and Michaels, following a lead."

I punched out a relieved breath. He was okay. But more than that, he was out of his compound with my team? Holy shit, hell might have frozen over.

There was still so much to discover about each other, but I knew Rowan rarely left his den—and even then, it tended to be to visit one of his safe houses. I also knew he struggled to trust anyone, especially government officials.

I didn't get the chance to ask about everyone else as Shaw explained, "Lucas is with Ethan, working on the sample they finally located in the Sydney storage facility. Though it's more a blueprint and schematics than a sample of anything. Callen and Chris have headed to Canberra, following some intel. We've also finally got the go-ahead from the director for the satellite. We should be good to go in a matter of hours."

I shook my head, trying to dislodge the overload of information.

"Shit, do you need to lie back down? You look ready to pass out."

Fuck it. I scooted back and pressed my head into the pillow. *Better.* When I lay like this, the room didn't spin as fast.

"Why did it take so long for approval?" Might as well go with the last piece of information I received.

"Some red tape that's worrying as hell. It's the reason why Callen and Chris have headed to Canberra."

I let that sink in. If they'd gone to Canberra, where the government offices were located, they really were concerned.

"Oh, and the director's gone with them."

"Fuck, really?"

"Yeah. We still don't know what's going on, but clearly someone higher up in the chain slowed down the application process. No doubt it'll make the whole operation to check the satellites and use the drone pointless, but with the hold-up, it shines a spotlight on a possibly bigger, even more corrupt issue."

The thought filled me with horror.

"And what about you?"

"Me?" Shaw's grin was wide and, for the first time, relieved. "I got Smythe duty and can now finally take a piss, as I've been too terrified to leave you alone."

I eyed the door to the en suite. It was a few steps away. We'd heard each other piss more times than I wanted to even think about.

"Okay, so I also really need to shit, and I couldn't do it with the door open, as it's all levels of wrong."

A hoarse laugh erupted from me, scratching my wombat-abused dry throat.

Shaw shoved a bottle of water in my hand, so my throat must have sounded dreadful. He then handed me a mobile phone. "I'm going to shit in one of the ten toilets out there. You call Hart or Kent and let them know you're awake. I'll get in touch with Lucas."

Okay, I could do that, especially because as soon as I glugged water, the dryness immediately eased.

"And Jada?" I wiped a drip of water from my chin.

"On a medical recon mission." With that, he squeezed my shoulder and headed towards the door. "Hey, Smythe?"

I looked away from the phone and at him.

"No sleeping while I'm gone, okay?"

I bobbed my head, managing a smirk. "Okay."

Alone, I peered at the phone, opening the contacts. Kent and Rowan were together, which yeah, it still sounded odd, but more to the point, who the hell was I meant to call?

I squirmed a little self-consciously, calling bullshit. While Kent was one of the most important people in my life, and I absolutely loved her, my gut twisted, my heart thudding with the desperate need to hear Rowan's voice.

Pressing on his name before I could doubt my

decision, I held my breath and practically swooned when he picked up on the first ring, saying, "Shaw, everything okay?"

Hoarse with unexpected emotion, I rasped, "It's me."

A short intake of breath reached me. "Fuck, Flynn, you're awake. We're coming now. Give us thirty minutes."

"Twenty," Kent said, her voice coming through loud and clear.

I huffed a quiet laugh, feeling out of sorts with all I'd learned. But hell if hearing their voices wasn't incredible. "Okay. Twenty minutes. I need to eat. My stomach feels like it's going to dissolve itself." I hoped getting some calories in my system would help clear my head too.

"Okay, food. There should be plenty to heat up."

Standing as the feeling finally came back to my legs, I left Rowan's room, listening to the opening and closing of a vehicle door. "I'll let you g—"

Rowan's "No" startled me, and I paused on my journey to the kitchen area. Before I had the chance to question him, his voice was low, a vulnerability to it I hadn't heard yet as he said, "Just stay on the line. Keep talking to me."

Hummingbird wings fluttered to life in my stomach, light and airy and travelling so fast, it was a possibility my feet would leave the ground.

Did he miss me? Was he worried something would happen in the few minutes it took for him to return? Maybe he just wanted to make sure I didn't burn his kitchen down.

"Okay," I finally answered, aware I was saying that word a lot, but with my mind going a mile a minute, I was simply relieved I remained on my feet and could communicate.

"Good." A soft, breathy sigh escaped him. "That's good."

Moving again, I took in the surprisingly tidy kitchen. Not that it hadn't been before, but with so many people now coming and going, I didn't quite expect such order. A mountain of containers filled up half of the fridge, their contents labelled with Jada's neat and swirly handwriting.

"Has Jada been on a cooking spree?"

Kent's snort reached me as Rowan answered, "You could say that. I didn't even know I had a slow cooker."

I focussed on his steady voice and the touch of amusement carrying his words, pretty certain he was keeping things light for my sake. More than okay with that, I asked, "Where are you guys travelling from?"

"We just finished meeting with the former CFO of Kitsuma Corp," he explained.

Wide-eyed, my finger poised over the microwave timer, I murmured, "No shit? Did you get anything?"

"Maybe. Michaels has stayed behind."

I grinned despite Rowan not being able to see me. I had wondered why it was so quiet and Michaels wasn't shooting his special brand of love from the back seat of the SUV.

"As soon as we're back, we'll organise Shaw to join him," Kent said. "Where is he now? Why isn't he with you?"

"He's just washing up," I landed on. While things between me and Rowan seemed to be moving at light-ning-fast speed, there were some things we didn't need to disclose till we knew each other better. "And I can handle a microwave. And seriously, this spag bol smells almost as good as—" I stopped abruptly. *Shit, my parents.*

"What's wrong?" Panic strained Rowan's words.

"Sorry, nothing. It's just... it's Thursday, right?"

"Yeah. You've been out for two days."

The confirmation sucked.

"I'm meant to see my parents tomorrow night."

The line went eerily quiet—so much so, I pulled the phone away to check we were still connected.

Kent finally spoke, her voice tight. "For your birthday. That's not until Monday."

Pleased they couldn't see me wince about my complicated feelings for my parents, I huffed out a breath, gathering my thoughts. "They could only manage Friday. Something about an event at the golf club and a spa day."

That I'd planned to fit in dinner around their schedules both frustrated and embarrassed me. There'd been no invite, not even a polite request. Instead, a summons, along with a time and date and the name of a five-star restaurant in the city.

Every year, I showed up, compelled by the last semblance of a connection I had with them. No other formal holidays were celebrated together; they hadn't been since I was fourteen.

"And I need to tell them about turning." *Oh hell*.

"You don't have to tell them anything, and you absolutely can't go tomorrow." While I couldn't see Kent, the tension in her voice sounded tight enough to snap. I didn't think I'd heard her sound so much like a mum before.

She was also right. Cancelling made sense, but my parents were not the most understanding people at the best of times. Not attending wasn't a possible choice... unless cutting off all contact was my plan.

The ache in my heart was sudden and painful. And I hated it. Hated wanting to keep the fragile thread between me and my parents intact.

After a moment of silence, Rowan said, "With everything going on, do you think it's safe for you to be seeing your parents tomorrow?"

"No," I answered immediately, a heavy exhale escaping my lungs. I was thankful Rowan asked the question and offered me the choice and opportunity to be rational.

"Okay, then. We're about ten minutes out. Have you eaten yet?"

"No." The microwave had finished, though, and as soon as I paid attention, I inhaled the scent of garlic and herbs. My stomach reacted immediately, grumbling loudly, pleased I'd gone for the spag bol rather than the lentil soup.

"Damn, I thought the bear had returned." Shaw sauntered into the kitchen area, an amused grin stretching his lips. "Eat before that growl in your stomach tries to escape."

I snagged a fork and the steaming-hot container of spag bol.

"Shaw," Kent interrupted as soon as the first mouthful of food was crammed in my mouth. I barely held back my moan of satisfaction. "Will you be ready to move and join Michaels as soon as Hart and I return?"

Immediately alert, Shaw's smile slipped. "Yes. Where is he now?"

Impressed at his ability to keep his cool considering he knew his boyfriend was by himself, I wondered how I'd behave if the roles were reversed.

While my feelings for the unicorn hacker had been admittedly intense over the months we'd been inter-acting—maybe irrationally so—since the moment I'd heard his voice, my heart hadn't stopped trying to jump out of my chest.

And while I wouldn't dare put a label on what Rowan and I were, I wanted more with him. Every-thing, if he'd give it to me.

His history didn't matter. All I cared about was our future and a possibility of happiness.

Also, who wouldn't want a chance to blow a unicorn?

Fork poised close to my mouth, I froze, only half listening to the conversation between Kent and Shaw. What if the only reason for all that had transpired between me and Rowan was the side effects of the gene transfer?

The hard slam of my heart against my ribcage was enough to draw Shaw's attention. I shook my head, but it didn't deter the concern etched on his face.

"Hey, I'm going to get kitted out. Smythe's all hamster-like at the moment, eating so fast. I'm going to end the call, okay?"

A weird sort of silence followed, which I somehow knew was because of Rowan and his earlier reluctance to stop the conversation.

"I won't let him out of my sight," Shaw reassured.

It was Kent who answered, "Copy that. ETA seven minutes."

When the call ended, Shaw indicated for me to follow him. "You can walk and eat, right?"

I nodded, managing to shove another mouthful of food in despite the ache and worry in my heart.

"Good."

He led the way to his quarters so he could get ready to leave when Kent and Rowan arrived. I followed obediently.

When we reached a bedroom I'd never seen before, I leaned against the doorframe as Shaw got ready.

I didn't have to wait long before he asked, "What's got you worried?" He flicked a glance at me before he rummaged through a bag he dumped on the bed. "Not your parents."

"Not so much," I responded honestly.

"So, what?" He tugged on a fresh black T-shirt before strapping on his holster.

Finishing chewing, I studied him. Shaw was in a relationship that had started out during a mission, and it had definitely been hot and heavy and absolutely fast. "You and Michaels, you're happy, right?"

If he was surprised by my question, he didn't show it. "Yes. It doesn't mean we don't piss each other off, but we're in this, and he makes me so damn happy."

I couldn't help but smile. It had taken knowing Shaw for almost two years before we'd become friends. The undercover mission I'd all but stumbled into—though I argued I'd been dragged into it by Shaw—had changed everything for me. Changed my life in the best of ways.

He'd helped me find a family, a team, and his friendship meant the world to me.

"I really am sorry for not telling you about Row's communication."

Studying me, he tugged on his boots. "I get it, and I'm glad you didn't. It meant I didn't have to lie to Michaels. Which I totally would have, by the way. I've got your back, Smythe. You know that, right?"

I swallowed the emotion trying to crawl up my throat. "I do. It means...." Fucking emotions and the stupid damn feels.

Shaw, like the perceptive guy he was, softened his smile before saying, "You're going through a lot. Between keeping secrets, and the whole becoming a badass lion shifter, and getting hot and sweaty with Hart, it's a lot for anyone to deal with. You've got the added bullshit of the nanogenes."

I stilled, eyes widening. "Nanogenes? What are you talking about?"

I would have laughed at the "oh shit" expression staring back at me if I could breathe properly. Of course I knew what nanogenes were. Just like I knew the case files of some of Hornell's previous experimentations.

It was really fucking happening. What I feared.

Accepting that the change might have worked, and by some miracle, it hadn't killed me, but it *was* going to kill me.

Two days had already been lost. What if the next time I closed my eyes, it took four? After that, eight? My body couldn't survive that.

A trembling started in my hands, travelling up my arms as my breath quickened. Shallow gasps pushed past my lips as I struggled to catch enough air. My heart pounded fiercely, erratic and out of control while the world around me distorted. As my thoughts raced, each one louder than the last, my eyes blurred, discolouring and warping the room I knew I should be able to see.

It spun mercilessly, like lines of code going haywire and glitching.

I needed to take control. Needed to anchor myself to the floor I knew existed beneath my feet. But as my palms turned clammy, my whole body shivering, I couldn't find a hold. Couldn't latch on.

I fought the suffocating panic that gripped my throat. The hold was strong and so damn alien, I didn't know how to pry it away. Didn't know how to make it stop.

"Breathe."

The word prodded me.

"Flynn, I need you to hear my voice, and I need you to breathe."

Floating words draped over me, warming me up, but I couldn't see. Why couldn't I see?

I clawed for something. Anything. A hold. To tear away whatever constricted my sight, my ability to draw in air.

"Hey."

The soft voice, hands holding mine. Fingers interlaced. A squeeze.

"Open your eyes and look at me."

That made sense. To see, I needed to fucking look.

I fought my eyelids.

A bubble of emotion and hysteria caught in my throat.

Open your eyes, Flynn.

My eyelids peeled away, revealing a blinding light that had me wincing. I shut them immediately.

"Not a chance. Look at me. Let me see your eyes."

Rowan.

I tried again, greeted by two arctic-jade orbs so dazzling and pure, a sob broke free. There was no catching it as it escaped, but Rowan was here, holding me, pulling me back from oblivion and the mess of spiralling colours. And while my trembling cries continued to float away, Rowan anchored me to this world. To him.

"What's happening to me?" My muffled words were spoken against his chest. Realising I was truly safe in his firm hold, I inhaled deeply. Vanilla and rainforests. A stuttering breath later, I snuggled in closer, taking comfort in how he stroked my hair and placed soft kisses on my temple.

"We're getting answers," Rowan said softly. "I promise you're going to be okay."

The conviction in his voice had me angling away and making eye contact.

"More than okay," he clarified, his gaze roaming my face.

"I had another panic attack."

"You did."

"I kind of feel sorry for Prince if this is what he had to deal with."

A complicated wave of emotions seemed to sweep over Rowan.

"You don't?" As soon as I released my words, I wanted to take them back. "Shit, I'm sorry."

While Hornell had been pulling the strings, Prince had been boots on the ground betraying Rowan and his team. He was also responsible for so much death and chaos... and Rowan's injuries.

With a shaky hand, I cupped his damaged cheek. At the contact, Rowan held his breath. When he didn't stop me, I danced my fingertips lightly across the damage, feeling the tight skin, its unevenness. The whole time I kept eye contact, refusing to sever it.

My eyes were sore, and I was confident I looked a mess, but that was okay. He'd seen me at my worst and hadn't run. He'd scooped me up, sat me on his lap, and cradled me. If I thought too hard about that right this second, it could send me spiralling, but I couldn't let it.

Instead, I opened up and let him see me vulnerable and a mess.

"What's happening between us isn't because of the changes to my biology." I pushed truth into my words. Dead-set conviction. Perhaps this should have been the last of my worries considering what Shaw had revealed about the nanogenes, but this mattered.

Rowan mattered.

As if knowing I had more to say, Rowan remained silent, slow breaths now escaping as his gaze fixed on mine.

And still, I traced his skin, absorbing everything. These scars still pained him, and while I wished I could take that away, I appreciated every millimetre of damaged skin. They told me some of his story and reminded me how lucky I was he was alive, and that I'd found him.

Though technically, he'd found me.

"I'm still me." *Just a fiercer version.*

"I know you're you."

I studied his face, still palming his cheek, seeing the honesty in how he stared at me.

"You're incredible," I said breathily. "Beautiful."

His eye twitched.

"You don't believe me?"

"It's not that," he said carefully after a moment. "I think you believe it."

"And you don't trust me?" *Bullshit.* I knew he did.

The fight, if that was even what it was, went out of him. "Of course I do."

"Which should be crazy, right?"

This time his lips tilted, my own miraculously following suit.

He didn't confirm how strange it was that we trusted each other implicitly. What was the point? Too much had happened for there to be any doubt of our absolute faith.

For the first time, he leaned into my touch. "Obsession should be crazy."

That shouldn't be sweet, right? I was sure it said something about me that talk about obsession sent my pulse skyrocketing, and the affectionate tone behind it certainly contributed.

But I felt it. Could relate to his words.

Rowan Hart was an addiction I never wanted to conquer.

Despite the way my heart tripped over itself, I answered honestly, "Love is an obsession that captures a heart willing to be imprisoned." Short, unsteady breaths followed.

Spouting flowery words and putting myself out

there terrified me. While I didn't know where those words came from—maybe I'd heard or read them somewhere—they felt true.

I'd wrap my heart up in a box, tie it with an elaborate bow, and give it to Rowan. Hell, maybe that was what I'd already done.

"You matter to me. More than anything." The tremble in his hands as he gripped my waist settled me more than his words did. He meant them. Believed them with a conviction that scared him.

It was no wonder I could relate.

I also grinned. Relief and joy, which were so at odds with my earlier breakdown and the potential death sentence hanging over my head, barrelled through me.

There was only one thing I could do.

Capture his lips, like he'd imprisoned my heart, and show him just how beautiful he was.

WE FOUND KENT AT THE BANK OF COMPUTERS with a headset on and her gaze dancing over the screens.

It had only been when I'd come up for air after making Rowan mine and pushing my cum deep inside him that the reminder of Kent being in the den had horror slamming into me.

Again.

But at least this time, I hadn't lost complete control. Every bite on Rowan's skin had been deliberate and just the right amount of possessive.

Taking off her headset, Kent turned in the chair and eyeballed me. The pounding music of some sort of country song—honestly, I struggled to get my head around the fact that Kent listened to country music—vibrated through the headphones.

Her nose crinkled a little and her lips straightened, but she didn't say a word. I was grateful as hell.

Surprise jolted me when she pushed out of her chair, my eyes widening when she tugged me into a fierce hug. Two hugs in a handful of days. Shit really had gotten real.

Easing back after one tight squeeze, she eyed Rowan at my side, then me. "Jada's on the way back. She has the equipment and meds."

Reality crashed into me.

Nanogenes. I needed to know what was happening.

"Do we know why I was out for two days?" I sat on one of the free office chairs and angled towards both Kent and Rowan, who'd since sat in his usual spot at the control centre.

Rowan's jaw clenched—unsurprising, as he'd been legit freaked out. Rather than answer, he peered at Kent, letting her take the lead.

As she explained what Ethan had shared with them, my heart turned from steady beats to fast hammering.

"From the moment we couldn't wake you, everything's been at warp speed." Kent didn't conceal the pain in her expression as her gaze roamed over me. "But we've got some answers, just more of them than we envisioned."

"More as in the reason why Callen and the director have travelled to Canberra?"

"Definitely. But our team is focussed on you and making sure you're okay. Once we know you're safe and healthy, we'll then support Callen however he needs."

It made sense, and I appreciated it more than I could likely ever express. "Thank you," I said sincerely. "So, what can I do, and what answers do you have?"

Kent launched immediately into an explanation of what had happened since I'd fallen unconscious. "We tentatively believe Ethan didn't know the full extent of what was going on, nor that the chip was for Hornell."

I snapped my attention to Rowan, trying to get a read on his thoughts. Judging from his clenched jaw, he was clearly still pissed off, which honestly, I understood. Felt it. I wished I'd witnessed him socking Ethan.

"Is that what you think?" I pushed.

Sure, the team and Rowan were putting all their effort into making certain I didn't need a shot in my arse every few weeks to keep breathing, but he faced his scars every day. And I thought maybe even had a semblance of peace knowing at least Prince had been put in the ground.

When Rowan had discovered Prince had lived— had been brought back to life—his world had tilted. The wounds freshly aching, a painful reminder that Prince, the man who bore a hell of a lot of responsibility, had been allowed another chance at life.

Yeah, that would have sucked.

And discovering that Ethan, a man he'd once trusted, had been involved—in even the smallest of ways—would have been another sucker punch.

"Beyond everyone in this room, I'm struggling to know what and who to trust at the moment."

It was wrong to silently celebrate the win, but his trust meant a lot.

"And Jada," he tagged on.

A glance at Kent and I understood why he'd added to the list.

"Fuck's sake, your whole team. Grudgingly. Okay?"

Unable to resist, I smirked, relishing the smallest hint of joy at Rowan's exasperation and Kent's stare down. With the future ahead of me precarious, I'd celebrate them when I could.

Even though he rolled his eyes when he caught my reaction, his lips twitched.

Kent ignored the exchange, getting back on track.

"You're not going to need the dose of Genosyntik booster." Before I could ask what that was, she explained, "It's the shot Prince needed to ensure the nanotech in his system continued to function and do its job. It's a chemical compound combined with microscopic nanobot technology. We were able to secure the prototype Hornell was after. Four hired hands showed up at the Sydney storage facility. Callen allowed them to slip right in, and once they had the sample chip, which included a storage device connected to a gene editing machine, he and his team were able to take them down."

A rush of breath escaped me. "And the vaccine information was on the gene editing storage?" So much had happened in two days, and I focussed hard on retaining all the new information.

"Yes."

That was great, but what the fuck about me?

When Kent's expression shuttered, my stomach tumbled.

"Jada's returning with some meds for treatment that need some fine-tuning."

While her gaze remained steady, it was what she wasn't revealing that sent my heart into overdrive.

"And that means what, exactly?"

Kent didn't answer. Instead, Rowan, while touching my back, said, "Jada's been working really hard at studying your genetic makeup. She's pulled in some favours from old colleagues with genetic specialities who've been helping her. Nothing on the market, or even in existence, will wipe clean or even help the coding in your blood. You need something that will override the nanogenes. It may take some trial and error."

They might have to experiment on me? The thought made me cold.

"The Genosyntik booster we've discovered has been helpful, and Jada and her team have a plan."

Taking a calming breath, I fought back the panic threatening to cripple me. "And something permanent, right?" Fuck, if I was going to be treated like a damn guinea pig, I needed the outcome to eventually be permanent.

"That's the goal here."

There was no reassuring smile, no false promises, just a warm, comforting hand on my back.

"Okay," I managed, shoving my fear as far away as possible. "And what can I do, beyond being prodded and poked?"

After searching my gaze, Rowan finally tilted his lips, forming a soft half-smile. "How about we see if the permission's come through for satellite imagery and try to take Hornell down for good?"

Relief expanded in my chest. I couldn't have handled being coddled. There'd been enough inaction. "Fuck yes."

The smallest of movements from Kent drew my attention to her. She stared at me long and hard, and while I wasn't sure what she was thinking, when she squeezed my arm, I had a pretty good idea.

"Let's find this piece of shit." She followed up with a wink.

The three of us settled ourselves in side by side at the workstations. Despite the worry, the fear trying to wind its way through my body, having Kent to my left and Rowan to my right loosened the tight boulder sitting on my chest.

As soon as my team was back, I suspected it would disappear completely.

It took fifteen minutes of prodding from Kent before the permission finally arrived. When it did, a thrill had me sitting straighter. Eagerness pulsed inside me.

We all suspected the delay had provided some sort of warning to Hornell—or whoever was located at the facility in Glenorie. If they'd cleared out, it would suck, but that would also mean we were a step closer and, for the second time, had foiled their plan.

The first being the two-day deadline to get the sample from the storage facility.

Each win was its own kind of balm to our frustration.

With our eyes glued to the screens, Kent took control, manoeuvring the satellite by setting the coordinates. It took long seconds to reposition. Meanwhile, tension buzzed around us as I sat with my heart in my throat, waiting for the image to become clear.

The footage snapped into focus, the grainy image settling after Rowan hit a few keys.

A sprawling facility lay before us, the visual currently too far away to take in anything beyond the general layout. Rowan zoomed in to cut off the surrounding area, and our attention snapped to the screen at the sudden movement to the far right of the facility.

We exchanged surprised glances that there remained boots on the ground. Keeping half an eye on the lone figure, we scrutinised the feed, discovering defensive devices guarding the compound. This was what Lucas had suspected: devices capable of detecting and neutralising drones.

This was definitely no ordinary setup. They were prepared for unwanted visitors.

Swiftly, we were documenting every detail—the buildings, the multiple guards—when a figure emerged, striding purposefully towards the helicopter. My heart skipped a beat as I recognised him: Hornell, the man responsible for so much chaos and death.

"Fuck."

I nodded and looked at Kent, silently agreeing with her outburst.

Hornell was there. What the fuck?

"We need to scramble a team," she said, throwing on her headset and reaching out to Lucas.

It would arrive too late. By the time anyone touched base, Hornell would be long gone.

"No chance we'll get anyone there in time," Rowan said, mirroring my thoughts.

"Agreed."

"We need to hack into the helicopter, stall its departure. Fuck, force it to crash for all I care."

Lucas's voice then reached us—Kent having adjusted the controls, no doubt after hearing Rowan's suggestion.

"That would be risky and would bend the rules of engagement." His voice was tight, but he wasn't saying no.

"There's some red tape we need to burn to the ground," Kent responded.

Rowan shot her an up-nod, unsurprisingly agreeing with her statement. I was right there with them.

"If he leaves, we're going to lose him again," Kent continued.

"Fuck." Lucas went quiet after biting out the word. This would be entirely on him. Even if Rowan took over and made the call himself, Lucas would be taking responsibility. As for consequences, that would all depend on what was happening in Canberra.

"Do it."

And we moved into action, frantically trying to take control.

"Kent, get a drone out there so we can track the helicopter should it move."

"The compound is set up with takedown devices," she responded, although she worked on arming a drone and getting it in the air from the closest SICB facility to Glenorie. "I'll need to keep it on the outskirts until it's needed."

I glanced at Rowan's screen, recognising the software that was absolutely illegal as he punched in code that I knew would hack into the helicopter's controls.

"Smythe, I've reached out to a secondary team and asked them to head out there on standby. I need you to coordinate with them. Channel seven. It's Jamison."

"Roger that." I focussed on my screen and opened up what schematics we'd found of the Glenorie compound, then pulled up Jamison's information—a panther in a special ops unit the team had worked with several times.

Rowan's "What the fuck!" grabbed all our attention. A thunderous red bled into his cheeks. "Someone's blocked me."

My brow bounced high in alarm.

Someone thwarted Rowan's takeover?

"I can't get back in. Someone's locked it down and kicked me out." His expression turned murderous. "Lucas, where's Ethan?"

Oh shit.

"Right here beside me."

"And he's not on any devices?"

"No."

"So who the fuck has blocked me?"

I could see him racking his brains as he continued trying to bypass the system. His frustration grew, his whole body vibrating with anger. It rolled over me, the emotion thick in the air, pressing down on me.

Anger scratched at my skin, doubling down as the helicopter took off.

"The drone is still five minutes out." Kent clenched her fist.

The urge to break free, to defend, to tear apart everyone who hurt Rowan and Kent grew deep in my belly, growling and pulsing.

My vision turned hazy, a blur of colour. A screech of a chair had me wincing. Loud voices rose. I cringed at the sound, my ears sensitive.

I needed to cover them but couldn't. I couldn't move. Couldn't think.

Couldn't—

A scream, thick and loud.

Heat, a too-heavy blanket threatening to melt my bones.

A soft purr, a whisper, and I blinked my eyes open.

The world had shifted. Come into sharp focus.

The fuck was happening?

Rowan knelt before me. Why was he on his knees?

When I parted my lips to ask, a loud roar shook the room and vibrated my body.

It had happened.

I'd turned without meaning to.

I was a motherfucking lion.

CHAPTER 12
ROWAN HART

HE WAS MAGNIFICENT.

But this was bad. Oh so fucking bad.

I wanted to punch myself. So focussed on being pissed off, my ego bruised by being jolted from my task, my attention on Flynn had slipped.

Who did that? How selfish could one person be?

I'd known he was progressively getting worse. Had known his protective instincts were at an all-time high. Objectively, I'd suspected, if triggered, it could push him over the edge.

So what had I done? Been a selfish fucker and done just that. Just like I was making this all about me while I stared at the huge lion before me, hoping like hell he was still Flynn.

Stepping over the one computer screen smashed on the ground, I edged towards him, wide-eyed and trying to take control of my emotions. "Flynn, you're going to be okay. Can you change back?"

He roared in answer, pushing warm air my way.

Movement in my periphery had me glancing that way. Still seated, Kent, the epitome of calm, simply looked at him. Her expression was on the soft side of neutral.

Already knowing she wasn't going to intervene and was letting me handle this, I returned my attention to Flynn. He sat on his haunches, his bright golden gaze on me.

"Is that a no, as in, you can't change back?"

He chuffed, not severing eye contact.

Shit. If only there was a way for me to understand him. What I wouldn't give to be able to mindread right about now.

The beep of the access road alarm triggered. I didn't move, trusting Kent to take control of the console.

"If I shift, do you think it'll help you?" I had no idea if it would or even why it would, but I was not a fan of feeling useless.

Another chuff, and I suspected Flynn was in agreement, wondering why he'd latched on to someone so useless.

Before I could respond, Flynn moved, taking slow strides towards me. While it wasn't quite a prowl and there was not an ounce of menace in his steps, I still froze, wondering what his intentions were.

I didn't have to wait long. He rubbed his large head against my chest, the movement firm, his mane brushing my chin, almost tickling. He huffed again before he purred, drawing a laugh out of me.

Wrapping my arms around him, I buried my face in his mane, inhaling his fresh scent that smelt of the desert after a much-needed storm. The soft purr increased, vibrating along my skin as he allowed me to hug him.

The arsehole was comforting me. Not for the first time, I wondered what I'd done to deserve him.

Flynn was everything kind and generous in the world. Beautiful and smart, he absolutely brought me to my knees.

"Jada's just parked. She has two colleagues with her. They've been vetted and pose no threat."

Since I already knew about the two scientists supporting Jada, the reassurance was intended for Flynn. I understood the need for her to share, but the implication that he could be losing himself dragged fresh fear to the surface.

I couldn't lose him.

A world without Flynn wasn't a world I wanted to exist in.

And since I was sure my brother would kick my arse and never forgive me for leaving him, I would fight for Flynn. For us. For his whole team if I had to.

I pulled away from the embrace, keeping one hand in his mane. The coarse hair between my fingers helped ground me. Reminded me Flynn was still here.

"Jada will help you." I forced steel into my voice, not leaving room for misunderstanding or argument. "We'll get through this."

Golden eyes stared me down, all but imploring me to understand.

"Together, okay? Always together."

I'd sell my damn soul if I had to.

Another chuff, and a wet tongue dragged across my face. Light infused my chest, burning brightly and completely fracturing the last semblance of harsh barbed wire. It melted away, leaving my heart exposed, vulnerable.

I smiled.

For him. For me.

For how ridiculously perfect Flynn was, in every single form he took.

When I heard Kent greeting Jada and new equipment being hauled through my den, I placed my hand over his furry cheek, my hand seeming small and fragile. "Let's go to the lab."

With a chuff, he nudged me to take the lead, following me closely.

Jada's eyes were aimed our way as we entered the lab. Her gaze softened as she stepped up to Flynn and swept her hand over his golden mane. "You're handsome in every form."

Grinning in agreement, refusing to let my worry bleed from my pores, I peered at Flynn. After he pushed his head against Jada's palm, he focussed on me.

"Ready?"

A slow blink and I knew he was.

"Here's the plan." Next to Kent, Jada held court. "It's actually perfect that you're in lion form. Can we take a blood sample while Tumnus" —she indicated a lion shifter who worked for the local university, specialising in gene coding—"and Kirke"—she pointed at a middle-aged human with greying hair and a kind smile who was a genomic scientist, currently working on an aboveboard contract for the government—"set up what's needed?"

A huff and an attempt at a nod showed Flynn was in agreement.

"Excellent." She turned to her wife. "Ivy."

"I need to get back in touch with Lucas. We cut him off. Then I'll do whatever's needed." She squeezed Jada's arm before leaving the lab.

I remained at Flynn's side, not wanting to stray too far. Unsure which one of us needed the comfort of proximity the most, I didn't question it.

Jada and her team set to work taking a blood sample and hooked Flynn up to a range of monitors.

His temperature was running high, but not alarmingly so, while his heartbeat remained steady, the regular thump doing wonders to help ease my own racing pulse. The whole time, Flynn kept his amber stare on me as I sat slightly off to his side to keep out of the way of the working doctors but close enough to touch him and make eye contact.

We sat together quietly, with the occasional interruption from Jada explaining what she was doing and looking for when she shared the large screen with us. The doctors milled around, talking in hushed conversations that we could hear but I chose not to listen to as I fixed my gaze on Flynn.

We were almost eye to eye, Flynn on top of an overly large examination table big enough to support a bear shifter. If necessary, it provided plenty of room for me to curl up next to him. I'd do so in a heartbeat if Jada needed him here for the foreseeable future.

Kent saying, "Lucas is on his way with Ethan," had me turning her way. I kept my sneer at bay, still struggling to come to terms with Ethan's involvement. Over the years, I'd been far from innocent, taking on some illegal jobs and absolutely gaining intel to squash corrupt individuals in the government—and the Alliance—but always for the greater good. Not only that, but I'd always done my due diligence—especially when taking on high-paid jobs.

I never wanted my skills used to harm the innocent, and I especially never wanted them to help the corrupt.

I hadn't thought Ethan would want that either.

"What about Michaels and Shaw?" It was what Flynn would have asked if he had the ability.

"They're just finishing up. Shaw indicated they had information to share."

I frowned, wondering why they hadn't already passed on the information over the network. Then again, neither had Ethan.

Everything in my den was secure. The system to

identify breaches was a program I'd fine-tuned myself. Nothing was infallible. I knew that. But I trusted the program and my skill.

The hair on my arms stood on end, a shiver meaning that I was missing something pulsing through me.

Immediately on alert, Flynn sat on his haunches, a low warning growl rumbling out of him.

"What is it?"

The concern in Kent's tone caught the whole lab's attention.

"Something's off. I need to check the mainframe." I shot out of my seat, Jada's shout for Flynn to stop not enough to deter me. Breaking free from the wires attached to him, he prowled behind me.

Kent was already at the area of the workstation she'd claimed as her own. "What are we looking for?"

I didn't glance her way as I said, "Check everything for security breaches."

"On the network?"

"Everywhere," I answered. "Firewalls, check the intrusion detective systems are in place, scan for vulnerabilities."

"On it."

Meanwhile, I entered the management software,

diving into the data security banks, looking for anything amiss.

Behind me, Flynn prowled a steady route back and forth behind where Kent and I sat. He'd be able to see the screens, watch what we were doing, and I suspected he was super annoyed he wasn't helping.

My fingers flew over the keys as I delved deeper into my system. Every line of code, every firewall, every encryption layer had been meticulously crafted by my own hands. But doubt gnawed at me. I needed to ensure, beyond a shadow of doubt, that my systems remained impenetrable.

Ego could get a person killed and put us all at risk. Not a chance I'd let that happen.

As I initiated the first series of tests, my pulse quickened with each command entered. The system responded flawlessly, routines running without a hitch and the alarms in place staying silent.

Reassuring, but the knot in my gut didn't loosen.

As I probed deeper, the lines of code blurred into a complex maze, a labyrinth designed to keep out unwanted trespassers. Nothing jumped out as being impacted. No broken string. No slight hole.

But the lingering fear remained.

At my side, Kent scanned through log after log, looking for anomalies. It might have been my system, but she'd notice a breach, even a slight attempt at infiltration.

A rush of anticipation mingled with dread when I saw her pause. I left my post, peering over her shoulder. "What is it?"

"This. The string in the power supply has coding I don't recognise."

Panic surged, gripping me as I zeroed in on the code. "Can you trace it?"

With a nod, she worked in silence, her focus never leaving the screen. Nor did mine. She dug deeper, tracing the origins, an eerie calm surrounding her as she dominated the keyboard.

"Here."

My brow creased as I focussed. "What's the time stamp?"

More lines of code appeared, finally revealing the information. Three months ago.

Some of the panic eased in my chest.

"Three months." She glanced at me. "What happened three months ago?"

With a heavy sigh, tension dropped from my shoulders. "A thunderstorm. There was a flicker from the mains before the generator kicked in." Once it had, I'd done a system check then, not noticing anything out of the ordinary. I frowned.

"What is it?" Kent asked just as Flynn nudged my hand.

I peered down at him and dug my fingers into his mane, taking comfort. "I checked at the time, but there was no glitch, no breaches." I glanced at Kent.

"Which begs the question, why is this anomaly showing up now, after three months?"

"Exactly. It wasn't there before."

She didn't ask if I was certain.

"Let's shut off the main network." I didn't like the blip in the coding. Just like I didn't like the strange feeling that something was off.

Kent set about closing the mainframe. It would mean we'd have limited access until I opened up a secondary network, but we needed to remain secure.

Jada's "Holy shit" jolted me. I spun on my heel, eyes widening and heart immediately pounding at the bright grin she shot our way. "I think we've got it."

As Kent said, "Done," indicating she'd shut down the mainframe, she spun in her chair, too, the breach threat momentarily forgotten.

"Got what, exactly?" I asked slowly. The lightning-fast pulsing of my heart meant my attempt to not get my hopes up was failing.

"The solution to reduce the nanogenes. We don't think we can erase them completely."

"Why not?" Kent asked.

"They've become part of Flynn's genetic markers. Erasure would put his life at risk."

Nausea swirled in my gut at the very thought. Thank fuck they'd discovered that and spent the past forty-eight hours deeply investigating and testing.

"All we need to do is reduce the nanogenes so they're no longer dominant. It'll ensure Flynn's in full control." When she paused, her lips pulling together, I narrowed my eyes. There was more she had to say, and I didn't think we'd like whatever it was.

Flynn's loud chuff had her nodding.

"So, we think it'll just be this one course of treatment, but we'll need to keep a close eye on you for a week. Then we'll need to run regular blood tests to ensure the nanogene count remains the same. The more extreme side effects will be greatly reduced." She paused there.

"But not gone completely?" I clarified.

Frustration morphed her features as she shook her head. "No. We may eventually be able to reduce the symptoms more and more, but it'll take time and testing. But the positive take on all this is that he'll regain control over his shift. That's the more extreme and worrying side effect. The others will be vastly reduced and are completely manageable. Plus, they're not life-threatening."

My brain immediately latched on to his side effects. How protective he could be. I deserved a sucker punch when my lips twitched. Maybe his life wasn't at risk, but if anyone pissed him off enough by putting someone he loved in—

Loved.

The thought smacked me in the face.

Of course I loved him back. That it was such a surprise meant I needed a nut punch too.

Flynn nudged me, dragging me out of my spinning thoughts.

When he chuffed, his gaze intent on mine, fresh amusement sprinkled with a shitload of joy flooded out of me. The arsehole was laughing at me.

Which meant.... I barely held back my groan of embarrassment. Getting a hard-on at the thought of Flynn being protective and horny and mine was not something I wanted to share in any company. Especially not in front of Kent and Jada.

"Life was so much simpler before I was overrun by the ITU," I groused with a hint of a smirk. A grunt punched out of me when Flynn knocked his head into my gut. "Jokes. I'm joking." I caressed his head, wanting him to shift back so I could hold him close, do my own protecting, and tell him I was absolutely gone for him.

"So," Kent interrupted with an arched eyebrow aimed pointedly at me.

I got it. I could hardly believe I was joking around. Period. Let alone with agents. I swore that Vinnie wouldn't recognise me. His being called in to calm me down when I punched Ethan a couple of days ago and struggled to keep myself in check was the version of me that he'd been used to since my injury and the betrayal.

We peered over at her.

"How do we do this?"

Kirke addressed us. "There's one more thing."

He might as well have said an explosion would be detonating in the next few seconds with the way hope seemed to be sucked from the room.

Undeterred despite the daggers being sent his way, he looked straight at Flynn. "We suspect the suppression of the nanogenes will be violent."

The already tense room tautened, close to the snapping point.

"Violent how?" Kent's tone dropped five degrees below deadly.

"We've only trialled this on a few drops of blood, so we can't be completely certain of the overall impact on your entire system. From what we've witnessed, the suppressant aggressively fights the nanogenes in the bloodstream, overpowering them within five minutes."

"How do you know it will be violent, though? What does that actually mean?" I pushed.

Flynn nudged at me, and I peered down, looking into his bright amber orbs. He wanted me to shut the hell up and let them get on with it. If I were in his position, I suspected I'd want the same thing.

But we had to know. Be prepared—regardless of what that looked like.

"The way the suppressant appears under the microscope is very similar to the reaction experienced by patients needing Genehalt."

Jada explained, "It's a treatment still undergoing testing, used to suppress shifters from converting back to their human form."

Horror slammed into me. "What the fuck?"

Jada shook her head. "It's legit and could prove invaluable in the healing process for shifters who've been badly injured. While shifting can help speed up healing capabilities, when unconscious and in so much pain, the body tends to react on default—returning to the biped form."

I knew this all too well, having had first-hand experience when trying to heal years back.

"As soon as that happens, it slows the process. This trial has been amazing. The data phenomenal."

My muscles twitched as I heard what she said and even agreed with her, but still.... "That's until it's used for something nefarious, like preventing shifters from turning into biped form to keep them quiet or to punish them or whatever the fuck else government officials or insane fuckers like Hornell want to use it for."

Anger buzzed through my body. Of course the government would fund something like this. It didn't matter how honourable people's intentions were, it would undoubtedly be used for the wrong reasons.

Yet another way to control shifters.

Flynn's soft whine broke through my spiral.

Making eye contact, I caressed his mane and took deep, unsteady breaths.

Jada was good. I knew that. Was sure of it.

Whether she was involved in the trial or not, and regardless of her positive intentions, she was naive if she thought for one second that once the treatment was approved—and I wouldn't be surprised if it happened before that—it wouldn't be used to the detriment of shifters.

Looking into Flynn's eyes, I knew it wasn't the time to be fighting this.

Would I be doing all I could afterwards to investigate and potentially shut the project down myself? Quite possibly.

"Back to the violence," I said. "Explain."

Kirke bobbed his head. "The impact on the body can be stressful. Increased blood pressure, heart rate. Patients have to be strapped down to stop them from injuring themselves as their body tries to fight the suppressant."

I glanced at Kent. "And you're okay with this?"

She attempted a neutral expression, but the firmness of her jaw and the tightness of her limbs let me know how much she was battling her reaction. "It's not up to me. This is Smythe's decision."

While she was right, letting him do this grated. I didn't want him in pain. Nor did I want him lost forever.

"Flynn." His attention was already on me as I spoke. "What do you want to do?"

For five long seconds, he stared at me while a slight tremble shook my hands. He then nudged my shoulder, burying his nose near my neck.

Fuck it all to hell. Of course he was doing this.

Before I could react, he backed away, bounded over to the overlarge gurney, and jumped up, landing effortlessly before he settled down on his stomach.

I couldn't look. I wanted to run away. Hide. Perhaps leave altogether, not sure I was strong enough to hear, let alone see what happened next.

My own screams from my injury, from my repeated, painful treatments that never worked remained a companion when I least wanted it. My cries, the sounds echoing around my den, would often wake me up at night.

Would I be adding Flynn's to the chorus?

I took two long strides to reach his side. I touched his shoulder while the team set about strapping him down. As they did, I stood rigid except for the single motion of my hand, soothing his fur.

I blocked out Jada's words as she spoke to her team and then to Flynn, focussing completely on him.

He had to be okay. The alternative had never been an option, and it was even less of one now.

In my periphery, I saw a line being organised, the needle puncturing his skin. A flash of red followed. More movement, and then Jada let him know they were going to begin.

And still I stroked him, refusing to look away from his face.

Flynn lowered his head, resting it on his paws, his eyes now focussed on me.

He twitched. Spasmed. Settled.

Until all hell broke loose.

He roared, all agony and distress, his body undulating against the straps. My heart wrenched, the sound biting at my skin and burrowing deep into my chest. He growled, a desperation to the ear-piercing bellow as his muscles strained against the straps holding him down.

My hand having broken away from his writhing form, I wanted to reach out, try to offer some comfort. But it would be meaningless when he was like this. Maybe even painful.

As it was, it seemed like liquid fire was pulsing through his veins, heightening his agony as each second passed by. Unable to do anything more, I settled as close as I dared, whispering soothing words, hoping they would somehow be heard and offer some solace.

"I'm here. It's going to be okay. It'll end soon. Just a little longer." Whether I lied or not, I didn't know, but I continued, pushing truth into each word. "It's going to work. Almost done."

His body lurched, an agonised roar tearing from him. His features twisted, tearing at my soul. Another convulsion, another tortured moan, and pain stabbed my heart.

This had to end. The torment needed to cease.

I didn't dare look away from him, not willing to withdraw my attention when he needed me most. I sensed Kent close by, a quiet vibration pulsing from her that fractured my focus. Jada stood at her side, neither saying a word as Tumnus and Kirke monitored his vitals.

Try as I might to tune out the frantic beeping of the machines, they joined Flynn's roars. Each sound, each second threatened to be my undoing.

How the fuck was he still alive, still here?

I was utterly helpless. My eyes stung with unshed tears. This incredible lion, the most incredible man I knew—body and soul—was reduced to an agony beyond his control. The sight tore at me, encouraged me to glance away and cover my ears, and yet I remained. A silent sentinel bearing witness to his mounting suffering, my own distress blooming at the first trickle of blood coming from his nostril.

"He's bleeding. What the fuck is happening?" For the first time, I tore my gaze away, searching the room frantically, looking for answers, for reassurance.

Kent, with a single tear staining her cheek, looked ready to tear off heads. A stoic Jada appeared to be blocking her way.

The doctors continued quietly monitoring Flynn's vitals, alert but not panicking.

"Jada, please." The words wrenched out of me with a sob, my tears finally spilling over.

"Just a while longer," she whispered, sorrow clinging to her words.

Lurching from the table, the straps barely keeping him contained, every muscle in Flynn's lion body turned rigid. Then silence. Brutal and terrifying silence as his body collapsed in a heap on the gurney.

No, no, no.

Fresh agony crashed over me with the force of a deadly wave.

He couldn't be.

I shook my head, my trembling hand reaching out.

I couldn't—

A beep.

Snapping my head in the direction of the monitor, I watched a wave peak. And another. Another. Until a steady stream of waves danced across the heart monitor.

"His vitals are improving." Kirke pressed a couple of buttons, and I dragged in a shuddery breath at the gentle beat of Flynn's heart. "He's going to need to rest. I'm going to take a sample."

I didn't respond, too focussed on crawling onto the gurney to wrap my arm around Flynn. I needed to feel his heat, his heartbeat. Every single breath.

The group watched silently, but my whole attention was on Flynn. He was so much bigger than me in lion form, but I pressed every inch of my body I could manage against him. When I had answers, I'd shift. It would make curling up beside him easier.

My attention flickered to Kent. With a tissue, she wiped the blood from his face. Tears danced in her eyes. A blink and one escaped.

Rather than wiping it away, she made eye contact. "Love him more than you've loved a single thing in the world."

"Always."

She blinked again, releasing another tear. She let Jada lead her away after they each pressed a kiss on the fur between his ears.

As I waited for news from the doctors, I traced patterns in the fur between his shoulder blades, desperate for him to wake and huff out a laugh, letting me know it tickled.

"It worked."

I snapped my focus to Tumnus and was met with a wide, relieved grin.

"The nanogenes have been suppressed. His bloodwork looks excellent. He's going to be okay."

He's going to be okay.

I let the words settle into my brain before an exhale

pushed past my lips. "Thank you," I said shakily. "Thank you so much."

He nodded, his smile softening.

I sat up so I could strip and shift. I'd stay by his side for as long as it took, and from the murmured voices and quiet work happening around me, nobody expected anything different.

CHAPTER 13
FLYNN SMYTHE

Soft rumbling and warm fur—both were welcome sensations as I woke. I kept my eyes closed, not recognising the mattress beneath me, but the familiar scent of gentle vanilla was enough to calm any potential panic.

I blinked my eyes open while taking stock of my limbs. Legs and arms, a bare torso, pale, peachy skin. Human form.

The throb of an ache hummed in my veins, almost like a phantom memory more than acute pain. But I couldn't think about that. The desperation in my growls still echoed in my ears, the agony too close to the surface for me to spare a thought for them.

All I wanted was the softness of Rowan's fur and his familiar comfort.

Angling my head, I drank him in, barely catching my gasp when I remembered just how incredible he was like this. With soft light slithering through the partially shuttered windows, the rays danced over his white fur, making the strands glow almost ethereally, like pure, freshly fallen snow.

Nestled snuggly at his side, I hesitated to move, not wanting to destroy this moment. Not when he appeared so peaceful. Even asleep, he exuded grace, but it was his tranquillity that mesmerised me.

With every soft breath, he emitted a gentle, rhythmic purr. My lips twitched. I was convinced it was the sweetest sound I'd ever heard.

Unable to hold back, I ran my fingers along one of the narrow stripes curving his shoulder. The fur, softer than I expected, shifted as his muscles twitched. I did it again, enjoying the slight movement and the silk under my sensitive fingertips.

Ice-green eyes appeared as he blinked them open. Rowan remained still, his soft breaths increasing slightly, his piercing gaze fixed on my face.

A smile formed as I trailed a final path over one of his ink-black stripes, and finally, slowly, he angled his large head closer. I tilted my neck, knowing he wanted to settle in the crook. He did so immediately, inhaling deeply, his huge body wriggling closer.

My smile turned into a huff of laughter, so relieved that he was here and I was too. And holy shit, truly in human form.

"I'm okay." The statement felt true.

His purr vibrated against my neck, and I fidgeted some more, loving the sensation even though it tickled.

"I have no idea what time it is." I reached out with my senses, listening intently. Movement in another part of the building caught my attention. It was far off, and there were no voices.

Pulling away, Rowan looked at me for a few long seconds. And I got it—his unwillingness to glance away. But we both needed to change.

"I'm okay," I reiterated and indicated for him to jump off the gurney. As he did so, I took a surreptitious glance around the lab. Nothing had changed, with the exception that the monitors were off and the medical equipment was no longer whirring.

In the time it took me to take in my surroundings, Rowan was back on the thin mattress beside me, his eyes wide and assessing.

"You," he croaked and cleared his throat. "How are you feeling?"

I took stock. The ghost of sensitive skin and achy muscles still tingled, but beyond that, my head felt clear, and I was confident that while my legs might be a little jelly-like, I could walk.

"Good. Better." I stared into his gaze, aware he wanted more. What I wanted, however, was to wrap myself up in him and never let go. Ideally not on a thin mattress, though.

The sound of quiet conversation, too low for me to make out, was taking place a few rooms away.

I huffed out a frustrated breath. "You want to kiss me before we're descended on?" I angled my head in invitation, placing my hand on Rowan's hip.

With a sliver of a smile, he leaned towards me, slanting his lips over mine. I sighed into the touch, opening willingly as he took control, kissing me deeper. My head spun in the best way as I held on tight, pressing my body against his even knowing we couldn't take this further. But I needed the safety of his embrace. The warmth of his kiss.

Our tongues tangled, slow and exploring, and another soft sigh escaped me. I felt his smile against my lips and followed his lead as he slowed the kiss further, pulling away a fraction between each press of his mouth to mine until eventually we stopped.

With our faces close, he whispered, "I thought I was going to lose you."

I heard his pain, felt it like it was my own. "But you didn't."

He pressed another soft kiss to my lips. "I kind of lost my shit."

A heavy thump knocked against my ribcage as I remembered his cries, his pleas between my foggy brain and the burning sting of pain I hadn't thought would end. "But you stayed."

"Always."

Another heavy thump and emotion lodged in my throat. I struggled to swallow it down, even though it shook my voice when I admitted, "This thing between us is more than the predator in me wanting to protect you." While I'd said something similar before, I needed him to know, to understand the depth of my feelings.

"If by 'thing' you're referring to how much I love you, then yeah, it's the whole of me that feels that way too."

As those words tumbled from Rowan's kiss-swollen lips, it felt like the air had been vacuumed from the room, leaving me light-headed and gasping for breath. My heart, already pounding a thunderous tempo, skipped before settling into a steady beat in perfect synch with his.

I smiled, all teeth and amazement as elation swirled around me, tingling the tips of my toes and running all the way to the depths of my soul. And still, I grinned, wanting to kiss him senseless and hold on for dear life.

I settled on saying, "I've loved you for a long time. Impossibly so at times. Even when I thought you were a magical genius unicorn, and I didn't yet know the depths of your soul or the story in your eyes. But I do now." I cupped his scarred cheek, stroking my thumb over the sensitive, marred skin. "I think I was made for you."

Watery eyes peered back at me, or maybe I was just looking through my own teary gaze. But it didn't matter, as beyond the hazy sheen, witnessing his love for me that I felt in my gut was everything I hadn't dared to dream of. Not ever.

Rowan's soft "I love you so fucking much" ghosted against my lips as he kissed me. More gentle presses. More tender touches. Until a knock on the wall of the doorless room pulled us apart.

"There're sweats next to the cooler."

I smirked at Kent's exasperated tone and, on shaky legs, stood with Rowan's help. We dressed quickly, some of the ache in my limbs already easing by the time I let her know we were dressed.

Entering together, Jada and Kent practically charged me, their eyes wide and filled with emotion. All Kent's usual aloofness—even her exasperation when she'd spoken from outside the room—dissipated in a giant hug that snatched my breath.

Sensibly, Rowan stood to the side, amusement clear in his expression as he didn't take his eyes off the rib-squashing vampire hugs I was receiving.

Pulling back first, Jada cupped my face, her smile sincere and her cheeks damp. She didn't say a word as she scanned my features, then pressed her palm against my forehead. My lips twitched in grateful amusement at her parent-like check.

"I'm so happy you're okay," she finally said. "How are you feeling?"

Meanwhile, Kent, as if realising she was still putting on a show by hugging me, eased away, her back straight, her carefully constructed "eat shit and die" expression forming.

"Honestly, I'm feeling better by the minute." No lie. For as much as being turned had been one cluster-fuck after another, it was nice to start to feel some of the added benefits—healing being just one of them.

She took my answer as truth and bobbed her head, glancing at Kent. Her smile appeared, just for a second, before she reschooled her features. "You look better." Her soft tone was at odds with her rigid posture, but this was Kent; she made the best kind of cuddly viper.

"Thanks. I feel it."

Since the hugfest was over, Rowan returned to my side, close enough that our arms brushed. "How long did we sleep?"

"Just an hour," Jada responded.

An hour? Hell, it felt so much longer than that.

"Where's the team?"

I pressed my lips together, eyes widening as I looked at Kent and deliberately not at Rowan. "The" team, not "your" team.... That was a step in some sort of direction, right?

"Callen and Chris are still in Canberra with Director Durrant. They're struggling to get the truth out of anyone. But if anyone can make someone talk, it's Callen."

I huffed out a breath of amusement. I'd heard plenty of stories, so I didn't doubt it.

"What about Ethan and Lucas? Weren't they on their way over?" The tightness in Rowan's voice, I suspected, was absolutely because he'd be seeing Ethan again any time now. But at least this time, no one thought I was dying.

Hopefully that would mean no bloodshed when Ethan arrived.

"They got a lead. It turns out the memory drive hadn't been fully wiped. There's a second chip still in use."

Horror slammed into me at Kent's explanation.

Of course there was a second chip in play. Hell, there could have been a hundred. Though, from what Ethan had disclosed, he'd only made one, and the coding and creation had been complex and tricky. I suspected not just anyone could pull it off.

"Do we know if the chip's been implanted?" A hum of anticipation rolled off Rowan.

"That's what they're aiming to find out. They're heading to Brisbane right now. Should touch down in thirty-five minutes. Michaels and Shaw have gone with them."

It was good that Lucas wasn't handling this by himself. Rowan still didn't trust Ethan, and while the vampire was deadly—I'd heard the stories even if I hadn't seen the man in action myself—him having backup would help us all breathe easier.

"Why don't you go wash up." It was more of a directive than a suggestion from Kent. She eyed me. "Do you think you'll be up for support when they reach Brisbane? Rowan and I should be able to—"

"Absolutely." I bobbed my head. "We've wasted enough time."

"Making sure you were okay is *not* a waste of time," Rowan cut in, sounding pissed.

I held back my smirk and my eye roll even as my

heart fluttered. That he was just as protective over me as I was him was a hell of a thing.

"He's right," Kent added, and I couldn't keep my reaction at bay any longer. A wide, happy grin split my lips.

"Okay, but the sentiment's the same. We need to keep chasing the leads. We were so close before he boarded that helicopter." Which reminded me. "We weren't able to track it?" That was the point when I'd lost control, so I remained clueless.

"No." Kent sounded pissed. "It headed into restricted airspace, and our satellite feed was severed."

"No shit?" No wonder Callen and Director Durrant were on a mission in the capital.

"Get a shower, we'll get food, and then we'll get to work."

We nodded as Kent spoke.

"I'm going to reach out to Kirke and Tumnus," Jada said.

"They've gone?" The rest of Rowan's den had remained quiet, but they could have been sleeping.

"Yeah. I'll let them know you're okay. Kirke's going to help with your checkups and the regular monitoring you're going to need. He has much more experience in this field than I do."

"And I owe them and you so much." Without

them, I wouldn't have shifted back. I'd have lost myself completely. "Thank you."

"You'll have the chance to thank them yourself, and as for me, you know I'll do anything in my power to help and protect you."

Waterworks were imminent. Again. Not wanting to deal with the emotion, I cleared my throat and simply wrapped Jada up in a hug. "I love you, Jada. Thank you."

A sniffle and a squeeze and she released me. "Love you too. Now shower. You stink."

I chuckled, fully aware I smelt deliciously of Rowan. "Twenty minutes."

Without another word, I snagged Rowan's hand, and we headed to his room. He locked the door before we entered the shower. We turned it on, and then we tugged our sweatpants off one-handed—neither of us willing to let the other go.

Once under the spray, I dipped my head back, sighing as the warmth started to cleanse away the pain and chaos. Rowan's hands moved to my waist from where he stood sentinel.

With a content sigh, I turned my gaze to him, my breath stuttering out of me at the intensity staring back at me. "This is the first time we've really showered together."

He nodded in understanding. All those other times had been him taking care of me, cooling me down during my almost delirious episodes of high fever—though there had been that hot-as-hell time under the spray. We'd been so focussed on coming that time, could we technically call it showering? "It means I get the chance to put my mouth on you."

Desire fizzed in my stomach; just those few words of promise were enough to get a reaction from me. "So I'm not the only one constantly horny when we're together?"

In answer, he took my hand and placed it on his erection. The silky steel beneath my palm felt phenomenal. The hitch of his breath, though—that simple, beautiful sound—had a direct line to my cock. Rock hard in 0.2 seconds was likely a record.

"You are definitely not the only one who's needy all the damn time," he said gruffly. Rowan followed up with a kiss, moulding his mouth to mine as he slowly devoured it.

He kissed me until I was breathless. Until I panted. Until my hands were flying over his skin, tugging him close so I could grind against him.

Panting heavily, he slowed the kiss. A frustrated groan spilled out of me, not ready for it to end.

"We don't have enough time. Not right now."

While he sounded pained, I narrowed my eyes at the hint of a smirk he aimed at me.

"How about you let me take care of you?"

My gaze softened immediately as heat pooled in my stomach, more than okay with this plan. "Yeah, yes, fuck yes, okay."

He chuckled at the desperation clinging to me, even as he dropped to his knees. When his eyes darted up, I stilled, frozen in place with just how incredible and hot he was.

"You're fucking magnificent," I whimpered when he tongued my slit. He teased me some more, licking me and placing open-mouthed kisses along my cock. With each caress, my legs shook, my hammering heart picking up speed.

The whole time, Rowan drifted between closing his eyes as he worshipped me and flicking his gaze up, watching my expression.

He was also teasing the hell out of me.

"Suck me," I said breathily, my attempt at a growly order impossible given the sweetness of his mouth.

When he arched his undamaged brow, he knew I was going out of my mind.

With my head already going light and my cock desperate to fuck his mouth, I finally managed, "You know what would make you look even more magnifi-

nngh?" The last syllable turned upside down as Rowan wrapped his lips around me, leaned in, and sucked me to the back of his throat.

"Nnghh…," I grunted, more garbled words following as I latched on to him, palming his cheek gently.

Pulling back, he released my dick with an audible pop. "What were you saying?" He stroked my cock, slowly jacking me off.

I shook my head, fast and desperate, having no fucking idea what I was saying. All I knew was I wanted his perfect mouth on me.

Arching his brow, he was all smug amusement. "You want me to make you come? Swallow your load?"

Wordlessly, I nodded.

He rubbed his cheek over my sensitive glans. "You want me to suck you off so damn good, it's all you'll be able to think about before you're able to sink into my hole?"

Fuck, what he did to me. "Yes, that. I want that."

A seductive grin lifted half of his mouth, holding me captive. I didn't think he believed just how beautiful he was yet. But someday soon he would. I'd make it my mission.

Before I could beg, he traced his tongue around my

glans, then sank his mouth down on my cock, stopping when it met his fist that gripped my base.

"Fuck, so good."

He pulled off before sinking back down, sucking a steady, perfect rhythm.

"So hot," I grunted, unable to tear away my gaze.

When Rowan palmed my arse, I knew what he wanted, so I gave it willingly. I thrust into his mouth, and he doubled down. Soft, needy noises spilled between us, our combined moans the perfect backdrop to the bliss of the moment.

My breath stuttered, and I slammed my hand on the shower wall, going light-headed from the rush of sensation zipping through me.

"Fuck, fuck...." White-hot pleasure burst behind my closed eyes. It zipped around my body as my skin vibrated.

I couldn't last. Could barely breathe.

With jerky hips, I chased my release. Followed the sensation I knew only Rowan could draw from me.

My eyes sprang open, meeting his as my balls drew up with an intensity that blurred my vision.

Rowan didn't stop. Holding on tightly, he bobbed his head, my cock slipping effortlessly between his parted lips, the suction a close second to the most mind-blowing sensation I'd been lucky enough to share with him.

"I fucking love you." Each word fell from my lips with a heated, jagged breath.

Cupping my balls, he squeezed lightly, caressing and gently probing them before he slipped his spit-slick fingers behind them and rubbed against my taint teasingly, never quite breaching my crack, never dipping to my hole that fluttered with interest.

Until he did.

Just the slightest insertion of a fingertip.

My cock throbbed, pulsed as a groan passed my lips, and I came hard, fast, with unsteady jerks. My grip on his shoulder slackened as he drank me down, sucking every last drop until my legs shook and his arms curled around me, and he released my sensitive cock with a quiet pop.

Lowering me to the shower floor, Rowan reached for my face, dragging me into a kiss. Wet, slippery with traces of my cum, his mouth was perfection. His kisses needy.

I kissed him back as I trailed my fingers to his rock-hard cock and took him in my hand. A grunted moan was my reward as I jacked him off, kissing him with fervour until he wrenched his mouth away to look me in the eyes.

A heavy-lidded gaze connected with mine. Fuck, he was beautiful.

I shuttled my hand over his pulsing cock, not relenting, not even when he parted his lips.

"Come for me. Let me see you." Need filled my request. I was desperate to watch him unravel and let go.

He bobbed his head, pliant and with an urgency that I loved. And still I tugged his slippery cock.

"Come on. Paint my hand. Give it all to me so I can rub it into my skin."

Fuck, just the thought made my spent cock jerk. I wanted that so badly.

"Holy... fuck!" His whole body shuddered. Wide-eyed, he jerked, his lips parting as a feral groan tore from him.

At the first spill, I shifted my other hand to capture the cum, committed to following through.

Not a chance this would wash down the drain.

A slow up and down with my hand earned me another shot of cum. I caught it and smiled when Rowan pressed his forehead to my shoulder, leaning on me.

"One more, baby. I need more."

He grunted, hips thrusting once more, and a

ragged "Fuck" pressed against my skin along with a smaller spurt of cum.

I cupped my reward, pressing a kiss to his temple. Jostled, Rowan eased away, his blissed-out gaze connecting with mine.

Having his attention, I made a show of lifting my hand and licking my palm, allowing his cum to spill down my chin. The catch of his breath tightened my gut.

"Fuck, that's hot."

I smirked. "And it's mine."

Another lick and I massaged the spilled cum and my covered fingers over my chin and down onto my chest.

His swallow was loud, his limbs still shaking as he watched my every move.

"You'll smell like me."

I nodded, still massaging his cum into my skin. What he wasn't saying was that everyone on my team would smell him on me too.

I didn't give a shit. All I cared about was basking in his scent. It calmed something inside me: an uneasiness, my need to protect and possess.

A soft half-smile formed, and he leaned into me, pressing the gentlest of touches against my lips. As he pulled away, he whispered, "You can always take whatever you need from me."

Emotion, all warmth and love, flooded my chest. He understood.

I offered him my promise: "I'm yours."

We sat like that for a couple of too-short minutes before reality had us moving.

After we were dressed and I'd demolished three sandwiches, I sat at Rowan's side, with Kent close by, at the workstation I'd claimed as my own.

Satisfied in almost every way possible, I felt refreshed and ready for action. My clear head meant I could focus on Kent's words and the schematics of the chip I was looking over.

The comms beeped. Callen's voice came out loud and clear. "Shit's hit the fan."

I froze, knowing Kent would take the lead.

"What's going on?"

"Murdock and Jefferson have called into question the unit's integrity."

Shock reverberated through me. We were a covert team, our ops approved by Durrant herself, the SICB director. And almost everything we did, our day-to-day operations, were championed by Callen, our division leader.

Access to our unit was restricted. So the fact that

two government officials had even heard of us was not okay.

"I'm sending you something now."

Rowan opened the encrypted file Callen sent. "Oh shit."

My eyes widened in alarm.

Operation overviews, case files, and our agent profiles appeared before us.

As a covert team specialising in infiltration, it regularly meant going undercover. It also meant we often worked outside the rigid red tape imposed by the government and other SICB departments. The release of this information would put all that in jeopardy.

"This has been leaked," Callen explained, his voice tight. "We're trying to contain it, but it'll blow wide open. Some fucker will manage to get it out of the government walls."

"I'll work on making sure that never happens."

I looked at Rowan, saw the determination in his expression. If anyone could make it happen, it was him. And with our support, he could possibly make this go away.

"There's more."

Kent remained silent as Callen spoke, her body rigid and on alert.

"They're trying to bring us in to do a full investigation. There's talk about charges."

My heart bolted into a high-speed run inside my chest. And still, Kent stayed quiet.

"I want you to all go underground. You're all good where you are, right?"

"Yes," Rowan answered for us. "They're secure here."

"Why?" Kent finally asked.

"There's more at play than we originally suspected."

"Are we thinking Hornell's responsible for this leak?" she prodded.

"Yes," Callen said shortly, surprising me by not breaking into some sort of tirade.

This situation was legit serious if that was the case.

"We've been following leads of officials in his pocket. With Murdock and Jefferson coming out with this nonsense, we have two clear suspects, but we don't expect they're the only ones. The sort of bullshit they're spouting could result in criminal charges."

"Against us?" My brows shot high.

"That's not going to happen." Rowan's tone turned deadly.

"I'm with Rowan on this. We're not going to let it get that far, but we do need to shut this down."

Callen's words brooked no argument. "Chris is already somewhere safe. My name's not on the files."

I did notice that. Callen used to be in the unit—a couple of years or so before I joined. Chris was his replacement.

"The data they gathered hasn't gone too far back. They only have present-day intel—or at least from the last four months, it seems."

"There's nothing about me." Curiosity coloured Rowan's words.

I acted immediately, fingers flying over my keyboard to check. He was right, obviously. "Why would that be the case?"

He glanced at me. "I've set up a system to erase any mention of my name and aliases. I get alerts. The software has a wide reach."

"Through security and firewalls?"

In answer, he raised his brow, and I rolled my eyes.

"Fine. Stupid question," I admitted, so damn proud of him and his incredible brain.

"Lucas and the team will be landing soon, right?"

Kent answered Callen. "Eight minutes. As soon as they've landed, I'll—"

"I can reach him now. Break through their Flight Modes." Rowan didn't wait for approval.

"You do that. I've organised a car for them. They

need to leave from the tarmac, as I suspect officials will be waiting to take them in for questioning. I'll send you the vehicle's coordinates. Lucas has several places in and around the area. He'll go to wherever he deems safe."

My mind was whizzing at the craziness of this development. While I paid attention to every word being spoken, I skimmed the documents.

Thankfully they weren't as thorough as they could have been. The information was pretty basic, and all the "personal" information was on public record. What concerned me, and I suspected it did the whole team, was how the case files had been accessed in the first place.

Lucas was confident that the breach at the head office hadn't compromised mission files.

As Kent signed off from Callen and spoke to Lucas with an update and his instructions, I glanced at Rowan when he squeezed my arm.

"They'll be okay."

I nodded, hoping the team, a hell of a lot more vulnerable than us right now, would get to safety without incident.

"Do you trust me?"

"Yes." The word punched out of me fast and without hesitation.

"Hornell will not win, and I'll help our team. Nobody will be touching them."

My lips twitched and he winked. I appreciated his deliberate wording—he never did anything accidentally—knowing his using "our" would settle me just as it would make me happy.

"We'll do this together." I searched his stunning frozen-meadow eyes.

"Always, Flynn. I'll do anything for you." He latched on to my hand and pressed a kiss to the inside of my wrist, drawing in my scent as he did.

And while my insides turned to mush, my resolve strengthened, transforming from mere determination to an unyielding force.

Together, we were unstoppable, ready to conquer any challenge that dared stand in our way.

BONUS SCENES

TWO FUN BONUS SCENE TO CHECK OUT.

1. Want to see Kent giving Flynn's parents a dressing down on his birthday?

There are two ways to get access. One is via the link in my Facebook group

HTTPS://WWW.FACEBOOK.COM/GROUPS/ROMMANCEWITHBECCALOUISA/

The other is for newsletter subscribers.

HTTPS://LANDING.MAILERLITE.COM/WEBFORMS/LANDING/R9F0I4

2. Do you want to see Rowan losing his shit with Ethan when Flynn is unconscious and Vinnie has to save the day?

This is a Ream exclusive. The great news is available to followers (free to follow) and all tiers.

HTTPS://REAMSTORIES.COM/BECCASEYMOUR

If you do select one of the subscription tiers on Ream, more great news is there are lots of exclusive bonus scenes to come.

Be sure to head to Amazon to one-click STRONGER THAN FATE, Lucas's story.

About the Author

I live and breathe all things book related. Usually with at least three books being read and two WiPs being written at the same time, life is merrily hectic. I tend to do nothing by halves, so I happily seek the craziness and busyness life offers.

Living on my small property in Queensland with my human family as well as my animal family of cows, sheep, chooks, and dogs, I really do appreciate the beauty of the world around me and am a believer that love truly is love.

To check for updates head to my website:

https://beccaseymour.com

https://landing.mailerlite.com/

webforms/landing/r9foi4

Plus, join my Facebook group, which I share with the awesome Louisa Masters here:

https://www.facebook.com/groups/

rommancewithbeccalouisa/

www.ingramcontent.com/pod-product-compliance
Lightning Source LLC
Chambersburg PA
CBHW051002210726
48287CB00004B/1348